# KINSHIP COVE:
# HEARTTHROBS & HOLIDAYS

## THE COMPLETE COLLECTION

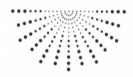

## ELLIS LEIGH

# REINDEER RIPPLE

## KINSHIP COVE: HEARTTHROBS & HOLIDAYS

**No one ever said working with Santa was all reindeer games, and some scars are harder to heal. Welcome to Kinship Cove by way of North Pole, Alaska. Holidays have never been so steamy.**

Being from the O'Rudolph family never had saved me from ridicule or given me any extra access to those reindeer games, but I'd made it through my childhood relatively unscathed. Or so I liked to tell myself. Truth be told, one herd in particular had been awfully cruel and gone well beyond just laughing and calling me names. But that was years ago. Right? I should be over it…right?

Over it or not, I was older. More mature. An adult. An adult with a job that took her to a shifter town named Kinship Cove, where the fates not only introduce me to a diner-owning, fox-shifting old lady who makes me the best cups of peppermint coffee ever, they also throw me a wild curve ball in the form of one Bennett Donderson. My fated mate and a man who can truly rock the white hair look. Unfortunately, he's also a man from the herd of my nightmares. One who had been unable—or unwilling—to protect me from his very own niece. How can I trust someone whose family takes being on the naughty list to an emotionally scarring sort of extreme?

What's a girl to do when her past slams headfirst into her present and threatens her future?

# 1
## RUBY

Kinship Cove. A shifter town, one where I—as a reindeer shifter —should have felt comfortable. One where others like me came together to live their lives without judgment or fear of outsiders trying to control them. The cove was beautiful, tucked deep into the forests of a mountain range with a rocky coast like the image on some Christmas card or the backdrop to one of those holiday movies everyone loved so much. It looked like the hometown of Santa Claus himself. It wasn't— that would be North Pole, Alaska, where I was from—but it sure could have been.

"Back again." The old woman who owned the little diner in Kinship Cove shuffled over to where I was sitting at the counter, her smile bright and her eyes sharp. Friendly, these local shifters. So darn friendly. "You've been here every day for weeks."

Friendly *and* observant. She wasn't wrong about that timeline. "What can I say? I can't get enough of your gingerbread French toast."

The woman—who kept demanding I call her Momma—shot me a sly grin and leaned a little closer. "Mayonnaise."

I had no idea what that was a code word for. "Excuse me?"

"We don't just use eggs in the wash for the bread—we use mayonnaise. My husband started that back when he ran the kitchen."

She smiled up at a picture of a handsome, dark-haired man hanging near the coffeepot. Assumedly her husband, and the display sure did look like some sort of memorial.

"I'm sorry—I didn't mean to bring up something that would make you remember his death."

"Death?" She spun around, laughing. "Oh no, child. He's not dead, just retired. The man is out on the golf course as we speak, the lazy git." She flicked her towel at the photo. "I leave that up there as a reminder to the customers—they always liked him. Me? I'm just glad he finally got out of my hair. It's hard to spend every day, all day with someone, even if they are your fated mate. Anyway, he's the one who created the recipe for our French toast. The mayonnaise adds a good fat to the bread without that oily butter drippiness that can happen. So when you finally go home and make your own, add a little mayo to the egg wash. You won't regret it."

Who would have thought? "Well, it's delicious. Thanks for the tip."

"You're welcome." She patted my hand, the chill in hers slightly sticking. What was that people said? Cold hands, warm heart—she must have had the warmest heart in Kinship Cove with those hands. "So, gingerbread French toast?"

I grinned, my mouth watering at the very thought. "Yes, please."

"No problem. And I'll have Jackson bring you a coffee. Make him blush for me, would you? It brings joy to my old heart to see my grandson so flabbergasted by a pretty woman."

If I'd been a lot younger, I might have been shy about her compliment. Might have brushed it off or stuttered my way through minimizing it. Thankfully, I was an adult with decades of learning to accept myself in the rearview mirror and a strong sense of self. Yes, I was a pretty woman—I could accept that as fact and carry on.

"You've got it," I said. "I might even give him a wink or something—really throw him for a loop."

Her returning grin was one I had so rarely seen. I had just made her truly happy, it seemed. "You're my new favorite customer. Keep coming to see me, okay?"

And then she was off, greeting customers with that smile of hers and snapping at her staff when they were too slow. She ran the place with an iron fist, but I loved it. Loved seeing her wrinkled face when I walked in. Loved knowing three generations of family had owned and run the place. There were antiques all over the dining room—pictures and little knickknacks that obviously meant something to them. There was also a bunch of pictures of the forest surrounding the town. Images of huge trees hanging off the cliffs above us, streams dividing pine groves, and individual lone-wolf trees that were likely long gone by now. It was one of the reasons why I came to the diner so much—other than the fact that the food was amazing. I got absolutely lost in the details.

Of course, I tended to get lost. A lot.

It wasn't really my fault, though. There always so much to *see*, especially in the forest. The lines in tree leaves, the crags of bark coating the trunk, a small bird perched high in the branches—a single tree could capture my attention for half an afternoon. I knew this about myself, and I adjusted my schedule to account for all of the distracting Mother Nature did to me during my workdays.

Thankfully, Kinship Cove was a lovely place to get lost in, and I worked with trees. Win-win for me.

"Good morning, Miss Ruby." Jackson—waiter, grandson to Momma, and adorably shy high schooler—turned over my mug and poured me a cup of coffee, already reaching for a peppermint candy for me to toss into the brew. Like I'd said—I'd been there. A lot.

I gave Jackson a grin. "Good morning. How went the studying last night? Did you figure out that problem you were having in calculus?"

He sighed. "No. I'm going to have to ask my teacher for help."

"Well. At least you tried."

"I know. It just sucks." His cheeks went red and his eyes flew open wider as he shot a glance around. "Sorry. I shouldn't have said that."

I shook my head and took a sip of my coffee, holding back a laugh. I'd gotten him to blush already without even flirting. Momma would love that.

"So," Jackson said as he exchanged my empty creamer pitcher for a full one. "What's the plan today?"

Because he'd learned my profession and was amazed someone got

5

paid to look at trees—which wasn't quite what I did, but that was the easiest explanation. "I'll be inspecting the trees up on the east ridge of the Christmas tree farm. The owner has some land he wants to clear, so I'm going to identify which trees are healthy and can be moved, and which should be harvested for their lumber."

"Huh," Jackson said, shaking his head. "That's one way to spend your day."

It was—my preferred way, to be honest. It may not have been everyone's cup of tea—or coffee, in my case—but being out in the woods, surrounded by nature and dwarfed by the local forests, was one of my favorite things. I'd been in Kinship Cover for almost three weeks, identifying trees that needed trimming, marking the ones that were too sick and needed to come down, and generally enjoying my time in the quaint little seaside village. I got lost a lot—even with the lovely signs the townspeople seemed to rely on to get around—but the beauty of the mountains on one side and the sea on the other was worth it. This little pocket of the world, this little shifter town where my inner reindeer and I felt comfortable to truly be ourselves, was a slice of heaven.

One I was getting awfully comfortable in.

"You should come by Grandma's house sometime," Jackson said as he refilled his coffee carafe from the huge brewer on the opposite counter. "She's got a whole back lot of trees. Growing up, we always used to shift to our foxes and go racing through the woods playing the predator game. It was a lot of fun."

Of that, I had no doubt. "Sounds delightful."

"Is there a reindeer version of predator?"

Such a casual question and yet one that made my fight-or-flight instinct flare. My skin went cold, and my stomach twisted as I forced myself to stay in my seat. "Sort of."

"Man, I'd love to know some of the reindeer games you used to play. I bet they were fun."

If only I'd been allowed to play them. "Yeah, so…I'm having the gingerbread French toast again today. I already told your grandma, so I assume that's in the works. This time, let's get it with a side of the fruit salad."

6

"No meat for the vegetarian. Got it. Let me just put this—"

The carafe he'd been holding—the one filled with steaming hot coffee—hit the edge of the counter, and everything happened in a sort of slow motion that defied logic. Jackson yelped, I reached to catch the container, and the coffee spilled all over my arm. The very, very hot coffee.

Ouch was not a strong enough word.

I grabbed my forearm, pain firing all the way past my elbow. "Holy ornaments."

"What happened?" Momma rushed over before I could even scream, reaching for me the second her eyes caught the redness of my skin. "Come with me, now. That's going to smart a bit."

Understatement. "It wasn't Jackson's fault."

"I'm so sorry," Jackson said, following us. But Momma wasn't having it.

"Back to work. I'll take care of her. And for the sake of the fates, don't fill the carafes so full—it makes them heavy and hard to handle."

She tugged me into the kitchen and directed me to the large, industrial sink in the back. Physically shoving me when the pain blurred my vision and had me stopping in my tracks

"Come on, child. Cold water will help." She pointed the sprayer at my arm—thankfully keeping the water pressure low so as not to cause more pain—and directed that cool water over my damaged skin. So much better.

"Your shirt's getting soaked," she said after a minute. "Take it off. I'll toss it in the dryer for you and get you a diner tee from the back."

"Thanks, Momma." I tugged off my work shirt and slipped my arm back under the cool water, wanting nothing more than for the pain to go away. At least until I heard a voice from behind me.

"Uh...t-there's a delivery," Jackson said. Obviously stuttering. Likely blushing. Lovely. That was what I needed—some young kid seeing me in my bra. I was going to be spank bank fodder for days.

Momma didn't miss a beat, though. "Answer the door, Jackson. Accept the order and tell the man I'll let him know if there're any issues."

7

I leaned farther over the sink, my stomach turning a bit but the pain in my arm dying down. Just a few more minutes, and I'd likely be able to turn off the water. The burn couldn't be that bad, though it was very likely the worst thing that had happened to me since I'd arrived in Kinship Cove.

"Ruby?"

I had obviously spoken—or thought, rather—too soon. That voice—I knew it. The tone sent me right back to North Pole, back to a time when I wasn't in control of my own life, to when things were just plain bad for me. My brain had to be playing tricks on me, though. No way could that man—that blast from my past—be standing in the kitchen at some diner in Kinship Cove. No way could he be right there behind me after decades of not seeing each other. It simply wasn't possible.

And the fates wouldn't be so cruel.

"Ruby O'Rudolph," the man said, which made him knowing me definitely possible. Who would have guessed such a name? "What are you doing here?"

And that was the moment when the full reality of my situation hit me square in the noggin. I was standing topless—bright red bra fully on display—in the back of the kitchen of a restaurant with my arm shoved under the industrial dish sprayer. Half naked and wet wasn't exactly how I'd intended to see a Donderson. Not that I'd ever wanted to see anyone from that family again.

I'd apparently been wrong about the fates—they were actually *that* cruel and then some.

"Ruby?"

He moved closer, so I had to make a decision on the fly. Not my strongest suit, but there wasn't much I could do. Fake it until you make it, right?

"Nope. Not Ruby."

Lies didn't come easily to me, though, and the way my voice cracked definitely gave me away. Likely as did the tattoo on my back of Santa's sleigh being pulled by a single, red-nosed reindeer. Family legends ran deep in our herds, but the proof of my lineage usually stayed hidden away.

*This was why I shouldn't ever be topless. In public.*

But Carter Donderson—reindeer shifter from the same region as my family, father to the woman who'd tried to destroy my life for years, and master manipulator in his own right—had never been known for being easy to trick.

"Uh...pretty sure you're Ruby O'Rudolph."

The know-it-all tone in his voice only made me want to dig my heels in deeper. "Nope. Not Ruby. Don't you think I know my own name?"

That was the moment Momma decided to reappear, burn cream and tee in hand. Completely destroying my disguise when she said, "Okay, Ruby. Let me deal with that arm."

A little late and a lot unhelpful, that one. Have you ever sighed so deeply, you felt as if your entire soul just blew right out of your mouth? Yeah. Me, too. I sighed a sigh as big as the sun.

"It's fine, Momma. Doesn't even hurt anymore." Another lie, though I told that one better. Still, I shut off the water and turned to face my humiliation head on. Sort of. I kept my eyes on the ground. "Hi, Mr. Donderson."

His dark-brown work boots were about the only thing I could see, which fit me just fine. Though...work boots had never been his style. He was more a suit-and-wingtip-loafers guy.

"Not Ruby, huh?" the man asked, sarcasm practically dripping from his words. "I don't remember you being a liar."

Carter Donderson was such a jerk, calling me out that way. That was it—the moment I moved past my embarrassment and grew too frustrated not to respond. I was still topless—still facing off against the father of my nemesis—but I was not one to take being called names I didn't deserve.

Not anymore.

"I'm not a liar." I squared my shoulders, and I took a breath deep enough to refill my soul and make me feel ready to go into battle. "So, you can just shut—"

The words caught in my throat as I finally looked up.

First thought—that was not Carter Donderson, though I still knew him. The man before me wasn't the father of the Donderson girl I knew.

9

He was the uncle of the one who had tried really hard to make me feel worthless. Bennett Donderson, whom I had never actually met but still knew far too much about simply because of my run-ins with his niece and who happened to be way older than I. Old enough to be my daddy, in more ways than one. Which brought me to my second thought—he was cuter than I would have expected him to be. I found him decidedly attractive, much to my dismay. How could I despise someone so...yummy?

Third thought—I was utterly and totally screwed.

My eyes met his, and the cold hand of fate grabbed my heart. The tug deep in my belly nearly yanked me right out of my shoes as I came face-to-face with none other than my fated mate.

Fa-la-la-la-fuck-la-la-la-la, but the fates were cruel mistresses. Me with a Donderson—with *any* Donderson—was just plain wrong.

"No," I said, stumbling over my own feet as I immediately headed for the door. "This can't be happening."

Footsteps sounded behind me, whether Bennett's or Momma's, I couldn't tell. Maybe both. Didn't matter, though—this was not my new reality. I was not supposed to be mated to someone like Bennett Donderson. His brother and niece had destroyed my childhood and sent me running from my home many years ago. I didn't want to be dragged back to that place. No way, no how. Didn't matter that from what I'd seen, he was likely the handsomest reindeer shifter I had ever run across. The white hair he wore loose and wavy accentuated his high cheekbones, and I'd even gotten a peek at some deep, green eyes that may as well have been colored with the needles of the cedar balsams I loved so much. Add a red hat into the mix, and he'd be one heck of a Santa to come crawling down my chimney.

Hot. The man was definitely hot.

And I was definitely screwed.

"Ruby," Momma yelled just before I reached the front door. "Your shirt."

Yup. Still topless and now standing in front of a restaurant full of people in nothing but my work pants and red bra. Wonderful.

"Thanks," I said, turning and grabbing it from her before spinning for that door once more. "I appreciate your help, but I have to go."

"Ruby, wait." That was Bennett, but I wasn't waiting for him. I tugged the cotton shirt Momma had given me over my head and swept outside, moving fast toward my car. Needing to escape.

Needing to get away from Bennett and fate and all that mishmash.

Coffee burn, being seen topless by half the town, and finding out I was mated to the uncle of my high school nemesis. This was totally not my day.

# 2

# RUBY

You know how people say things couldn't get any worse? They were wrong. Things could always get worse. How did I know that? Because somehow, someway, I had managed to make my painful exit from Momma's diner even worse. All because I hadn't paid attention. How in the holidays did someone get lost walking the same path they'd walked every single day for weeks? I had no idea, but somehow, I'd managed it.

My steps sounded hollow against the wooden docks of the cove—a place I hadn't yet been to and wasn't sure how I'd arrived at. Whatever— I'd simply call this the scenic route. And it was scenic. The cold of town was a bit more tempered here, the coming snow not as obvious. The water looked gray and rough and sounded harsh underneath me as the waves crashed into the pilings and rocks. Dark and stormy for sure, and yet the buildings and storefronts seemed downright chipper. Everyone was decorated or in the process of decorating for the season, every entrance lit all the way down the stretch of commerce. Wreaths and garlands, trees with angels, beautiful menorahs, kinaras, and even a Festivus pole—no one could say the docks weren't intersectional in their festive nature. I liked it.

What I didn't like was the way my mind kept wanting me to truly think about those years when Pansy Donderson and I had clashed. The ones that had nearly killed me. The ones I had never wanted to revisit. Apparently, I was going to have to, though.

"Stupid fates."

"Pardon?" An older man—seal shifter, by the smell of him—looked up as I walked past. Obviously having heard the mumble I hadn't meant to share.

"Sorry—just talking to myself. Happy holidays."

"Happy holidays to you, miss." He gave me a head nod and a toothy grin, then he was gone, and I was back to lamenting my fate.

How could I possibly be mated to Pansy Donderson's uncle? That just seemed so...wrong. True, I'd never actually met him before today. I knew his name and his reputation—everyone knew everything about all the families where I was from—but he'd been so much older than me that we had never interacted. If what I had heard was right, he'd been popular and athletic—a real jokester from an early age. Me? I'd been shy and quiet, tortured into hiding every single thing about myself by one girl. Pansy Donderson had been smart and manipulative, cruel to a fault as well. A wicked combination. She had said all the right things to the teachers, manipulated her friends, and basically gaslighted an entire community whenever anyone accused her of doing what she truly was doing all with the support of her widowed father. The poor, motherless girl and her single dad, or so everyone thought. Her behavior and the way she played everyone in that town had been impressive—terrifying, but impressive. I never wanted to run into her again.

Which would likely be a little tricky considering her uncle was my fated mate.

The saddest part was that, no matter how much the idea of having found my mate excited me, there was no way I could go through with it. Being with Bennett Donderson meant dealing with Pansy, and that certainly wasn't happening. Yet reindeer mates were few and far between, seeing as how we only mated with our own species. With just eight founding families of our specific breed and three generations running around the world, that didn't leave many options. The fates had chosen Bennett, and there was no arguing with them or do-overs. What was I going to do?

A car pulled up on the side street of the dock, a very loud and modern version of *"Deck the Halls"* blaring through the speakers before cutting out completely as the engine was quieted. Bright red with gold trim and a white interior, the car was impossible to miss. The man who unfolded himself from it even more so. Bennett stood beside the sled-on-wheels, his white hair positively gleaming in the lights strung from every flat surface, his sweater looking soft and cuddle-worthy. My lady bits sang for him, my body beginning to vibrate when he finally turned my way and smiled. At me. He looked like the handsomest Santa Claus ever conceived. He looked like a man out of my dreams.

Or rather, my nightmares, if I really gave that some thought. *Donderson...nope.*

"You might as well keep driving," I said, passing him by and focusing hard on the gray waters leading to the ocean. *Nothing to see here. Just keep moving.*

"Why are you so upset, Red? I mean...out of the two of us, I have many more reasons to be the upset party in this situation."

If he was somehow making a crack about my looks... "And why is that?"

"Because I've had all these years alone, and now I'm going to have to share my cool stuff with someone else." He sidled up beside me, his arm brushing mine. Intentionally. The jerk. "Alas, if I must..."

"No one said we had to share anything." And that was the moment I went to make a dramatic exit by turning onto a one-way street to escape from him...and ran straight into a man who smelled like a floating garbage pile instead. Gross.

"Sorry," I said, trying to move past him.

He blocked my every move. "Dockworkers only down here."

"But...it's a street."

"No, it's a loading dock." He pointed over my shoulder. "Can't you read the signs?"

I looked up, reading the words I'd missed along the way. *Loading Dock. Authorized Personnel Only. No Trespassing.* Oops.

"Sorry," I said, my voice a little softer and my steps changing direction. "I must have missed them."

"So, the rumors of the O'Rudolphs are true—you *do* get distracted easily." Bennett chuckled from behind me.

I saw red. "I'm better at natural navigation than man-made. As were my father and his father before him. We don't get distracted—we're simply looking for the way via other methods." Let it be said that this time, my lie came out surprisingly well. I *did* get distracted. A lot. But Bennett didn't need to know that, and he certainly didn't need to bring my family into the conversation. I wasn't bringing in his sociopathic niece or enabling brother.

"I'm sorry. I didn't mean to upset you." Bennett appeared beside me, grabbing my arm and directing me toward his car. "Come on, Ruby. Let me get you to wherever you're staying. I don't like the idea of you alone on the docks."

I stopped, staring at his hand on my arm. Loving the feel of his hold on me and hating myself a little for even admitting that. Still…I was tired of walking and had no idea how to get home. Who was I to turn down such an offer?

*Maybe he's not like them.* "Fine. You can drive me straight home. I've rented an house behind the library."

Bennett led me to his car and opened the passenger door for me, waiting until I'd slid onto the seat—leather, and the whole interior smelled like peppermint in the most delicious way—before running around to his side. He dropped into his spot much more gracefully than I had. But then he opened his mouth.

"I remember you as a child, Red. Still always buried in a book?"

I gritted my teeth. "If you're going to mock me for liking to read, you can let me out right here."

Bennett sat back, frowning. "That wasn't mocking. I was going to attempt to make conversation by asking what you're reading right now —since you're living right behind the library and all. Why are you so defensive?"

*Because your niece was cruel to me, and your brother helped her. Because everyone made fun of me. Because no one ever let me play reindeer games. Because...* "You were never nice to me."

"Hang on—I never knew you. We're what...two or three decades apart in age? I only knew *of you*. And I was always nice to everyone—I would have been nice to you had I ever met you before today." He leaned closer, invading my space as he started the engine and whispered, "I would have been very nice to you had I known you were my mate. Nice bra, by the way. Red really is your color."

I shivered, trying my best not to let him see it. O. Holy. Night. The man was a handsome one. Also, technically he wasn't wrong—he likely would have been exceptionally nice to me if he'd known I was his mate—which meant I had nothing to say. That didn't stop me from trying. "Yeah, well..."

Thankfully, he filled in the gap when I left him hanging with that stunning and well-articulated rebuttal. "So, here's the plan I've worked up so far. How about I drop you off, give you some time to freshen up, and then I'll be back to take you to dinner?"

The man was smooth, that was for sure. "Why?"

"Because the fates think we're perfect for each other." He pulled out onto the main road—the one I could never remember the name of—and turned toward the library. Or at least, I assumed he did. Why did all the signs look the same, when I could spot the difference in a tree from fifty yards? What kind of voodoo was that?

I hated feeling lost, which didn't help my mood a bit. "What if the fates are wrong?"

"What if they're right?"

"They're not."

"They might be."

"Never."

"Santa says never say never."

I snapped my jaw closed. He had me there. Santa didn't like finite decisions—he preferred to keep everything back home fluid. To have options.

Bennett had somehow become an option.

"I promise you," Bennett said, suddenly much more serious. His tone

17

much more forthright. "It's just dinner—I'd like to get to know you a little bit. If you hate me after it, I'll leave you alone."

It wasn't feeling hate that I was worried about. "Fine. This decision by the fates is as close to never happening as possible without being never. How's that?"

"Okay," he said, his laugh a sharp contrast to my grumpy responses. "So, we are probably never. Got it. Doesn't change my plans, though."

Bennett pulled up outside the house behind the library and hopped out of the car, coming around to open my door. To offer me his hand so I could climb out easily. To be kind to me. That was...unexpected.

"So," he said as soon as I was back on my feet. "What do you say? Dinner?"

How had he managed to stand so close? And why was I breathing so hard?

"Ruby?"

He smelled so good, and my entire body wanted to collapse into his. That had to be the mating bond tugging us together—I never would have inched a step toward him on my own. Nope, not even though he smelled like every good dream of home I'd ever had, or that he looked like my childhood crush come to life. I would not have fallen under his spell and reached out to grab his arm for support. Never...or as close to never without being never.

Stupid mating bond.

Did I mention he smelled really good? Seriously...I wanted to lick him like a candy cane.

But I wouldn't.

What I would do was argue. I was so tired and anxious and...scared. Nothing usually scared me in life anymore, but Bennett Donderson? He terrified me. "I don't know."

Bennett wasn't one for giving up, though. He leaned down, bringing his face closer to mine. Filling the air around us with that intriguing scent. "One shot. That's all I'm asking for. Please."

It was the please that broke me. I always had been a sucker for manners. "Fine. But if you even come close to mocking one thing about me, I'll leave."

"Why would I do that?"

I shrugged, not wanting to call him out for his niece's actions but unable to forget her reign. How could he not know how much of a horror she'd been? How could he not understand the depth of her mean-girl-ness?

As I stewed and avoided, Bennett pushed my hair behind my ear, staring into my eyes when I finally garnered the courage to meet his. *So very green. Like pine trees ready to be decorated. Positively spellbinding.*

"Who hurt you, Red?"

Spell broken. That wasn't a conversation I was willing to have. Not yet, at least. I just couldn't trust him with that memory. "I'll need an hour to get ready."

He nodded, looking quite puzzled but accepting my distraction. "Sure. Not a problem. Though, let's exchange numbers in case we need to get in touch."

I squinted a little at him. "Likely excuse."

"It's a legitimate reason, actually. I promise not to send you nudes... unless you ask nicely."

Deck. The. Halls. "Right." I coughed, pulling out my phone and fumbling to bring it to life while trying really, really hard not to think about Bennett naked. An impossible task. "What's your number? I'll text you."

Bennett offered up the ten digits I needed in that calm, sexy voice of his, then replied to my text with one of his own. A Santa-hat wearing emoji...of course.

"Got it?" he asked.

"Yep. Got it." I turned to leave, unable to stay with him a second longer. Hoping I could make my way into the building without any more embarrassing wrong turns. "And remember, any mocking—"

Before I could finish my sentence, I slipped. Not some gentle, easy slip where you stumble a bit and catch your balance again. Of course not. I slipped to the point that my leg flew high into the air in front of me and swung my body weight backward. I was going to fall flat on my ass right there on the sidewalk in front of Bennett Donderson. Stupid ice.

I didn't. Fall, that is. Not because I was somehow magically able to right myself. Oh no. Bennett must have rushed forward—without slipping—because suddenly his arms were underneath me and I was moving up instead of down. Up, up, up. Then in. He had me snuggled against his hard chest in no time, which did nothing for my desire to lick him.

He really needed to stop smelling like candy.

"Are you okay?" he asked, staring down at me. Locking me in his gaze. The world seemed to fade away. There was no town, no smelly old men blocking roads, no library in the distance or horrible children torturing others like in some sort of old John Saul novel. There was just him and me and the crisp, cool air of an upcoming snowstorm. There was only the green of his eyes staring into mine. There was us...and nothing else. For one single moment, everything seemed perfect.

"You're just so beautiful," he murmured. His lips were just out of my reach, not that I was watching them or anything. I mean...how could I not notice those plump, pink pillows of flesh. They were almost like a beacon to some sort of holy land that might have turned out to be hell itself. The apple on the tree. The promise of good when evil lurked. One stretch, and I'd be able to kiss him. One move, and I'd finally get a taste of that candy-cane smell that had been tempting me.

But I couldn't. "Bennett, I—"

"I don't know what the fates think I did to deserve such a mate," he said, letting his nose rub against the tip of mine. Warming me with the simple touch. "I don't know at all, but I'm thrilled with their lack of understanding about my past."

I couldn't hold back my smile. "Been on the naughty list?"

"Always. Fair warning—that's not about to end."

And with that, he kissed me. A quick, closed-mouth kiss, but still. Contact. His lips touched mine, and the world went spinning away. All that was left was him and me and the scent of peppermint on the air. We had no pasts, no jagged scars from times gone by, no pain hidden under years of avoidance. There was no bad in the world anymore...and there was no resisting him at that point.

Bennett clenched his hands, gripping me tighter as I melted against him. His warmth and energy making me want so much more. More than a simple kiss, more than a hug. More than anything we could have —or should have—been doing on a public street. The man was pure temptation. And I was succumbing.

When he pulled away—because, of course, he had to since my own thoughts had devolved into nothing more than grunts of *mine, want,* and *more*—I made the ultimate mistake. I licked my lips, and then I nearly died. Pure, sweet peppermint danced across my tongue. That scent would forever remind me of Christmas, which happened to be my favorite holiday. The taste forever tied to happy days with family and good memories. And now it was also tied to Bennett.

My mate.

What had the fates done to me?

"One hour," Bennett said once he set me on my feet and began to slowly back away from me. "You asked for one hour. I'll respect that but not a moment more." He grinned when he made it to his car. "And be ready, Red. I'm planning on pulling out all the stops."

I still hadn't quite caught my breath from that kiss, but I sure as heck wasn't going to let him know that. "So, I should be scared?"

"No. You should be prepared."

"For what?"

He opened his car door, leaning over the top of it toward me. Looking like a man who was on the hunt. "To be swept off your feet, of course."

He'd already done that in more ways than one, but I still wasn't ready to just admit stuff like that to him. "Good luck with that one."

Bennett laughed, slipping into the driver's seat and starting the engine. An old Christmas carol blasted from the speakers, and he leaned out once more to yell, "One hour. Don't keep me waiting, beautiful."

And then he was gone, and I was left to deal with…so much.

But I only had an hour, and I needed to get ready. He wasn't the only one able to do some sweeping.

## 3

# BENNETT

W hat fun it is to ride and sing a sleighing song tonight." Before the chorus could overtake me—because honestly, *"Jingle Bells"* always had been one of the most fun carols to sing—I fixed my bow tie and took one last look in the mirror. White hair on point, face clear, smile bright, eyes greener than the pine trees behind my cabin. I was one handsome reindeer, for sure. A mated one.

*Finally.*

So many years of waiting and wondering if it would happen for me, and then *Bam!* One look, and my heart was owned by a little reindeer from my hometown. Even with that connection, though, I'd ever met her. Pity, really. I could have spent the last few decades spoiling her in every way possible, but the fates hadn't been as prompt as I would have liked. Didn't matter—she was mine now, and I had every part of my personality set to woo. I may not have been prepared for the curve ball of Ruby O'Rudolph when I'd walked into the diner that morning, but I was going to knock it out of the park anyway. I had to.

I finished tidying the bathroom, still singing about bells and snow and sleighing song fun, then headed for the door. I didn't have much time—Ruby had only given me an hour, and the drive to town was a solid fifteen minutes. I'd rushed home, showered, brushed my teeth, gotten dressed, and straightened up my cabin. It hadn't been messy, but it wasn't *bring a lady back later to woo her* clean. If my mate was going to see my place tonight, everything needed to be perfect.

But perfect had been a little hard to come by in my woods lately. Not because of me or the woods themselves, but because of...others.

"Oh, Nijel. Oh, oh, oh."

As I made my way from the porch to my car, I did my best to ignore the noises coming from my neighbor's cabin. Impossible, but I tried. Nijel—my best friend—and his mate Lucy had only recently found each other, so the drive to bond physically was strong with them. I'd been around enough to understand it, though I didn't particularly want to hear it. The biggest problem was that she was a screamer. I'd taken to closing all my windows at night and sleeping with a fan on so as not to be disturbed, though there were nights when even that wasn't enough. Hopefully, they'd be on a break if I brought Ruby home. At least until I got her inside. At least until I got a chance to see if she screamed as well.

Goodness, these pants were too tight to disguise a hard-on.

Lucy's screams weren't helping my...situation. "Oh, oh, I'm gonna... I'm gonna..."

"Yes, child. We know. You're going to come." I shook my head, truly thankful my friend had found his one and only, settled into my car—a 50s Chevy I'd tricked out to look just like the sled my grandfather still pulled for the big man every year—and pulled out of the driveway. Radio blasting, of course.

*"Jingle bells, jingle bells..."*

Ah, Christmas. The holiday would be upon us in a matter of weeks. I was looking forward to it, but I always had liked the season. All the songs, the feeling of goodwill, the garland strung around town. Kinship Cove would soon turn itself into a picture-perfect seaside village whose pictures could grace advertisements and holiday cards sent around the world. The snow would fall, the white would blanket the city, and everything would smell like cookies and peppermint. I couldn't wait. And I especially couldn't wait to share the whole damn thing with my new mate.

*Gotta get my baby girl a stocking and a Santa hat.*

I pulled up at Ruby's place—two minutes early, I might add—and hurried to the door. I couldn't wait to see her again, to be in her presence, to learn more about her. I was like a kid on Christmas Eve—ready to unwrap my presents. Not literally—though if she gave me the okay to get her naked, I wouldn't turn it down.

Damn these tight pants.

I rang the bell, trying hard to think about things that wouldn't make my bulge any bulgier, and waited. The fight against the hard-on was fully lost the second Ruby opened the door.

Blond hair shining like the Christmas star, a green dress that hugged every naughty curve on her sinful body, legs for days and days, and... and peppermint. The scent enveloped me, becoming my entire focus. My mate smelled like my favorite herb, a fact which made my mouth water for her. Hard was an understatement.

This was going to be a long night.

"Stunning," I murmured, unable not to. Wanting so badly to reach out and pull her into my arms but waiting for a sign from her. For some sort of evidence of consent.

I didn't get it, so I kept my hands to myself.

She looked at me in a wary sort of way, almost as if she were somehow worried. "Shall we go?"

No way was I pushing her past her point of comfort, so I ignored my wants, sent a message of *behave yourself* to the bulgy part of me, and held out my arm for her to take. "Of course. Be careful on the sidewalk—there's a bit of ice."

Thankfully, she accepted my offer and placed her little hand just below my elbow. At least she allowed that level of contact. I'd take my wins no matter how small.

While trying to keep up a very casual sort of conversation—*how long have you been in town? Do you like the diner? The weather sure does seem to be getting ready for some snow*—I drove us to the fancy hotel overlooking the cove. There was an excellent restaurant inside, and the views were amazing. I'd even managed to snag us a reservation in the back room where we could be alone. Trying to impress her? Yes. Again...I was in full woo mode.

The restaurant proved just as charming and lovely as I'd remembered, and the staff was more than happy to bring us to our private little dining nook in the back. Unfortunately, Ruby kept a slight distance from me as we walked, which gave room for the waiter to assume he needed to assist her. I nearly shouldered him out of the way just so I could pull out the chair for her instead of him. I shot the man a quick frown, glancing at Ruby in a way I could only hope she didn't notice but he did. The man was no dummy—he nodded once at me in apology then moved to the other side of the table as I assisted Ruby. Discreet—I liked that. Kinship Cove *was* a shifter town, though—he understood a male's need to protect his mate and the danger of coming between them.

*Mate.* Holy holly balls—I had a mate.

Back to wooing. "Do you like wine, Ruby?"

"I do," she said, smiling up at me, thankfully oblivious to the power play that had just happened behind her. "In fact, I'd love a glass of Malbec."

"Let's get a bottle of your best Malbec," I said, addressing the waiter. He gave me another polite head nod, keeping his eyes firmly *off* my mate—smart man—before disappearing toward the bar. And then there was just me and Ruby, which was exactly how I wanted it.

"Thank you for joining me tonight." I leaned back, giving the waiter room to pour our wine when he appeared with it. Watching him like a hawk as he poured Ruby's. Thankfully, the man didn't linger. He whispered a quiet *I'll give you a moment to look over the menu* and disappeared quick as a trick.

Ruby simply smiled as she brought the deep red wine to her bright red lips, looking absolutely stunning in the candlelight. "Thank you for the invitation."

"It was more of a demand."

Another smile. "Somewhat."

"Well, I appreciate you submitting to me."

Her eyes darted to mine, a wicked glint appearing there. "I tend not to submit easily. Don't make this demanding thing a habit."

Pants. Too tight. "Never."

When the waiter returned—to my side, not hers—he quickly and professionally took our orders and left us alone again. Never outright avoiding Ruby but making sure he stood near me when addressing her. Keeping his eyes off the cleavage that teased me from across the table. My mate was a gorgeous woman dressed to impress, and that man was getting one hell of a tip for keeping his cool.

The conversation between Ruby and me flowed easily enough during dinner, though it stayed very surface—weather, books, pop culture. Safe topics. On that, I followed Ruby's lead, giving her the time she needed to grow more comfortable. Respecting the obvious boundaries she had when it came to me. At least until we had finished with dinner and were enjoying a post-meal coffee—peppermint-flavored, of course.

"So," I started as I set down my cup for the final time. "How is your family? Do you get home to see them very often?"

Her face went a little pale, and she looked away. Hiding. "They're fine. I don't really go home anymore—they come to me."

"Why's that?"

A shrug was thrown, one that looked to me to be some sort of distraction. "You know. Just...really busy."

Door closed and locked. Boundary line firmly drawn. That much was obvious. Time for a little tap-dancing to get me out of trouble. "Well, I hope you and I can make some time for each other. I'd really like to get to know you better."

Her response—a quiet *we'll see*—felt awfully...ambivalent. That definitely wasn't a good sign. My heart deflated a little bit.

Check paid, restaurant left, car ride back to her place over, and I was still stewing over her issues with the subject of home and her refusal to allow the conversation to go anywhere other than casual. Something wasn't right—something she likely wasn't going to tell me anytime soon. Our mating bond was definitely there, humming and buzzing in the background, but she seemed to be fighting it. Seemed to prefer to keep her distance from me. That bothered me to no end.

"The snow should be falling soon," I said as I led her to her house. I'd been forced to park two blocks away due to the weekly street cleaning, so I was thankful she was willing to hold on to my arm as we strolled. The O'Rudolphs were known for being a bit...distracted at times. Clumsy was another descriptor, though that seemed slightly harsh. Either way, I didn't want to take any chances with my Ruby. I had a feeling I'd find her distractions charming if she ever let me see her relax. "Are you ready for snowball fights and snowmen?"

"Not in the least," Ruby said with a laugh like bells. "I haven't been in the snow in years. I usually stick to warmer climates during the winter months."

That sounded—hellish. "My reindeer wouldn't be happy if I didn't let him out to play in the snow. How do you avoid the wrath from yours?"

It took her a long moment to answer, a pregnant sort of pause forming before she finally said, "I don't really like to shift, and the snow makes me want to. So, I avoid it."

I nearly stumbled. The idea of ignoring my inner reindeer, of distancing myself from him, seemed abhorrent. To him, as well. He definitely grunted at that particular comment. "You don't shift?"

"No."

I tried to keep my tone casual as I asked, "Why not?"

Another pause. Another feeling of something coming. A door into her mind opening. And then...

"I don't shift because of your niece."

There was no word strong enough to describe the panic that settled over me at that handful of words. No way to explain the dread that formed in my gut. I pulled Ruby to a gentle stop. "My niece?"

"Yes."

*Fa-la-la-la-fiddlesticks.* "Pansy?"

"Do you have another one?"

"Well...no." Thank the fates for that. Pansy was enough to deal with, and obviously, she'd gotten her claws into Ruby at some point. "What does Pansy have to do with you shifting?"

She looked away, hiding once more. "You probably know."

I racked my brain, trying with everything I could to remember... something. Unfortunately, my relationship with my niece was neither close nor something I thought about. She was...well, the nicest way to put it was…a horrible person. I'd long since broken my ties to her even though that left me without a relationship with my brother, which wasn't really the biggest loss considering how he allowed and even encouraged his daughter's deplorable behavior. The only things I'd heard about Pansy after I had left our hometown of North Pole, Alaska, had been her effect on the family and their continual efforts—and failures—to convince my brother to control her. I hadn't heard a thing about anyone else.

But apparently, Pansy's reign of terror hadn't been confined to my parents and grandparents. And me. A thought that truly laid me out.

"I promise you, Ruby. Whatever you think I know, I don't. What happened?"

She took a deep breath, finally gracing me with her gaze. Killing me with the sadness I saw there.

"I don't shift because I've never gotten over the torture your niece put me through in high school."

Concern turned on a dime into pure, unadulterated rage. "What torture? Did she hurt you?"

"I don't want to do this." Ruby released my arm, striding with purpose toward the little house behind the library, heading home. Without me. "Thanks for dinner, but I think the date is over."

She was leaving me behind. "Ruby, wait. Talk to me."

"No."

Another boundary thrown up. This one, I had to at least attempt to work around. For both our sakes. "Okay, then don't talk. Just… Stop. Please."

She did. Stop, that is. She even turned and gave me a long, hard stare. One that nearly killed me—the woman had built so many walls between us. Ones I had no idea how to tear down. But I was certainly going to try.

Santa didn't raise quitters.

Knowing there was nothing I could do to calm her, that this night was over and there were no more chances left, I did the only thing I could think of. I threw open my arms, wishing she would take advantage of my offer and snuggle me. Wanting to soothe whatever upset the conversation had caused her. "You're obviously hurting, and that's not acceptable to me. I don't want to add to it. I want to alleviate it."

"How do I know you're not just telling me what I want to hear?"

How, indeed. "I'm not a liar, Ruby. I'm not a cheat or a manipulator. You set a boundary, and I'll respect it. I give you my word as a man, as a Donderson, and as someone who survived his own experiences with Pansy."

She didn't say anything, but she also didn't move away. She stood stock-still right there on the sidewalk, continuing to watch me. Seeming to inspect me with her eyes. Obviously waiting for some sort of sign.

I didn't know what type, though, so I lowered my arms, and I shrugged a shoulder. "Let me walk you home, my mate. Give me a chance to say goodnight so I can know you're safe. I promise that's all I want."

She continued to stare at me, that wariness bold as ever on her face.

I couldn't leave things like that. "I swear to you, Ruby. I am not here to hurt you. I would never attempt it or allow it from someone else. Ever."

Nothing changed—for some very long seconds, there was not a single shift in her expression. Her body stayed tense, and every inch of her continued to look ready to run. But then she did the most amazing thing—she relaxed just enough to be noticeable, and she stepped closer. Walked all the way toward me and placed her hand on my chest. Slowly curled her body into mine as I carefully wrapped my arms around her and breathed her in. As I relaxed just a little bit at the fact that she would allow me to hold her, even if it was just for a moment.

One I could not waste.

"Whatever she did," I said, speaking into her hair. Keeping my arms around her even as she stiffened a little. "I swear, I had nothing to do with it. I have no knowledge of what happened to her outside of family stuff once I left town. She's been out of my life for a long time, but apparently still really affecting yours. I'm so sorry for that. When you're ready to tell me what she did, I'll listen. Okay?"

She nodded against me, pulling herself from my hold as she murmured a quiet, "Fine."

Which was obviously all I was going to get from her. "Good. Now, how about I walk you the rest of the way home? You seem like you need a bit of quiet."

"I'm right here." She hooked a thumb over her shoulder, indicating the house that truly was *right there*. "It's been a long night. You might as well get home yourself."

The rejection stung, it truly did, but the little reindeer wasn't being mean. No, she was broken inside, and me being in her life made all those rough edges scrape along her sensitive flesh. This mating was going to be difficult to get off the ground. Not that I wasn't willing to put in the work, I simply needed to reset my expectations.

She would be worth it.

"I'll wait until I know you're inside," I said, giving her what felt like a sad little smile. "Mate or not, I would never want anything bad to happen to you."

Ruby stared at me for a long moment then once again surprised the hell out of me. She rushed forward, practically jumping into my arms to give me a kiss. Not a deep, full-body one, but a kiss, nonetheless. She even opened her mouth and let me steal a taste of her—peppermint, just like I'd thought—before releasing me.

"I should probably go," she said, her voice husky and her words breathy. "This is all so…"

"I know." I kissed the tip of her nose and gave her one more hug. "It's okay, though. I understand you're hesitant and don't trust me yet, and that's okay. I'll work to earn it. There's no rush."

"You are not what I would have expected." She smiled, shaking her head, and brushed another kiss across my cheek. "Goodnight, Bennett."

"Goodnight, my beautiful Ruby Red. I'll see you tomorrow."

"Maybe," she said, walking away from me. Breaking my heart a little bit with every step. "I'll give you a maybe for that."

But her smile was present in the tone of her voice, so I tossed back a, "Definitely. That answer will be changed to definitely. Just you wait."

She laughed, climbing the steps to her porch and waving one final time before disappearing inside. A fun, joy-filled moment, even if it was a goodbye. But as I turned to leave, my mood soured once more. Craptastic candy canes—Pansy. The girl had nearly destroyed our family, had wreaked havoc in my life almost from her toddler days, and she'd somehow done it again without even being directly involved with my mating.

No way was I letting my niece kill my future.

I had barely slammed my car door closed when I had my phone in my hand, the contact selected. Dialing for backup.

Nijel answered on the second ring. "Bennett? What's wrong?"

No point in sugarcoating anything. "I've met my mate, and she hates my family—my niece, specifically—so I need you and your mate's help."

It took him about three seconds to answer. "You have a niece?"

Fuck, we had never talked about family, so of course he didn't know. "Yes, and knowing her, the hatred is justified. Can you and Lucy meet me at my cabin in twenty? I really need to talk this over with someone smarter than me to make sure I'm on the right path. That's your mate, by the way—not you."

"Understood and agreed with. We'll be there." No pause, no thinking about it. That was why I'd chosen the grumpy wolverine as my best friend.

"Thanks."

I ended the call, ready to get my Scrooge on. It was time to exorcise whatever ghosts from our pasts were getting in the way of our future.

4

# RUBY

I woke up to a lighthearted feeling that could only come after a wonderful date, a sense of surprise because of whom that date had been with, and a feeling that it was time to let go of the past, even if only for a little bit. Oh, and a message from Bennett on my phone.

*Have to work this morning but will be done by three. Want me to come over afterward?*

It took me a good ten minutes of staring at the phone to fight back my internal twelve-year-old. The one who wanted to squee and kick her legs in the air and—well, I might have lost that particular fight. In the end, I could only try to catch my breath as I typed a quick and simple response.

*Sure.*

There. Vague. Nothing too eager or disinterested. I was toeing the line of being just interested enough so he knew I was. Why? I had no idea. He was my mate—my perfect match as chosen by the fates. I could have brought him home five minutes after that first moment of connection and banged his antlers off, and he wouldn't have thought any less of me. Heck, he probably would have appreciated my enthusiasm.

Another message popped up, pulling me from the rabbit hole of what *enthusiasm* with Bennett Donderson might be like.

*I'll pick you up on my way home so you don't get lost.*

Well, wasn't that presumptuous.

*I wouldn't get lost.*

His reply? The laughing-crying emoji. The jerk.

Okay, not a jerk. It wasn't a secret that I tended to get distracted by what was around me—especially whatever local flora caught my eye. I understood that. Truth be told, my mother was actually worse. As had been my grandfather. Three generations of O'Rudolphs with absolutely no sense of direction and little ability to focus on tasks. We weren't exactly known for being the reindeer with the fabulous internal GPS—that was the Dasherwiczes. Our skill in life was more centered around emergencies. We were fabulous on dark and stormy nights when visibility was at a low point, what with our glowing noses and all. In a species full of cute, black noses, we'd instead been gifted—and I used that term loosely—with something much more distinctive.

Stupid ball of fire on the end of my reindeer snout was a gift, but I couldn't find my way out of a paper bag at times. A gift and a curse.

But alas, there was nothing I could do about my animal nose except not shift, which definitely didn't make the beast inside me very happy. Of course, she hadn't been happy in years. Had been too scared to come out and play, to be honest. Not that I could blame her. High school...it had been a real trial.

I sighed, rolling out of bed—tugging the quilt I'd kicked off in my excitement over Bennett's texts back onto the mattress—and headed for the en suite. It was time to start my morning exactly how I always did.

With a shower, coffee, and a mental plan of the work that needed finishing.

I spent the majority of my day out on the hillside, cruising the trees for a local farmer. He wanted to clear some of his pine to build a new barn, so he'd hired me to inspect the trees, pick some to fell that wouldn't damage the others, and calculate the stumpage of lumber he would likely get on the harvest. All things I was not only capable of as a silviculturist—tree and forest expert, in layman's terms—but also truly enjoyed. There was nothing in the world like being outside in the forests and feeling the energy of the trees. They were living, breathing beings just like the animals who nested in them or burrowed around their roots. In the simplest of language, wood was my thing.

By the way, never say *that* particular line in a bar full of men. They'll make assumptions.

I ended up talking to the farmer for far longer than expected, which meant that I pulled up at the little house behind the library well after Bennett had planned to pick me up. Thankfully, the man appeared to have some patience. He was sitting on a rocking chair on the porch when I stepped out of my car. And by the fates, did he look amazing in dark pants and a colorful Christmas sweater.

"I'm so sorry I'm late—I was talking pine sap resin with a farmer and lost track of time."

He rose to his feet, smiling my way. "I've heard that excuse before."

That stopped me. "You have?" Because not many people had ever heard of my job, let alone met someone in the field.

Bennett shook his head, chuckling. "Not at all. But I thought it sounded good. What is it you do, anyway?"

"I'm a silviculturist."

"Ah, an expert on forests. How are the trees in Kinship Cove looking?"

I hurried to him, wanting so much to hug him just for that answer. So, I did. I even snuggled into his chest and breathed him in. A little affection never hurt anyone, right?

"The trees here are beautiful and amazing. They make me so happy."

He ran a hand down my back, leaning in when I turned my face up to his. Brushing his lips against mine as he whispered, "I know the feeling, even if it's not the trees I'm looking at."

And then he kissed me. Slow and deep, the sort of kiss that built to more. The kind that made a woman's knees weak and her heart race. A kiss that spoke of promises of things to come.

But we had a long day and night ahead of us, and I wasn't yet in the mind-set to accept more than a kiss.

"I need to change," I said once we broke apart, trying hard not to show how befuddled his kisses made me. "I'm covered in forest."

"Sure. Would you feel more comfortable if I waited out here?"

The man was amazing. I nodded, backing away as I bit my lip. Unable to control my teenage-like obsession with him. Even my reindeer swooned whenever this man was around. We were goners.

Goners who needed a quick shower. "I'll just be a few minutes."

He dropped back into the rocking chair, shooting me a smile. "Take your time. I'm not going anywhere without my Red."

And somehow, I believed him.

It took me less than five minutes to change my clothes and wash the dirt from me. A little makeup, a brushing of my hair, some lip gloss, and I was ready to spend time with my mate. Even the knowledge that he was Pansy's uncle couldn't quell my excitement. Bennett had been proving his kindness to me, had shown his patience and his charm. I was going to enjoy my time with him today and let the worries of what the future could hold wait until tomorrow.

Which was why I was practically skipping when I found him in the same spot, rocking slowly in the shade of the wide porch.

"Ready?"

He looked up, a slow, sexy smile tugging the corners of his mouth. "I'm always ready for you, mate."

Goodness. That word said in Bennett's slow, sultry voice just about sent my entire body into overheat mode. My inner reindeer perked up, her interest obvious. This was our *mate*. Good, bad, or ugly—not that he was in any way, shape, or form ugly—the pull to him was solid and intense. Today was going to be...interesting.

Bennett helped me into his car as usual then rushed around to slip into the driver's seat. He had the engine roaring and his arm behind my headrest as he backed out of the spot when he asked, "Still okay with coming to my house? I cook a mean eggplant parmigiana."

As if that were the enticing factor of the offer.

Though… "Eggplant parmigiana is my favorite."

"You're in luck, then." He shot me a wink. "You, me, and some great food served right alongside an even greater bottle of wine. What more could we ask for?"

The first thought that bounced around my head was a bed, but really…did we even need that? I had a feeling it wouldn't be a necessity. And though the thoughts of the future and Pansy were still there, swirling like dark clouds on the horizon in the back of my mind, I refused to give in to them. One day. I wanted one day of pure joy with the man the fates deemed my perfect match. I wanted to see him in his element, to be charmed by him, and to make sure he was who he presented himself to be.

I wanted to forget the past and simply exist in the moment.

And if that moment happened to include some time spent between the sheets?

So be it.

# 5

# RUBY

Bennett's little cabin in the woods was absolutely adorable, well beyond my expectations in terms of charm. Neat, tidy, well-decorated—with a little snow on the ground, it would be like something out of a holiday movie. Of course, the fact that he had Christmas carols playing, candles burning, and a fire in the fireplace might have influenced that opinion. It could have been a movie set...home of the handsome and yet somehow still single man from town. Hallmark Channel, here we come.

"Would you like some wine?" Bennett asked as he headed for his kitchen. "I'm sure I have a Malbec or two in my collection."

"Yeah, that would be great." I planted myself on a stool at his island, turning to look around. This space was pure Bennett, and I wanted to learn all the details. Big, comfy furniture, the perfect rugs placed just so, throw pillows and blankets in rich colors adding a bit of fun—this was a house that was built to relax in, even if it was a bit too tidy. I had a need to mess a few things up, just like with Bennett himself. Nothing big—I would never do harm—but I felt the urge to make the cabin and the man less perfect.

Bennett with sex hair would be quite the awesome sight.

The man himself handed me a wineglass, giving me a sly smile as if he knew where my mind had gone. "What are you thinking about over there, Red?"

Had my cheeks reddened? Because they were certainly burning at the idea that Bennett might have been able to see into my mind and know I was thinking about him. With sex hair.

*Such good thoughts.* "Nothing much. Just wondering how you manage to keep this place so neat."

"I'm not the biggest fan of chaos. Plus, I live alone—I'm the only one to clean up any messes, so I try not to make them." He pulled a container from the refrigerator and set it on the counter. "Are you ready for something to eat? This won't take too long once I get my oven heated."

"Feeding me leftovers?"

"Not at all. It takes three hours just to make the sauce for this, so I tend to make it ahead and reheat it."

"You make your own sauce?"

He edged across the counter, leaning close. Very close. "If I'm going to do something, I'm going to do it right. Are you hungry, sweet girl?"

How could those words sound so dirty, and why was it so hot in there? I took another sip of wine, not backing away. Staying locked in that hypnotic stare as I melted inside. His green gaze was so intense, so all-consuming, that I couldn't look away even if I'd wanted to. Heck, I could barely blink. No way would my panties survive the night if he kept looking at me that way.

And I was pretty much okay with that. But first...the food. "It's still a little early for dinner."

"It is, so we'll wait on this." Bennett stepped around the island, reaching for my hand. "Come. We can watch a movie or something."

And get to rumple his perfect pillows and hair? "I love the sound of that."

He grabbed my hand—the one without the wineglass because no way was I leaving that behind—and led me to the couch. I sank into the soft, suede-like cushion, curling my legs under me as the seat was too deep to let them hang. And then I sighed.

"This feels like heaven."

Bennett dropped down at my side, angling himself until he was just slightly behind me. Cuddling us together with his front to my back. I wasn't unhappy about the position at all, especially not when he wrapped an arm around me to tug me closer.

"Athena," he said suddenly. "Please turn the living room lights to level three."

The lights dimmed, the room taking on a lovely sort of golden glow.

"That's impressive," I said. "Are you one of those tech people who has to have all the toys?"

"Not at all. My parents sent me a few smart lightbulbs as a Christmas gift last year, and I've been trying them out. I don't have any other smart stuff in the house. You?"

"Nothing. All that technology creeps me out."

"Why is that?"

"Because if the device can hear me, so could other people."

He grunted in what I had to assume was agreement. "I would hope whatever I was doing in my living room wouldn't warrant too much attention from outsiders."

"Like snuggling with your new mate?"

"Like that. Which reminds me—is this okay?" he asked, his voice soft. Such a gentleman.

"Yeah. It's...nice." I finished my wine, tipping the glass up to get the very last drop. Relying on a little liquid courage to keep me in line...or knock me right off it.

"Would you like another?" Bennett asked, his lips close to my ear, his voice a warm caress over my skin.

I shivered, handing him the glass to set on the table behind him. "I'd better not."

"Well, let me know if you change your mind. I'm at your beck and call."

Of course he was.

We settled in to watch a movie—*Bad Santa*, of course, because even reindeer shifters from North Pole had a sense of humor—the two of us cuddled together in a way that was decidedly couple-ish. Not that I was complaining or pulling away. I liked being in Bennett's arms. Enjoyed his touch and warmth. The man was an excellent snuggler.

He was also a vicious tease. He'd been running his fingers up and down my arm with the softest of touches the entire time. I liked it. A lot. Too much, really, if my plan was to stay on the not-getting-my-sex-on side of the line. I hadn't committed to one side or the other, to be honest, but he definitely seemed to be enticing me to let my guard down. And my pants.

Two could play that game.

I rolled slightly, almost lying on my side and using him as a pillow. My view never changed, my eyes still locked on the screen, but that didn't stop me from returning the favor of the arm rubbing. Instead of focusing on his biceps, though, I let my fingers play a medley or two on his thigh. Tickling, tapping, definitely teasing from his knee up, up, up... Go big or go home, right?

"What are you doing down there, Red?" he asked, his voice huskier than it had been. His legs slightly more tense, too. This was one reindeer game I was definitely winning.

"Same thing you've been doing."

He hummed, tapping my elbow. "I was touching your arm."

"I can't reach your arm." I dragged my fingers a little higher, nearly giggling when he groaned. "I can reach your thigh just fine, though."

"Well, thank fuck for that." He slid lower, turning me even more. Settling onto his back with me lying on top of him and staring up at me in a way that made my heart flutter. "Is this okay?"

I nodded, my inner reindeer mentally shoving me forward. Or at least, that was the excuse I would use if anyone ever asked me why I'd dropped down and kissed those plump lips of his. It was all instinct, you see...all animal need. Totally not my fault.

Our lips met again and again, our tongues sliding together as the intensity increased a notch or so. Thank the fates for that because holy holly balls, the man tasted like peppermint again. My absolute favorite. I opened my mouth to take him in, loving the way he didn't surge forward. How he continued to move slowly and with deliberation, how he seemed to be in no hurry.

But when he slid his hands over my hips and deepened the kiss, tugging my entire body closer to his while gripping my ass, I was done with the slowness. I wanted him—right there and right then. He had just taken me from the gonna-have-no-sex side of the line to the gonna-have-*all*-the-sex side.

And Bennett? Oh, he was ready. I rocked my hips into his, finding him hard as a rock. There was no way not to notice. No way I could resist rubbing myself over that ridge again and again. The man had a chimney worth sliding down, naughty list or not. Merry early Christmas to me.

But Bennett broke the kiss, groaning as I continued to move. Holding on tight to my hips even as he whispered a soft, "Ruby—"

"Don't try to talk me out of it," I said, diving in for another kiss. Wanting to turn off my brain for a little bit and just feel. Just take. Just… enjoy. "I know what I want."

Bennett nodded, a soft *okay* escaping from his lips in between kisses. Dropping his hands to my thighs and pulling my legs up to fully straddle him. Oh, he was right there. Just where I wanted him to be but with way too many layers of clothing in the way. Something that needed to be adjusted and fast.

I sat up slightly, reaching for the bottom of my shirt. Tugging it over my head in one fell swoop.

Bennett smiled, sliding his hands up my waist, over my rib cage, and right up to the bottom of my bra. His fingertips teasing ever so softly. "Red again."

As in my bra. Yeah, it was red. And lacy. And really, really sheer. "I always wear red. It's my favorite color."

"It's mine now too."

He groaned as I grabbed his wrists and moved him into position so he could cup my breasts. So he could flick my nipples through the sheer fabric, making my head fall back and my entire body arch into him.

"I like you touching me," I said, adjusting my position so I could once again ride that ridge. So he could tease me in all the right places.

But Bennett wasn't one to sit back and let me take over, it seemed. He jackknifed up, one hand coming to hold me by my neck as he kissed me deeper this time. Tangling his tongue with mine and groaning through the kiss. His other hand stayed on my breast, rubbing and teasing and slipping inside my bra to pinch my nipple. I jerked but pulled him closer, loving the little bit of pain with the pleasure. Adoring the way he was taking over.

What I wasn't prepared for was for him to swing us both to the side so he could stand up and carry me toward the back of the house, to where I assume his bedroom was located.

"Bennett—"

"You deserve better than a dry-hump on my couch." He kicked the door closed behind him before laying me down on what looked like a white cloud of the softest down comforter I'd ever touched. Sweater yanked off his body, pants dropped in a matter of seconds, the man stripped himself naked without care. Without a single bit of self-doubt. Not that he should have had any—he was gorgeous from top to bottom, thick and muscular and all man. He didn't move right away, though. He stared down at me instead, breathing hard, naked and primed with his heavy cock jutting straight out in my direction. Looking fierce and ready. Looking like the man of my dreams.

I couldn't wait another second, so I reached for him. Beckoning him toward me. "Come here, mate."

A dirty trick, using that word against him, but it worked. Bennett grunted and dropped to his knees, yanking me toward the end of the bed at the same time. Groaning loud and long as he gripped my thighs and slowly—oh, so slowly—began to spread them.

"You know once we do this, once I release inside of you, that's it. The mating bond will be set."

I nodded, knowing reindeer husbandry just as well as he did. How the ties of fate would bind us once we did this. No bite needed, no exchange of blood required—we *were* herbivores, after all. Just a round of unprotected sex, and we'd be bound together. I was ready for it. "No condom."

"I'm not going to try to talk you out of anything," he said, his voice gruff and low. His breath teasing my inner thigh. "But you can tell me to stop. Any time, any moment, any reason—doesn't matter. Okay?"

My smile was unstoppable, my hands reaching to grip that wild white hair of his of their own volition as I nodded my acceptance. Even my legs had begun to shake in anticipation of what was to come. I had lost control of my body, but I wasn't scared. This man would take care of me. I knew it down to the depths of my soul—he wouldn't hurt me.

What he would do was tease me relentlessly.

Bennett tugged my pants right off—leaving me in nothing more than my red bra and panty set that thankfully matched—then spent several minutes kneeling between my legs, working his wicked mouth from my ankles up. Stopping way too far from where I wanted him to be before turning to the other leg. I moaned and writhed as he kissed one leg then the other, tugging his hair as well, but he refused to be rushed. Every pass brought him a little closer. Every kiss growing a little longer. A little wetter. A little more luscious.

"You're so beautiful," he whispered as he finally brushed his nose along the front of my panties. "Smart, too. What did I do to deserve such a mate?"

"Maybe you haven't been as naughty as you thought." I groaned and bit my lip as he rose over me, his smile positively wicked. His fingers dipping into the waistband of the red lace still hanging on to my hips.

"Oh, I'm naughty, Red." And then he tugged the panties right down my legs, grabbing and lifting me as he needed to. Before I could do more than chuckle, he was right back where I wanted him to be. And he was spreading me wide for him.

"Please," I murmured, reaching for him again. "Stop teasing me."

He didn't answer, but he didn't need to. With one hand, he grabbed my ankle and placed my foot on his shoulder. He pushed my other leg wider still, then he did exactly as I had been wanting him to do. He dove in, kissing and licking and sucking my wet flesh as I yelped and arched almost off the bed. Oh, the man was good. So good. Every kiss had a strategy behind it, every lick placed precisely. He owned my body with nothing more than his mouth...and then he added in his fingers.

"Fuck, Bennett." I jerked as he slid two long, thick fingers inside me, biting my own wrist to keep from being any louder than I already was. "You're going to make me come."

"That's the goal." He curled those fingers inside me, making me want

45

to scream again. Making me want to beg him for more. Just a little more, just a—

"Fuck, I can't wait to feel you wrapped around my cock."

Maybe it was the way his fingers had found a spot inside me that made me see stars, or maybe it was such dirty words falling from Bennett's lips, but whatever it was—it worked. I came with a yell that may have been the loudest of my life, arching and twisting and trembling under him. My body sucking his fingers in deeper even as I grabbed his hair in my hands and held him still.

"So much," I gasped, still riding that high. Halfway between too much and not enough.

Bennett grunted then released my leg, rising over me. Covering me as he dragged me up the mattress. Dropping his weight onto me as he settled between my thighs. "This pussy is mine now, Ruby. I'll treat it good, though. Every greedy inch of it will be pampered and spoiled, I can promise you that. So soft and wet, all for me."

I chuckled, the possessiveness both a little funny and a lot hot. "And if you're not around?"

"Oh, I'll be around." He dropped a kiss on my lips as he began to move. To nudge his way inside. To thrust slow and shallow as I stretched around his length. "Where would I go when this greedy pussy needs my cock so much?"

I did need it. Too much to put into words. I groaned as he filled me, gripping his shoulders and tugging him in tight. Needing more and faster and harder to come again. And I would come again—I had a feeling Bennett would make sure of that.

Bennett held on to my hips, pinning me in place as he found his rhythm. Staring down at me with such a fierce determination in his eyes, it made me nervous. Made me worry for what was to come. Worry...and want.

"Take it off," he whispered, nodding toward my chest. "Fuck, Ruby—take the bra off so I can see your tits."

I did as he asked, twisting up so I could reach behind my back and unhook the red lace, then tugging it down my arms and dropping it off the side of the bed. Bennett didn't slow down; he simply groaned and kept fucking me. Kept driving himself deeper inside me.

"Better?" I asked, raising my arms to grip his neck. "Is this what you wanted?"

"One thing, yeah." He leaned down, dropping a wet kiss on my lips, still thrusting. And then he curved his body over mine so he could suck a nipple into his mouth. So he could bite it gently before rising once more. "Later tonight, after I get you off a few more times, I'm going to sit with you on my lap and suck on these beautiful tits until you beg for more."

Fuck me. I was going to die if he kept talking like that. "Thanks for the warning."

"Not a warning, a promise. As is this." He grabbed both my legs and pulled them up to rest on his shoulders, kneeling over me as he slid deeper. As he pounded me stronger than before. As he really began fucking me hard. "I'm going to make you come on my cock, Ruby. And then I'm going to cook you dinner, I'm going to get you a little tipsy on wine, and I'm going to eat that pussy again because I want more. So much more. You're going to let me spoil you tonight, aren't you, Red?"

Who could refuse such an offer? But Bennett didn't need an answer from me; he simply kept moving, kept pounding me. Kept pushing me higher and higher until I was nothing more than a writhing, moaning, senseless mess of a woman. Until my pussy was soaked and my clit was tingling and there was no place for me to go. No way for me to escape. No—

"Fuck, Ruby. Your greedy pussy just sucks my cock right in. I love the way you're soaking me right now."

I broke. Shattered, really. Came apart and got put back together by the man with the filthy mouth. The one who knew my body well enough to press a thumb on my clit and drive me higher, the one who chanted my name in my ear as he followed me into the abyss of pleasure with a heart-stopping thrust that nearly knocked my head into the headboard.

The man who owned my body with his.

My mate.

"Mine," I nearly whimpered, clinging to Bennett's shoulders as instincts I had never known existed pushed the word out of my lips. Bennett jerked and growled at my declaration, a quiet sound that spoke to the beast inside me. That pulled the rope binding us a little tighter.

"Yours. All yours." Bennett pulled me in tight, holding me just as firmly as I held him. Seemingly needing me just as much too. I craved his weight and his heat as I came down from the high of what had just happened, and he gave it to me without hesitation. Without fear of being too close. Blissful, that embrace was. Meaningful in a way nothing had ever been before. This was what the fates wanted—what they decreed when they linked us together. Bennett was my man, my fated mate, my forever.

But the thought that slipped into my head as I fell asleep, as I succumbed to the need to rest safely within his arms, was that he was also a Donderson.

And that herd hadn't been good for me in the past.

*But maybe...*

# 6

## BENNETT

I woke suddenly, something pulling me out of sleep in a way that was rougher than usual. Harder to resist, too. A need for something burned deep in my gut, for the physical connection I'd only just begun to explore. Moving on nothing but instinct, I reached for my new mate. For my Red, whose scent lingered all around me. For the warm body that had brought mine so much pleasure.

What I found instead was an empty bed.

My reindeer immediately howled his dismay, both of us moving from sleep into full panic in a blink. I was on my feet in a second, brain clear and heart pounding as I raced down the hall. Ruby was gone. *Gone.* What was I going to do? How was I going to find her? What if she was in danger? What—

"Hey." Her sweet voice coming from across the room when I rushed into the kitchen immediately soothed me. Okay, so maybe I hadn't been completely awake until then. Maybe I had been thinking I was living a nightmare. Or maybe I was so terrified of losing what I'd only just found that even her being out of bed for a few moments had stirred up the wild inside me.

My reindeer and I might have needed to relax a bit.

"You lost, sweet girl? The bed's this way." My voice came out cool and calm, almost completely normal. I was damned proud that I didn't sound like the raving lunatic I'd just been. Still, I couldn't help but hurry toward her. Couldn't stop my feet from crossing the floor as quickly as possible. I didn't want to be away for a second longer than I needed to be.

Ruby simply smiled over her shoulder at me. "Not lost—just nosy. I couldn't sleep, so I came out here." She tugged a book off the shelf, turning it over. Wrinkling her nose adorably. "So, do you actually *like* Hemingway, or is this some sort of showpiece?"

"Empty books. My shelves are filled with them." I chuckled when her startled eyes met mine. "Kidding. I actually like reading Hemingway, though he can be a bit dry."

"Indeed. You're naked, you know."

"And you're not. We should fix that."

She chuckled, putting the book back on the shelf, rising onto the balls of her feet to reach another. The shirt she wore—my shirt—rode up those luscious thighs of hers, teasing me. Giving me a bit of a show.

One I wanted more of.

"So, you couldn't sleep," I said as I moved closer, crowding her. Sensing her body come alive as mine made contact. "And instead of waking me up to entertain you, you came out here to judge my book collection."

"Somebody has to keep you in line."

She wasn't wrong there. "And you think the way to do that is to insult what I read?"

"No." She turned, pressing her back against the shelves and grabbing my biceps. "I think the way to do that is to figure you out. Once I know you, I'll know how to handle you."

"Oh, my sweet Ruby." I leaned closer, my lips brushing hers. Settling into a quick kiss that only left me wanting more. "I think you know how to handle me just fine."

And then we were more-than-kissing—my body against hers, her lips tangling with mine, our hands tugging each other closer. No space between us, no words necessary to set us into motion. Our drive to be together—to bring each other pleasure—was based on instinct. Easy, it was. Natural. And so fucking hot.

Ruby sighed and panted my name softly when I moved to kiss her neck, and I was a goner. Restraint—what little I had—destroyed. I grabbed her thighs, lifting her. Wrapping her legs around my waist and pinning her in place against the rows of books. Trapping her. Controlling her.

*Mine.*

"Bennett, I—"

I cut off her words with the sudden rock of my hips into hers, with the tease of my cock against where she was so hot and ready for me. The thin cotton of her shirt rode up, granting me access. Giving me her pussy to play with. And play was exactly what I wanted to do.

"Do you like this? Me pinning you up against the wall because I can't wait the three seconds it would take to carry you to the bed or the couch? You like pushing me to the point that I have to fuck you right where you stand?"

I couldn't stop myself. I spread her thighs wider, twisted my hips, and slid inside, so fucking thankful that she was as into this as I was. That she was wet enough—aroused enough—for this to happen right there and then. That she clung to my neck and arms and panted my name, making sure I knew she wanted me. And she felt so good. So hot and wet and soft. So perfect for me.

My mate. Fuck, that sounded good even just in my own head.

"Are you mine, sweet girl?" I asked, needing to hear her say it too. Craving her acknowledgment of our connection. "Tell me, Ruby. Tell me who owns this pussy. Whose job it is to take care of it."

"Yours." Ruby groaned and gripped me tighter, burying her face in my neck as she panted and rocked with me. As her pussy soaked my cock and welcomed me home. "I'm all yours, Bennett. And you're mine. My mate."

And if that wasn't the greatest thing I'd ever heard, I didn't know what could be. I may not have been a predator, but I was still a man with a beast inside him. I let out a growl that shook the walls, that had my Ruby gasping and rocking and trying to make me fuck her harder. That told the universe to back the fuck off because no way was anyone coming between this woman and me.

Ruby gripped my shoulders, her nails digging into my flesh, and I lost my fucking mind. The pain, the marks I knew would be left behind, the claiming of me—that one move had my inner leash snapping.

"Fuck, Red." I plunged into her over and over, nearly losing control. Trying hard not to hurt her against the shelves but unable to completely control my desire for her. At least until she squeaked and came for me, until that pussy squeezed my cock like a vise and then trembled all around me. Until I had her pussy juice literally dripping down her legs. Fuck, I loved to make her come. And I was going to do it again.

"Hang on," I said, gripping her ass and carrying her to the bedroom once more. "I'm not done with you yet."

I never would be, but I couldn't say that right then. I didn't want to scare her. She was mine and I was hers, so there would be no coming between us. No ending of things. This was it—my fated mate had accepted me, and I would do whatever it took to keep her happy and sated. To make sure she knew I was hers and hers alone. To care for her.

I would be the best mate possible so long as she let me stay with her.

"I need more," I murmured as I laid her down on the bed, stealing a kiss simply because I could. "Can I have it? Will you give it to me?"

Ruby stared up at me, her eyes a little glazed and unfocused. "Yes. Of course."

Permission granted. I grabbed her by the hips and flipped her over, smacking her ass once she was on her stomach. Crawling up behind her as she lifted her hips like a good girl. Like a woman who knew what was coming and wanted it as badly as I wanted to give it to her. Like my perfect match.

"Fuck, this ass makes me want to do bad things to it." I smacked it again, not as lightly this time, then bent to give that soft curve a bite before rising over her once more. "I'd take coal in my stocking for the rest of my life so long as I could keep my hands on this ass."

Ruby shivered, moaning. Spreading her knees so I could see everything. So I could catch sight of my come dripping out of her swollen heaven. Fuck, she was beautiful in every way, but this...this image was something I'd never forget.

Utterly and totally mine in every way.

Unable to resist for another second, I slid inside her in one long, slow drive. Pushing deep as I gripped her hips. As I yanked her body against mine and began that age-old rhythmic rocking. As I yanked and released and used her cunt to jack myself off. Not that I wasn't also focused on her pleasure. Fuck no—everything was about her. About getting her off. Which was why I licked two of my fingers before wrapping an arm around her hip and finding that little clit. Rubbing it. Pressing that bundle of nerves until I had her going positively wild on my cock.

My girl was so damn responsive.

Ruby groaned loud and long as I fucked her good, her face buried in my pillow. Her hands tangling into my sheets. Submitting to the pleasure I was giving to her. To me. I simply *had* to smack that ass one last time in appreciation.

Coal. Every. Fucking. Year.

"That's it, beautiful," I whispered as she twisted her hips and began to fuck back onto me. As she started to take over in the race to find her pleasure. "Take me. Every inch."

And she did. She took me inside and rocked her hips against mine, refusing to be still. Wanting to participate. And I loved it—adored the give-and-take of the act. Became obsessed with every grunt and groan and hissed curse she spewed. With teasing and fucking and giving until I had her just where she needed to be. And when she came, when her entire body clenched on mine and she lost herself to her pleasure, I finally got her to scream my name at the top of her lungs.

Take that, Nijel.

Sensing she was close to crashing, knowing my own muscles were already screaming from exertion, I thrust a few more times, my rhythm off but my body chasing that final high as she pulsed around me. As her orgasm pulled my own from my body. Coming inside her when I couldn't hold off for a second more. Claiming her as mine again and again as I filled her. As I lost myself to the whole-body effect of us together.

When it was over, when both of us had finally stopped coming, we collapsed onto the bed, her giggling as I clumsily tugged her into my arms. As I clung to her, craving her warmth. Both of us sweaty but happy.

I was so fucking happy.

"I'm so lucky," I said, still trying to catch my breath. Completely blissed out on Ruby and me and our mating bond. "The fates were so generous with me. I don't deserve a woman like you, but I'll do everything I can to earn my place at your side."

Ruby didn't hold back, stretching to kiss me again. Tangling her tongue with mine and making parts of my body wake up once more even though we both needed a break. "I'm the lucky one."

She wasn't, but I'd let that slide. Whatever made her happy. Because that was all I wanted—a happy life with my mate.

I wanted it...and I'd do anything to protect it.

# 7

# RUBY

"You can't be serious."

Bennett—my darling, sweet, amazing mate—stood at the front door of his cabin, dressed in his winter, Christmassy, Fair Isle sweater best. With an ax casually thrown over his shoulder as if that were the most normal thing in the world.

Why was that so sexy, by the way?

"Of course I'm serious. The first snow will be here soon, and I want to get my Christmas tree up before it comes."

Yup. That was what he'd proposed we do the morning after completing our mating bond and spending a full day wrapped up in each other—go out into the woods and chop down a tree. For Christmas.

He was still so...North Pole. "Fine. I don't know how well my shoes will hold up out there, though."

"We could always shift—run through the forest in our reindeer forms. I can carry a bag around my neck."

That would be a solid nope from me, though. I hadn't shifted in... well, long enough that the beast within me sounded a plaintive sort of moan in my head. But today was not the day.

"I'd rather hike. Axes and reindeer don't seem to be a good mix if you ask me."

"Whatever makes you happy, Red." He grinned and reached out a hand for me. "Don't worry. We're not going too far, and I'll carry you on my back if I need to."

"What about the ax?"

"You can carry that."

I eyed the blade at the end of the thing, more than a little concerned. "Sounds like a bad idea."

He sidled closer, smiling in *that* way—the way that made my breath come faster and my heart pump a little harder. The way that made my skin burn for his touch and my thoughts scatter.

*Such a naughty reindeer.*

"You planning on chopping me up, Red?"

He was just so handsome and kind and...not at all what I'd have expected. I was definitely falling for the man.

So, I grinned, and I rose on the balls of my feet to give him a quick kiss. "Not at all, mate."

That smile dropped and his eyes grew heated. I had quickly figured out that he loved it when I called him mate. Such a little thing, but apparently that term turned him on. Something I was definitely keeping in my pocket to play with later.

"Good." Bennett kissed me again, deeper this time, grabbing a handful of my ass and tugging me against him before giving me a smack when he broke the kiss. "Let's go before I toss that sexy ass back on my bed and keep you there for a week."

"That sounds way better than trekking through the woods."

"But at the end of the trek, I'll still be throwing you into my bed, *and* we'll have a Christmas tree."

Which apparently was today's goal and not something I was going to talk him out of.

As I should have known, Bennett made trekking much more fun than I would have thought possible. We didn't just walk or hike through the woods. He chased me through the trees while we played a subtle sort of hide-and-seek. We checked out trees, and he let me rattle on about species and hardiness and stumpage of the ones that should be harvested for the overall health of the forest. We had *fun*. He never strayed too far away from me, left me behind, or complained when something in the woods caught my eye and I got distracted—he simply joined me in checking out whatever it was before we moved along.

And the trees! Don't get me wrong—Bennett was the highlight of the hike—but the trees of the forest were just so astounding. Big, tall, old-growth pines and firs mostly, with that wonderful scent people paid good money to recreate with candles and air fresheners. This was natural, though. This was what came with decades of time given to the trees to grow to their full potential.

Happy trees made a happy me, and these giants were definitely happy.

"Look at them." I rushed to the two huge Scotch pines with thick, heavy branches and the most beautiful dark-green needles I'd ever seen. "They're so healthy. They prefer to grow in pairs, did you know that?"

"I did." Bennett tugged me into his arms from behind, nuzzling into my neck as he held me close. "It's why I don't plant them in my Christmas tree crop—I'd hate to break up a pair one year, and I really don't have room for two Christmas trees."

"They've probably been together for a hundred years." I stared up at the top branches of the trees. The ones that had been around the longest. "Can you imagine all they've seen and been through."

"I can't, but I bet it's been a good life. And they've gotten to spend it together."

I spun in his arms, hearing a wistfulness in his voice. "Are you okay?"

He stared down at me, serious for once. "Just wishing I'd crossed paths with you earlier. If we would have met when we were still in North Pole, we'd have had all these years together."

But back then, back when I was still living at home, his niece had been terrorizing me. I likely would have run away from any sort of tie to their family out of pure survival instinct. Something I couldn't tell him—not yet. I wanted one last day of not dealing with all that history. A few more hours of just Ruby and Bennett before we brought in...others.

So, I ignored the panic his words caused and pushed down the worry once more. *Just one more day.* "The fates had their reasons for not bringing us together then—we have to trust them. Now come on, show me how you swing that ax."

He led me the rest of the way through the forest, holding my hand and chatting aimlessly. At least until we arrived at his Christmas tree farm. Then he became all business. And I...well, I fell in love with the short, little trees.

Bennett had planted balsam and Douglas firs, mixing the two together and obviously working out how to group them for better growth. He didn't plant them in rows like a lot of farms—he planted them in families.

"So," I said as I ran my fingers over the branch of a balsam fir, loving the fragrance it gave off. "Which one is this year's winner for your home?"

"Help me pick."

So, I did, pointing out a balsam that looked a little heavy and full, that would make a beautiful tree. That would have made a gorgeous addition to the forest if it had been given the time to grow up.

"Your farm is so full," I said as Bennett went to work chopping down the tree. He'd taken off his sweater so the view was especially nice, but I was distracted by the trees. As always. "What sort of conservation are you practicing?"

He swung the ax a few more times—damn, the man had some nice shoulders—before stopping to examine the trunk. And answer me, of course. "I do a three-for-one. For every tree I chop down—which is only one a year for my decorating—I plant three." He picked up his ax, striking the trunk once more. "I figure, that way..." Another chop. "I'll always have a tree for decoration." Chop. "Always have backups in case one gets sick before I can utilize it." Chop, chop. "And I can keep the forest around us healthy by repopulating it with trees I have no intention of ever cutting down."

One last chop and the tree fell, leaving a very satisfied—and sweaty—Bennett standing over it. I wasn't sure what was sexier in that moment. Him being all lumberjack-like or the fact that he'd thought about the health and longevity of the forest around us and was doing something to protect it.

Definitely the latter.

Though the lumberjack vibe certainly got my attention.

"How are we going to get this back to your house?" Because I wanted to go home. Now. Immediately. There were very naughty things I wanted to do to my mate that needed privacy. And a bed. The floor would do in a pinch, so long as it wasn't covered in fir needles.

Bennett chuckled, obviously in tune with where my mind had gone as he slipped closer. "I'll drive out with Nijel tomorrow to grab it—he has a Gator, so it'll be easier. Let's get you home and cleaned up."

"I think you're the one needing cleaning up," I said, gripping those biceps. "You're sort of sweaty."

"Does it bother you?"

"Not in the least." A quick kiss and a little trailing of my lips down his neck and over his chest—a tease of what was to come—and we were moving. Bennett wasted no time, tugging me along as we rushed through trees and over hills.

Picking up a rock for some strange reason.

"What's the for?" I asked, pointing to the large stone in his hand.

"It's an agate."

"A what?"

"An agate." He stopped, holding out the orangey-brown rock for me to look over. "They're from volcanic eruptions long before there were any people on the earth. Agate."

My blank look must have worried him, because he frowned.

"You really don't remember this? Didn't you have to take geology in high school?"

High school. With Pansy. My stomach dropped, and my heart raced for an entirely different reason. I'd been in geology with his niece and her cohorts, hiding in the back and hoping against hope every single day that they'd just leave me alone. I definitely hadn't been worried about fancy rocks in that class.

"I must not remember," I said, keeping my voice low. Trying hard to shove all those memories away. One more night—just a few more hours

—then I could tell him. I could let him know why I never wanted to be a part of the Donderson herd. I could lay out my reasoning for needing boundaries and space from them. I wanted a little bit more time to be just Ruby and Bennett—and not Pansy's favorite punching bag and her uncle—before I dealt with any of that.

Bennett, still not having any idea about the full horror of my past with his niece, gripped my hand tighter and started us moving again. "No worries, my sweet mate. I really enjoyed the class, so I remember. You may not have been as interested."

Sure. That sounded logical.

I stayed quiet the rest of the way back, my reindeer and me both growing more and more anxious. I was going to have to tell him everything—the teasing, the humiliation, the years of skipping classes to avoid her. How much I despised his niece, and how I would never—ever —choose to be in the same room with her. I was going to have to make him choose between his family and me.

And I was seriously worried I wouldn't win.

"Come, my beauty," Bennett said when we made it back to the cabin, pulling me from my spiraling thoughts. "Let's take a shower."

"Together?"

He grinned and dropped a kiss on my lips before holding the front door open for me. "It saves water."

Somehow, I doubted that would happen, but I was never one to turn down a chance to be naked with my mate. Even if I did feel as if I were going to throw up from the stress of remembering. Of fearing what was to come. Of worrying that this connection might not be strong enough. "Sounds like a plan."

"Why don't you grab a bottle of wine from the kitchen?" he asked. "I'll get the water going."

Another kiss, another handful of skin and tease of what was to come. Another attempt to lock those bad memories up where they belonged. "I'll hurry."

"I'll be waiting." He sauntered toward the back of the house, looking so damn good. Confident and sexy, that one. For sure.

Me? Not so much…but Bennett made me feel beautiful and wanted. He made me feel valued and special. He was a wonderful mate…

With a horrible family.

I had just selected a Pinot Noir from Bennett's collection when his computer—a fancy desktop model that sat in the living room—lit up and started sounding an alert. The screen said incoming call from "The Boss."

"Bennett," I yelled, staring at the screen. "Your boss is calling on your computer."

"Can you answer that? Just click the green circle."

"Are you sure?"

"Absolutely. He already knows about you, so don't worry—he'll be thrilled to meet you. And I'll be right out."

Okay…so I was meeting his boss over a video call. This wouldn't be awkward at all.

I did as he'd instructed, clicking the green circle to answer and waiting with what I hoped was a strong smile on my face as the screen grew and adjusted.

As a single face—definitely not a he and likely not his boss—appeared on the screen.

As my nightmare became a reality.

"So, it is true," Pansy Donderson said, giving me that same sneer she'd perfected all those years ago, Taking me right back to that place and that girl. "Well fuck, this is going to be fun."

# 8

# RUBY

S o, the rumors are true—you *did* end up mated to my uncle."
I couldn't breathe, couldn't speak. The room had turned hot, and the air had dried up like it would in a furnace or an oven. I was being roasted by this woman over the internet, and my body wasn't prepared. I had slid into full fight-or-flight mode, and I'd never been a fighter. Especially not when it had come to her.

And she knew it. "What...not going to talk to me?" She stuck out her bottom lip in an exaggerated pout and tilted her head, the mocking strong. "We're family now, Crash."

I winced. That nickname. Always that nickname. I'd been clumsy as a child—forgetful and distracted by everything around me as most O'Rudolphs were. Pansy had taken that and twisted it as if something had been wrong with me. She'd used my differences against me. Unlike my grandfather, the great Rudolph of the red-nosed reindeer, there'd been no eventual acceptance of me by my peers, all because of Pansy. She'd laughed and called me names every single day of my life until I'd finally left town. It had been horrible.

And apparently, I was about to relive it.

"Ruby?" Bennett yelled from the back of the house where I could still hear the shower running. I turned toward his voice almost on instinct, my heart breaking at the sudden knowledge of all that I was about to give up. What I never should have let myself pretend I could have. I'd pushed my fears aside to live in the moment, and I was about to pay the price for being so cavalier. So was Bennett, because I couldn't do this. I'd completed the mating bond, I'd fallen head over heels for the man, but I couldn't deal with *this*. Not her and her enabling father—Bennett's only brother—being in my life. Not again. Those scars ran too deep, and I wasn't strong enough to go through it all another time.

So, I slipped my shoes back on, grabbed my purse, ignored the words coming from the computer screen. I turned off all my thoughts while locking down my heart.

And I walked out the door.

Not having said a single word to Pansy Donderson.

It hadn't been a truly conscious decision, my sudden exit. I'd simply acted on instinct, following the path my reindeer played out for me, which was away. Away from the danger Pansy Donderson represented, away from the pain she inflicted. And if that away also meant from Bennett, then we'd have to deal with that particular heartbreak once we were safe again.

I heard Bennett's voice yelling my name once I hit the road, but I didn't stop. I couldn't. Even my reindeer—my sweet, quiet animal form —couldn't resist the need to escape. She wanted us to run, and I was determined to follow her lead. I was actually contemplating shifting so she could take over, so my human brain could settle and give everything over to her. This was pure survival. I'd wanted to die many times growing up, wanted to cease to exist to stop the pain Pansy had caused me. I wouldn't—couldn't—do that again.

I kept walking. At least until a fancy sports car—not as flashy as mine but still quite nice—pulled up beside me.

"Ruby?" Momma from the diner leaned over the passenger seat, eyeing me from behind some seriously stylish sunglasses. "What are you doing out here on the road?"

Running scared. Escaping. Dying a little with each step. "I need a ride back to town."

She frowned but nodded, ever the caring parent. "Get in, child."

So, I did. And then I was gone. Speeding away from Pansy and the Donderson herd. Away from the horribleness of my past. Away from those memories.

And away from Bennett.

## Bennett

The steam billowed around me, the water hot and ready for the two of us. Talking with my boss was going to be quick because I had a mate to get clean. Once I dirtied her up even more.

"Ruby?" I yelled, expecting her to yell back a *yeah* or *what* or, my favorite option, *coming*.

I got silence, which sent a chill straight up my spine.

Something was wrong.

That was when her words came back to me. My boss had been calling—but she didn't know his name, which meant the caller ID on my computer had said Boss. Not my boss, *The Boss*. Which had nothing to do with work and everything to do with the motherfucker who'd destroyed our family with his enabling of his sociopathic daughter. The one whom I would have never—not in a million years—wanted to have access to my mate.

Ruby had likely just answered a call from my brother, Carter—The Boss who'd run our family straight into the ground.

*Fuck.*

I hurried out of the bathroom, looking around. My skin going cold when I didn't see my mate anywhere. Reminders of that morning, of waking up with her not in bed with me, danced through my mind, but this was worse. The house was quieter, the feeling of emptiness definitely overtaking everything else. She was gone. *This cannot be happening.*

"Ruby?"

"She's not here."

That voice coming through the speakers was not a welcome one or even one I'd been expecting. Pansy. Of course, she'd somehow inserted herself into my life and screwed things up. Wasn't that what she'd always done? She and her father, who had never once attempted to rein in her cruelty.

I made my way around the kitchen island, heading straight for the computer with my stomach slowly falling into my feet. Pansy stared back at me from my monitor—thirty-two inches of hate-fueled brat. That's what Ruby must have seen when she'd answered the call as I'd told her to. Lovely.

"Why are you calling? You're not supposed to contact me directly, and you know it." Because she was a manipulative liar and a thief. Because she purposely wrecked everything good around her so she could always be the center of attention. Because I'd grown tired of her bullshit and my brother's support of her years ago and truly wanted nothing to do with any of them. I'd learned the hard way that she and Carter couldn't be trusted, so I didn't.

"I just wanted to talk to you, Uncle Bennett. Wish you happy holidays," she said, her tone tempered. Controlled. Fake. "Daddy says Great Grandpa's getting too old to pull Santa's sleigh anymore and that he'll be asked to step in soon."

Yeah, that wasn't going to happen. "There are three Donderson men in line before him, including our own father, so I doubt he'll be tapped any time soon."

Those dark eyes flashed, the anger obvious. But then she smiled in that fake way she'd perfected and shrugged a single shoulder, sweetening her voice as she said, "Daddy told me different, and I believe him. Don't be jealous that you'll never get a chance to pull the sleigh."

Fa-la-la-la-fuck this shit. "I think we're done here, Pansy."

"I heard about your new mate."

There was a bite to her tone, an inflection on the word mate that sat wrong with me. As was the statement itself—I hadn't spoken to anyone about Ruby. No one except Nijel and his mate, and neither of them would have mentioned a word of it. Especially since they didn't even know my family or have access to anyone in North Pole. No, if Pansy knew about Ruby, it was because she had been snooping somehow. I'd need to run some scans on my computer and check my phone—one of those had to be the weak link. My niece may have been a horrible person, but she was also fucking brilliant. A horrible combination.

And she'd had minutes to unleash her psychological games on my mate.

Ruby and Pansy alone together was not something I'd ever have allowed. Never. I'd obviously screwed up by telling Ruby to answer the call. But before I could fix whatever had happened, I needed some information.

"What did you say to her?"

Pansy laughed, throwing her head back as if her interaction with Ruby had been the funniest thing ever. "Me? I said nothing. I didn't need to. Good old Crash O'Rudolph couldn't even look at me, let alone have a conversation."

"Pansy," I said, keeping my tone hard and harsh. Not giving her a fucking inch.

She shrugged and began picking at her fingers, barely giving me her attention. Playing games as usual. "Look, Uncle, it's not my fault your mate is a little soft in the head. She always was." Her smile returned, a horrible glint in her eye as she met my gaze. "All I did was mention how we were family now, and bam...out the door she ran."

*Fuck.* "Pansy, I've told you—I don't want you calling or talking to me. All communication needs to go through my lawyer."

I got her full attention with that one, not that I wanted it.

"But you're my uncle, Bennett. Family's for life."

And sometimes family has nothing to do with blood and everything to do with choice.

"We're not family, child. Not anymore. You've proven yourself untrustworthy over and over again, just like now. How'd you really know about Ruby?"

She shrugged, twirling her hair with a wicked sort of half smile on her face. "I told you—I heard a rumor."

"Stop lying, Pansy."

My niece could bluff with the best of them. She was also a really good manipulator of others' emotions—she could even cry on command. Which she did right then. "How could you accuse me of that? Why are you so mean?"

"Pansy, I—"

"Everyone is against me," she wailed. But I'd heard that before. I'd been convinced that maybe—just maybe—if I gave her another chance, she'd stop being so cruel to me. I'd been wrong.

More than once.

She hadn't changed a bit and likely never would, which was why I lived so far away from home. Why I set ground rules with her and her father and the rest of my family about using my lawyer as a buffer for any necessary communication. Which was why I knew I'd never get a chance to pull Santa's sleigh because I couldn't commit to being anywhere near her and Carter.

I didn't want to deal with her ever again, so I'd cut myself off from everyone and everything. Until today.

"Tell me how you knew about Ruby, or hang up. I have nothing else to talk to you about."

The tears stopped instantly, her face slipping into her angry mask. Her eyes practically glinting. "It's amazing the things you can have access to when people are sloppy with their network."

That...didn't really make sense to me. "Pansy, I swear—"

"How're you liking those smart lightbulbs Grandma and Grandpa sent you, Uncle?"

And there it was. The answer I'd been waiting for. The only thing I needed from her. I knew she'd eventually give me the information. She couldn't help but want to prove she was the smartest person in the room—and she may well have been. But she was also the worst and had likely influenced my parents in purchasing the gift for me just so she could spy. By the fates, I was an idiot at times.

And Ruby had been right to worry about other people listening in on us. My mate was far smarter than I, and I needed to find her.

"Don't call me again, Pansy."

"But Uncle Bennett, I have so many things to talk about with you."

Another lie, and one I was falling for, much to my chagrin. She didn't need to talk to me—she needed to keep me busy so Ruby could get away. So she could run to the point that I might never find her again. Pansy wanted to screw up my mating.

And she was.

*Fuck.*

I didn't even respond to her. Instead, I hit the key to end the call and hurried out the front door, yelling as soon as I reached the porch. "Ruby!"

No answer. No sight of her either. Just the sound of cars on the road and a lot of trees to hide behind. Shit. She could be in trouble. She could be so far ahead of me that I'd never catch up.

She could be gone. Forever.

I jumped in my sleigh car, revving the engine before peeling out of my spot. Heading down my long drive for the highway. When I reached it, I turned toward town. That would be where she'd go, right? She would know at least that much...right? The other way was nothing but dense forest and empty roads for miles. She wouldn't...

I spun through a U-turn and slammed the pedal to the floor, screaming down the highway toward the mountain roads. Needing to make sure she wasn't lost or scared or hurt. Wanting so badly to be in ten places at once. I drove for a few miles, not seeing any sign of her, before the bond between us—the tingling feeling of her presence nearby —weakened. Okay, fates, wrong way. Thanks for the tip, finally.

I flipped another U-turn and headed toward Kinship Cove, following the feeling of her to the best of my ability, which was sadly lacking.

It wasn't an exact science, tracking a shifter by the mating bond. All I knew was I was headed in the right direction. At least, that's what I hoped I knew. Since I wasn't really sure, I had to put in the work. I checked the roadsides, stopped at the gas station, drove through town and to her house behind the library. Sadly, I came up empty. There was nothing to see and no sign of her at any of those places. I drove for what felt like hours, looking and asking and trying my hardest to find my mate. Our bond was there, tingling inside me the entire time, but it wasn't in tune enough to use it as a beacon. She was close, but where?

I finally stopped at the diner, hoping she'd gone there for some coffee. Knowing Momma would take care of her. Praying the old lady was working since she was likely my only hope.

Momma was there, all right. She spotted me the second I walked through the door, though she didn't greet me with a smile. Instead, she glared my way and stalked closer. Looking ready to fight. The fox in her right at the surface and staring me down as if I'd stomped on her tail.

Uh oh.

"Hi, Momma," I said, trying my hardest to stay calm and be polite even in the face of her obvious rage. "Have you seen—"

I didn't get to finish my question. Not because Momma interrupted me. Oh no, she'd never be that rude.

She smacked me upside the head instead.

# 9

# BENNETT

My brain rattled around in my head for a good ten seconds before it settled back into place. Momma really had held nothing back.

I cupped my ear, wishing it would stop ringing. "What was that for?"

The little fox shifter leaned closer, dropping her voice so our conversation stayed private but not softening her angry tone a bit. "Your niece tortured that poor girl, and you just let her invade your house over the computer? You're not so smart, reindeer."

Fuck...she knew about Pansy. That meant my Ruby had to be there —or at least she had been. "I don't know exactly what you're talking about, but I didn't let my niece do anything. She's not supposed to contact me, ever. Not directly."

"No?"

"No. She's...not kind."

"Yeah, I figured that part out." Momma sighed and nodded her head toward the counter. "Come. Let's see if you can fix this."

That *if* certainly didn't infuse me with confidence. Still, I followed her to the counter, taking a seat as she made me what turned out to be a huge mug of hot cocoa with whipped cream, sprinkles, and even a candy cane for a little touch of mint.

Sadly, my favorite beverage did nothing to buoy my mood. Only one thing would—Ruby. "Do you know where she is?"

"Everyone comes to Momma eventually."

"So, she's here."

Momma shot me an irritated look. "Your mating is complete, yes? Can you not feel her?"

I focused deep, really trying to give that little tingling under my skin all my attention. Trying to understand it.

I didn't, but I tried. "I feel a tingle, but it's no stronger or weaker than what I felt back at my house."

"It'll grow. As will you and Ruby, but not like this." She grabbed my mug right out of my hands and stalked toward the kitchen entrance, shooting me her trademarked glare. "Come with me. Now."

I did as I was told.

Thankfully, when I reached the kitchen, my compliance proved to be the right decision. Ruby sat at the stainless-steel worktable, her head in her hands and an identical mug of what I had to imagine was hot cocoa before her. She looked so lost and sad, though. My heart broke for her.

Momma coughed, catching Ruby's attention. My mate's eyes met mine, and everything inside me thumped. My inner reindeer was ready to break free and go on a rampage, to destroy whatever had put that sad, haunted look on our mate's face. Momma, on the other hand, was calm as a cucumber. She simply pushed and tugged and huffed until she had me exactly where she wanted me—sitting across the counter from Ruby.

"You two," she said, pointing her bony finger at us in turn. "Talk."

Ruby shook her head, making my heart clench in horror that she'd given up on us, but Momma smacked the counter and forced us to look at her.

"Don't be stubborn—talk." She shook her head, walking toward the door to the dining room. "I didn't make it through over a century of a mating with eighteen children in the mix without learning a few things. You can't solve anything if you can't talk about it. Now, talk. I have cleaning to do."

With that, she left us alone.

And silent.

But if it meant figuring out exactly why my mate had left me so suddenly and fixing that, I'd be the one to break the ice for sure. "Ruby, I—"

"Your niece was the biggest bully in high school," she said, her voice quiet and pained. Honesty screaming from every word. "But not like a regular bully—a vicious, destructive one. She made me miserable to the point that I still get sick thinking about it. She made me want to give up on life to get away from all that torture. Seeing her face on that screen—"

"That shouldn't have happened." I reached for her hand, unable to not touch her. Needing so much to soothe her. "She's not allowed to contact me directly. She's not supposed to know anything about my life."

"But she's your family."

I sighed, not really wanting to go down this path—into a conversation that was never easy and not something I liked to think about.

Before I could speak, before I could say a single word, she shook her head and yanked me right out of my own thoughts. "I don't know if I can do this."

My reindeer roared, and I sat up straighter. Fuck this—I couldn't lose her. Wouldn't. Not now, not ever. I just had to figure out how to save our mating, and if that meant talking about the worst, darkest days of my life, so be it.

Ruby was worth every moment of the pain I knew was to come.

## RUBY

Heartbroken. That was the only way to describe how I felt. My heart was literally broken into a thousand pieces in my chest, and I just wanted to cry. I had finally—*finally*—found my mate, the one person whom the fates deemed perfect for me, and I had to walk away because I couldn't handle being in his life when it was tied up in Pansy's. So not fair. And all too much.

I rose from my seat, intent on leaving, but Bennett jumped to his feet and grabbed my hand.

"No. Please." He came to sit next to me, dragging his stool with him. "Just give me a minute, okay?"

His eyes were too soft for me to deny, his closeness too much of what I wanted to ignore. I had a minute for him. "Fine."

He stayed silent for a good ten seconds, looking at our joined hands. Frowning in a way that surprised me. He was such a happy man normally. This was definitely unusual.

"I knew something was wrong with Pansy from a young age," he said, his tone somber and his voice quiet. "Her mom died when she was just a baby, so my family—especially my brother, Carter—coddled her, completely spoiled her as their little princess. But her bad behavior was more than just standard only-child stuff. Nothing we did was ever enough, and she was positively cruel to everyone around her. She never showed a single drop of empathy for another person and was always completely selfish in the things she did. It got worse as she grew older, but my brother claimed not to see it. I tried to tell Carter something was really wrong, but…"

"He refused to listen."

"Exactly. To him, Pansy was perfect in every way, just as his mate had been to him, and he never allowed anyone to speak against her."

"It was the same way in high school when Pansy got into trouble. No matter how many students and teachers would say she did something wrong, her dad would deny it. He'd lie and make excuses for her, blaming other kids and convincing the staff that everyone was against his daughter."

Bennett sighed. "My brother enables her bad behavior."

I knew that much. "I avoided your herd as much as possible. I simply couldn't handle being around all of you."

"Them, not me. We hadn't met." He grabbed my hand tighter,

tugging me closer. "Not until you came to Kinship Cove. I knew who you were, of course. Knew your family. We'd never truly been face-to-face before."

Right. We hadn't, but his family... "Bennett, I just—"

"I didn't know she was being cruel to you," he said, his words fast and his tone a little more desperate than before. "I would have stopped her. My parents stepped in with some others she was mean to when she was younger since my brother refused, so I always figured she'd learned her lessons and had taken to only tormenting us. We never knew about you or anyone else from high school."

That caught my attention. "They stepped in? They didn't just gloss over her behavior?"

"Of course. My brother enables her, but the rest of us don't. Knowing their grandchild was hurting people with her attitude and her words—it gutted my parents and embarrassed my grandparents. We all tried to reason with my brother, tried to convince him to take her to see experts on her behavior, but it didn't work. None of it worked. My parents left North Pole just like I did—to escape the daily lashings her words caused—though they still stay in contact with Pansy and my brother. I don't. I can't."

And he never would be able to if he stayed mated to me. I pushed him away, my head still spinning. My heart still broken. "Right. And that's why I can't stay in this mating. I don't want to be around her. Ever. At all. I can't. She's just...horrible."

"That's fine." Bennett inched closer, his eyes wide. Earnest. "We never have to be. She is not in my life."

"But she's your niece, and her dad is your brother. They're your family."

"Family in name only. Carter and Pansy aren't supposed to call me, they aren't allowed on my property, and they are in no way allowed in my home. Obviously, she broke a couple of rules there, and I'll be ripping those fucking smart lightbulbs out the second we go home—"

"The lightbulbs?" Because that was definitely a subject switch I hadn't seen coming.

"It's how she knew about you. She must have hacked my living room lightbulbs to listen in."

Oh. *Oh.* "She heard us…"

He winced, his face pulling up in what looked almost like a scowl. "Yeah, she likely did. I'm sorry about that. I never even thought she would do something like that."

Funny, but it sounded *exactly* like something she would do. I wouldn't be surprised if she'd recorded us having sex against the bookshelves. The thought made me sick.

"Bennett, she heard us—"

"I know, and I'll deal with it. And I'll make sure she never interrupts our lives again."

The right words, but they were far too easy to say and really hard to live up to. They also put a ton of pressure on me. "I don't want to come between family."

"You're not." He tugged me again, almost clinging to my hand. Looking completely desperate and in pain. "Sometimes the family you end up with isn't the one you were born into. My parents are lovely people—you'll like them—but I had to cut ties with Pansy and Carter a long time ago because she manipulates and destroys everything she touches. That disconnect is not on you—it never would be something we saw as your fault."

But it was still so hard to believe… "And if she comes back?"

"I'll kick her ass out."

Easy. Too easy. "What if you get the call? What if you're needed to pull the sleigh for Santa?"

Something we all—every reindeer shifter from North Pole—wanted deep down. Like a royal title, the position on the team was an honor and a family right. Eventually, Donder would stop flying for Santa, as would my great-grandfather Rudolph. Then the next in line would get their chance. Blitzen and Dasher had already stepped down, allowing their sons and daughters the chance. Pulling that sleigh was every reindeer's dream job, and if Santa called Bennett back to North Pole…if the big man needed Bennett to deliver all those presents…well, that would be a really hard thing to turn down. I was ready to do it so I never had to go back there, but Bennett... I could never ask him to kill that dream. I could never—

"I will never pull the sleigh," he said, interrupting my cycling thoughts. "I don't want to."

"Of course you want to."

He huffed what sounded like a laugh. "Fine, of course I want to, but Carter will make sure that never happens for me, and I've long since accepted that fact. It's not an option or a consideration in my life, and if some twist of fate brought that chance to me, I'd turn it down and allow someone else to take the spot."

"Losing that possibility would kill you."

"No. Being offered that and turning it down would sting. Losing *you* would kill me."

I shook my head, trying hard to absorb his words. To accept them. "Bennett—"

But the man stopped me, grabbing me and yanking me right off my stool and onto his lap. Holding me to him. Bringing us together with a sigh and a shiver that I felt all the way inside me.

"You're my mate," he said, his voice rough. His emotions clear. "My sunshine. My perfect match. My future is with you, Ruby. I know it will take time for you to accept and understand the dynamic here, but I'm begging you to try. I can swear to you, Pansy is nothing more than a ghost from both our pasts. I hadn't spoken to her in years before this morning. I have no intention of speaking to her again unless it's to tell her to leave us the hell alone. And pulling the sleigh is a dream I've long since adjusted to not having a chance at. I would never put the blame on you for any aspect of my refusal to go back to North Pole. I swear it."

I shook my head, wanting so much to believe him. Terrified to find it all a lie.

"I promise to protect you from her," Bennett whispered, soothing me. "Always."

That vow gutted me; it broke me apart and did its best to put me back together. It opened up those old scars and reknit them. "No one ever could."

"I can. And I will." He kissed the top of my head, still holding me.

Soothing the ache of too many years being afraid of someone had caused.

But I'd have to see if it lasted.

"Those lightbulbs have to go."

He nodded. "Consider them gone."

# EPILOGUE

## RUBY

December in Kinship Cove was an almost magical affair. Everyone joined in the holiday spirit—lights illuminating entryways, boughs of pine garland decorated shop fronts, and signs of the various holidays being celebrated could be seen in the homes around town. Add in the light snow that would soon be coating everything, and the place might as well have been a postcard.

I loved it.

Know what else I loved? Walking down those gorgeous, charming streets with my mate's hand holding mine. Bennett and I had worked a lot on our relationship since the day of Pansy's intrusion, and while I wouldn't say we were perfect or that everything had been settled—especially in regard to his family—I could say we were trying. His parents were even coming to visit us for the holidays. I was almost looking forward to it.

And this time, they weren't bringing him any tech gifts that could be hacked. We'd just have to turn the lights on and off the old-fashioned way.

"She's going to fall," Bennett said, frowning as he looked across the street at the bakery. He wasn't wrong. Ginger—one of the three Chance sisters—stood high on a ladder, hanging lights along their stylish awning. As I watched, she did indeed begin to fall, but thankfully, her dragon-shifting mate was there to catch her. The two laughed and snuggled together, looking ridiculously happy.

I had a feeling Bennett and I looked much the same to outsiders.

"I'm glad he was there to catch her."

Bennett raised my hand to his mouth, kissing the back of it. "That's what mates are for."

Something I was slowly learning myself, thanks to him.

"It's going to snow tonight," I said, unable to hide my excitement.

"We should head up into the woods. We can shift and let our reindeers have a little fun."

My inner beast perked up, her nervousness mirroring my own.

"I'm still not too comfortable shifting."

Because we weren't—but I was trying. For him. And for a healthier relationship with myself as well. With my past. Being an adult meant healing some hurts instead of running from them. Something that was definitely a work in progress for me.

"I know you struggle with feeling safe in your reindeer form, but I promise to take care of you. And I really want you to run with me." He tugged me closer, wrapping an arm around my shoulders. "I want to see your rack."

I nearly guffawed at that one. "You see *my rack* every day."

"It's never enough." He yanked me to a stop, nodding toward where a sprig of mistletoe hung above us. Bringing his face to mine to give me one deep, sexy kiss right there on Main Street. "That's never enough either."

"The mistletoe?"

"The kisses." He tugged me toward his car, spinning me around as the first snowflakes began to fall. "Come on, Red. Let's go home and let our reindeer have a little fun."

How could I say no?

We made it to the little cabin in the woods in no time, both of us laughing as we tumbled out of the Santa mobile. I was already half naked before he even made it around the corner of the house, ready to shift. Ready for a little fun with my reindeer side. I rarely let her out, so her excitement was damn near palpable.

"You'd better run once you shift," Bennett said, yanking off his coat and shirt. "When I catch you, it's game over."

I was looking forward to that. I finished pulling off my clothes and shifted, not even giving my reindeer time to shake out her fur before running up the hill and through the tall pines. The forest called to us, the scents and sounds another form of home. As was simply being in her body for a while. Surprisingly, there was no fear in Bennett's woods —no worries or stress. Nothing but the absolute joy that came with being a reindeer on the cold, wooded mountainside with my mate right behind me. Supporting me. Never leaving my side. Bennett was right— being with him in the woods was fun.

We ran for a long while, cresting hills and sliding into valleys along the way. Enjoying every second out in the wild and the weather. It wasn't until I reached Bennett's Christmas tree farm—until the snow in the air grew thicker, falling faster—that the man chasing me finally stopped. His reindeer stood on top of a small hill, looking like a beast. Like the leader of our herd. I nearly shivered at the thought of that. And one day, he would be leading our herd. Our family. The one we would make ourselves. Though I'd definitely take Momma's advice.

Three children would be more than enough for us.

I shifted human once more, giving Bennett time to approach me. Running my fingers over his soft muzzle when he reached me and letting him rub his head against me to scent my skin before dropping a kiss between his ears.

"Shift, my mate," I said. "We can do more than just run through this snow."

He shifted human, his naked body wrapping around mine immediately. Warming me in the chill of the air. Without warning, he picked me up and carried me beneath a heavy bough of one of the trees to a spot not yet covered in snow. The fallen needles cushioned my back as he settled on top of me, the roughness a nice dichotomy to the solid man above me. This moment, this place, this feeling—all of it came together to fill me with a sense of rightness. Of belonging. This was where I was meant to be, and Bennett was who was supposed to be with me.

"I really do like your rack," Bennett said, leaning down to kiss my right breast then my left. "Thanks for sharing it with me."

I chuckled, pulling him closer. Needing to feel him everywhere. To be surrounded by him. "Thanks for keeping me safe."

He grew serious, his green eyes staring into mine. His earnestness such a turn-on to me. "Always, Red. That's what I'm here for."

I shifted my hips a little, feeling him slide into place. Ready for more than just a snuggle in the cold. "Love me, mate. Make me yours."

"Mine," Bennett said, then he kissed me long and deep, nudging his way inside even as his tongue tangled with mine. Spreading my legs wide and filling me with himself. Claiming me as his once more.

"Yours." I gripped his shoulders, pulling him closer. Closing my eyes at the initial sting of him entering me. At the stretch I loved so much. "I'm yours."

"Forever. I'll take care of you, my mate. Always."

And just like every other time he'd told me that, my trust in him grew a little bit more. He would keep me safe—physically, mentally, and emotionally. I still had my fears and my memories to deal with, but Bennett never wavered in his support of me. Never broke from his promise that he'd put me first.

I had him on my side.

I had my mate.

Forever.

What more could I ask for?

# PEPPERMINT PRANCER

## KINSHIP COVE: HEARTTHROBS & HOLIDAYS

*It's the holidays for our Kinship Cove friends, which means treats, hot cocoa, and kisses.*

Being an elf in North Pole, Alaska, means one thing to me: baking to support my fellow elves who are responsible for making toys. When a fellow kitchen elf takes a tumble days before the big gift run, I'm assigned to the reindeer shifter side of town. Carb-loading is my specialty, after all. No way would I let the reindeer team fail after a solid year of work by elves and reindeer alike. I know my role—get in, bake, get out—but while delivering delightful pastries to the hungry sleigh-pullers, I run into a problem. One by the name of Prancer.

Yes, he's a reindeer shifter. Yes, he's an OG on the sleigh team. And yes, he's just as obsessed with me as I am with him. But each species has its rules, and everyone in North Pole knows we have to work together to pull off the Christmas run. Which means keeping the secret of our fated connection from everyone—elves, reindeer, Santa…

Even Prancer himself.

Christmas is coming whether we're ready or not...and it's going to be a battle to keep my ho ho ho on the down low low low.

# 1

# LOLLY

H ot behind."

"If only every elf thought that," I mumbled under my breath as I leaned forward against the counter, still kneading dough and making sure whoever needed to run past me had the room required to keep us both from getting burned. The kitchen buzzed with energy, breakfast for Santa's elves a big affair with all the best foods to start the day—French toast, cinnamon rolls, snickerdoodle bread, and lots and lots of peppermint hot cocoa. Only the best for the workers at the North Pole. Especially since their jobs of researching, buying, and making toys were over. Over the next couple days, they would complete the final organization of the magic sack for Santa to pull from and then...Christmas. The best time of the entire year for Santa's elves.

Lots of vacation time coming up after a year of hard work.

"Lolly."

I jumped, my focus darting to the older elf by the office door with a clipboard in his hand. One of the bosses. "Lolly, I need to see you."

Odd—I wasn't usually an elf who got into trouble. My stomach sank, but I dropped the dough we needed for the lunch service in a bowl and covered it with a clean towel before hurrying his way, calling out the usual alerts that kept the kitchen safe. You had to make sure people knew you were there, but it still got annoying. I would likely be yelling *corner* and *behind* in my sleep until the day I died.

Which could be today because—again—I never got into trouble. Ever. I just hoped I didn't throw up all over myself when he started yelling at me.

"You wanted to see me?" I gave the elder elf—Balthasar—a small smile, wanting so badly to wring my hands but holding firm. *No fidgeting. No fidgeting. No puking either.*

"Good morning, dear." He looked at me over his glasses then shifted his gaze back to his clipboard. "Maeve—you know Maeve, right—well, she took a bit of a fall last night and will be requiring time off. I need someone who can bake at that level to send to the reindeer kitchen. Would you be interested?"

I blinked. And again. The reindeer kitchen was quite the promotion. That honor had never even occurred to me in all my years baking for the elves. "And you're sure you want me?"

Balthasar gave me a hard look, frowning slightly. "I wouldn't have called your name if I did not. You're one of the best bakers we've got, and we have a duty to Santa to make sure his team is well fed and fueled up for the big night. Maeve is unable to do her duty, so are you interested in stepping into her place?"

"Yes." I nodded, finally giving in and wringing my hands—in excitement, not nervousness. "I would love to bake for the sleigh team. When should I go?"

"Now, dear. Arthur is already on his way over with a few trays of cinnamon-date buns. Make sure they're served the second you arrive so the team isn't late for training." He scribbled something on the paper clipped onto the board and then stabbed me with a hard, icy stare. "No distractions, no mistakes. We only have a few days before the team flies out for the big trip, and they're going to need some major carb-loading to be able to make it through the night. I expect you to help with that. Your cinnamon-date buns are the best and most nutritious breakfast pastry we serve—even the Queen thinks so."

I grinned, unable not to. No one had wanted me to try sweetening the buns with dates instead of sugar, but I'd done it anyway and they had been well received. Far more accepted than I'd even known, apparently. "Yes, sir. I'll do my very best, sir."

And with that, I spun around and hurried out the door, racing across the snow-covered brick walkways toward the kitchen on the opposite side of our downtown area. Shops were just opening up for the day, grocers and bakers and creators setting out their wares to attract elf buyers as they took their breaks from work. The entire area would be buzzing like the kitchens by lunch, but I would be busy. I would be baking *for Santa's reindeer team.* I still couldn't believe it.

"Hey, Lolly." Jackson, owner of the little bookstore I frequented, waved as I rushed past, his bright smile a constant in the alley. I would have to stop by later—maybe pick up a book or two—maybe tell him all about how I ended up cooking for the reindeer.

*The reindeer.*

That might not seem like such a big deal to some, but the team that pulled the sleigh were practically celebrities to me. True, most of the original reindeer had moved on—mates and families didn't get along with Santa's scheduling—but two of the nine were still flying. That duo was legend. I'd never met any of the team, especially not the two old guard, but I wanted to. To bask in their presence for even a moment would be such a gift. Something that could actually happen if I was able to serve the reindeer on time.

Which meant I needed to stop daydreaming, run faster, and get my *hot behind* to work.

I did just that, rushing through the door leading to the training center kitchen in no time. Elves scurried about—chopping, frying, prepping, rolling, slicing. Every station looked neat and tidy, every person shouting as they moved just like they should. The sight was the organized chaos of a well-run kitchen, and I couldn't wait to find my station and jump into the mayhem.

"You must be Lolly." An older, female elf I'd never met approached, her eyes sharp but the small smile on her face soft. "I'm Miss Cici, and I'll be running this madhouse today. Your buns were already delivered and are in the warming ovens, and we've set up a station for you." She pointed to a space toward the back—one surrounded by plastic bins of white powder. Flours.

"How long until I need to serve?"

She clicked a button on her pen, which lit up at the top to show a tiny digital clock. "Three minutes. I know we're rushing you, but as soon as those buns are delivered, I'm going to need you to start on the rolls and things for later. These reindeer go through a lot of bread."

"Carb-loading," I said.

Miss Cici nodded, her smile growing. "Exactly. I set up your station, but it's been a number of years since I've baked for the team. If you need anything at all, you call me. I've also assigned an elf named Arthur who's going to stick around to help you carry and serve your breakfast buns. Got it?"

"Yes, ma'am."

"Good. Now, go—the sleigh and backup teams are waiting on us."

With that, I was off, racing across the kitchen to the area I was about to claim as my own. On the way, I grabbed some butter and eggs from the refrigerator so they had time to come to room temperature. I also snagged a bit of star anise—every elf who worked in the kitchens had their tricks, and I was about to show those reindeer one of mine.

"Ready to serve?" Arthur asked when I made it to the baking corner. He had his eyes glued to a timer, his hand on the door to one of the vertical ovens. Always prepared, that one.

"I need thirty seconds." I grabbed a grinder and dumped a few of the star anise inside, then hit the grind button. Once done, I tipped the now-ground spice into a bowl and added a heaping cup of turbinado sugar. I whisked those together until it seemed blended, then added a tablespoon of cinnamon and some nutmeg. More whisking, more watching the clock. Just seconds left.

"What's that?" Arthur yanked open the oven a moment before the timer went off, pulling out trays of cinnamon-date buns and placing them on a cart we'd wheel into the dining room. Beautiful, thick buns with a sticky, sugary top. *So perfect.*

"This is my secret—it adds a little boost of flavor directly to the palate. It's like a sweet and spicy supercharger for the buns." I sprinkled the mixture over every roll, knowing they'd come out as perfect as ever but still worried. This was it—Santa's team, and possibly the big man himself, was about to eat something I'd made. "My hands are shaking."

"These buns are the best breakfast pastry at the North Pole and healthier than any other option because you use dates in them. You have nothing to worry about." And with that, Arthur pushed the first trolley of buns toward the door to the dining room.

"Nothing to worry about. Right." I didn't buy that line, but there was nothing I could do about it now. So, I took a deep breath, and I raced after Arthur.

And I really, really hoped the reindeer liked my buns.

The second I opened the door, though, I was met with only one thing. Noise. A wall of noise slammed into me when I entered the dining area.

*Holy peppermint sticks.*

The reindeer—so many more than the nine who pulled Santa's sleigh —were talking, yelling across tables, and generally being a bit rowdier than I would have expected. Still, I kept my chin up and didn't falter. I had a job to do—feed these beastly men and women so they could bring a little joy to people around the globe. Santa needed me to do my best. I would not let him down.

"Start here?" Arthur asked, indicating the end of one of the long tables. The one at the front of the room. The one that sat a little quieter than the rest.

"Is that the lead team's table?"

Arthur nodded, grabbing plates and putting on his game face. "May as well feed the most important ones first. They're a nice group— normal folk like the rest of us, from my past experiences with them."

"Normal. Right."

I followed Arthur as he delivered cinnamon-date buns to the reindeer shifters at the table. They were so much bigger than either of us, so much more muscular. I was forced to sprinkle the magic mixture over the roll before we served it or else I would have had trouble edging my way in between some of them. Not that I would have minded—there was certainly no lack of good looks in their gene pools. While the reindeer were a mix of genders and ages, the couple of the old guard reindeer left at the table were easy to spot. The originals could be identified by their graying hair and broader shoulders, the slight wrinkles at the corner of their eyes and their air of experience. The men who had been the ones to first haul Santa around the world with a touch of elf magic were very...daddy-esque. Not something I was going to complain about, for sure.

Sadly, the reindeer paid me no mind. Not even to say thank you. But I was okay with that—shifters and elves didn't really mingle except in situations like this, where we did some sort of quick, quiet service. Their ability to overlook us was completely normal.

I was just about to serve the last bun, just about to give the man in the end seat his sweet breakfast treat, when he turned and looked down at me. His lips twisted slightly, and his brow furrowed, his curly graying hair flopping slightly with his motion. Deep brown eyes met mine, and I froze. Locked in place by the energy in that gaze.

Sexy. The only way I could describe him was *sexy*.

*What now?*

"Sir, I..." I stopped and licked my lips, trying to find my voice. "Sorry. I have hot buns for you."

The corner of his mouth kicked up, a sparkle developing in those soulful eyes. "You do now? And what sort of buns are we talking about?"

Burial by snowballs could not have stopped the burning sensation racing through my body. Why did I have to say hot buns? "It's a cinnamon-date bun, sir."

He leaned a little closer, keeping his eyes on mine and dropping his voice as he said, "And what if I told you I don't like cinnamon rolls?"

My answer came quick—without thought or planning. "They're not cinnamon rolls—they're cinnamon-date buns. Besides, you don't know a cinnamon roll unless you've had mine."

He gave me a nod, still staring. Still holding me in place with his gaze. How did he do that?

"Then I guess I have to give you a try." And with that, he sat back, giving me room to place his plate on the table. I didn't pre-sprinkle this time. I stepped onto the rung of his chair, bringing my body closer to his, and gave him a quick smile before sprinkling the sugary-spice mix on his bun right in front of him.

"What's that?"

"My special topping. Trust me."

He grunted, the sound making my heart jump a little.

"Ready now?" he asked when I was finished sprinkling and had stepped off the rung of his chair.

"Yes. Give it a try—you won't regret it."

I waited, watching with more anticipation than the time I'd fed the big man himself, as the man slowly lifted my bun to his lips. He kept his eyes on mine, kept a sense of intimacy in the moment, as he took a bite. A big bite. As soon as the pastry touched his tongue, he jerked, his eyes darting from it to me and back. His chewing quickened, and he sat a little deeper.

Death by cinnamon-date bun. *I win.*

My almost arrogant shrug came naturally, my pride something I was unable to hold back. "Told you they were the best."

He nodded, still watching me. His stare intense. "What's your name, little one?"

"I'm Lolly. And you are?"

"Prancer."

I nearly stumbled backward. I'd known because of the gray hair and the daddy aura, but hearing him say the name, knowing this was one of the originals, still stunned me stupid. "You're...Pra...*the* Prancer."

The man across from him—the one who had been completely silent so far—laughed. "Yes, ma'am. That's the prancing man over there. Just out prancing all the time in his prancing shoes."

Prancer rolled his eyes, finally letting me escape that magnetic gaze. "Shut up, Cupid."

Two originals. Holy Christmas trees. "I'm sorry—I shouldn't be taking so long to serve these."

Cupid—the other original left. Tilting tree toppers, this was all too much. When the two started sparring verbally, I scurried away from the table so I could drop off the rest of the buns and hide in the crowd. I couldn't get Prancer off my mind, though. Those eyes, that slight smile, the depth in his voice. That man was sexy.

Too sexy to want anything to do with me.

Completely out of my league for a lot of reasons.

The first being that reindeer and elves didn't mingle like that.

Still, as I raced into the kitchen to begin working on the bread for lunch, I couldn't help but look back to the table where Prancer sat. Where he seemed to have been watching me from. My eyes met his, and an electric charge shot through me. One more reminder of the weird connection between us.

*If only...*

# 2

# LOLLY

From sweet to savory—from warming spices and sugar to herbs and aromatics. Such a fun flip to be a part of. Lunch for the team would be pasta with a thick cream sauce and lots of buttery garlic bread. The latter was my responsibility, and I took great care in making sure the dough had enough time to proof, that my garlic-butter sauce was applied at just the right time so no one ended up eating burned garlic, and that the crust was good and crunchy while the insides stayed super soft. Exactly as they should be.

"These are good, child," Cici said as she came to inspect my work. "Well done. We'll be serving in ten if the team stays on time."

"I'll be ready." I double-checked my pans, baskets, and counts, knowing I'd made too much but wanting—needing—to feel as if I were contributing to the team's success. And I couldn't lie—a certain brown-eyed reindeer may have been on my mind as I'd drenched the bread in butter sauce. I hoped he'd like it. Dreamed of hearing that little grunt of approval again.

*Focus, Lolly. Focus.*

"Anything else we need?" I asked as Arthur came to roll out a cart of the bread a few minutes later.

"Nothing, Miss Lolly. I'll handle this part."

A stab of disappointment zinged through my chest. I'd hoped to be the one to deliver them. "Of course. Thank you for that."

He nodded and set upon his job, carrying trays stacked high with baskets of hot garlic bread, while I grabbed a towel and began the process of cleaning my station. I'd still need to finish the dinner and dessert baking, but no one wanted garlic in with their Italian cream horns. Everything had to be refreshed before I could move on.

I was in the middle of stretching to reach a container of the more obscure extracts we had available when someone slipped in beside me. Someone warm and smelling like balsam and so very exciting.

"Allow me." Prancer—all well-over-six-feet of him—grabbed the container and set it on the counter, staring down at me in that intense way of his. "Anything else I can do for you?"

Oh, the places a woman's mind could go when presented with such an open-ended question.

Places not at all appropriate for the moment.

"That's all I needed. Thanks."

He made that grunting sound, the one that did strange things to my heart and my stomach and...other places. The one I'd been dreaming about while making the garlic bread. My memory and imagination had not done the sound justice.

"What are you doing back here?"

Prancer shrugged, leaning back against the counter and taking up more space. "I never got to say thank you for the cinnamon roll."

"Cinnamon-date bun, and there's no need to thank me. It's my job."

A nod, a slight frown. What *was* he thinking?

I laid my hand on his arm, looking up at him. Unable not to sidle just a little closer. "You look pensive. Is there something I can do for you?"

Those brown eyes burned a hole right through me, his intense stare making me tremble with something too strong to think about. But honestly—the way he *looked* at me. How did the women in his life survive such gazes?

"I would very much like it if I could walk you home, Lolly."

His words danced through my head without rhythm, not quite making sense. I cocked my head as I tried to make heads or tails of him.

"You remembered my name."

"Of course."

"And you want to walk me home?"

"Yes."

"But I'm not done with work."

"I meant after work. When you are done. I'd like to be the one to escort you home."

Again...no sense. "But it's safe around here—no one needs to take me home."

His grunt turned frustrated, and he kicked off the counter, stalking closer. The man pinning me against the prep station behind me. "Need and want are two very different things. I very much *want* to walk you home after work. Would that be acceptable to you?"

I could only nod, only stare into those eyes and try my hardest not to drool.

"Good. I assume you finish up while we eat dinner."

Another nod from me.

"Fine. I'll come back here once the meal is served."

"Don't miss dinner," I said, suddenly worried about his strength and conditioning. "It's been a heavy carb day, but dinner will be more protein-focused."

"I'll be fine. I don't usually eat dinner anyway." He made as if to move, perhaps to walk away, then he stopped and gave me another solid stare. "Are you making dessert?"

My turn to nod. "Italian cream horns. Not my specialty, but very yummy and a favorite of the elf kitchens."

His lips turned up into a smile as he began to back away from me. "Save me one. See you in a few hours."

And with that, he was gone. Back to the reindeer world, while I worked away in the elf one and tried to understand what in the flickering fireplace had just happened. If anything.

My entire body vibrated with the energy he'd left behind, so *something* had definitely happened.

Something that left me reeling and with so many questions. How could he make me tingle so much when he hadn't even touched me?

And what would happen once he actually did?

Prancer was nothing if not true to his word. And prompt.

"Just about done?"

I glanced up as I scrubbed my station, smiling at the man who'd just walked in through the kitchen doors at the same time the last serving cart had been pushed out of them. "Almost."

I tried not to think about the fact that he was standing off to the side, waiting for me. Tried not to notice the other kitchen elves watching us. Staring, really. Instead, I focused on making sure every inch of my station was cleaned and ready for the next morning because there was nothing I could do to stop their questioning. This was all...unusual. Reindeer didn't enter the kitchen—it simply wasn't done. And yet, there he was, way too tall and big and taking up so much space. Because of me.

Lords a-leaping, I had no idea how I was going to survive this night.

I put the last dirty bowl in the industrial washer and tossed my towel into the bin to be laundered before taking a deep breath and approaching him. No more wasting time.

"I'm ready for you to take me home now."

His eyes darted to mine, and his smile grew. "Then let's go, Miss Lolly."

I led him through the kitchen and out the back entrance, allowing him to hold the door for me as we stepped outside. A cold wind raced through the brick-paved alley, but that wasn't the only thing making me shiver. Prancer had put his hand on my lower back to lead me. No skin on skin, no actual flesh touching mine, and yet I shivered. The man had some sort of serious power over me.

"How long have you been working in the kitchens?" Prancer asked as we casually strolled toward the elf side of town.

"Most of my life. I was never good with tools and building things, so I bounced from different areas of service through my training. Once they put me in a kitchen, I knew I was home."

"So, you like to cook."

"No, I like to *bake*."

He frowned, his brow furrowing under his graying curls. "What's the difference?"

"Cooking is gut feelings and guesses and tossing things together to build the flavors. Baking is chemical reactions and experimentation and precision—it's science. I really like science."

"I like science, too."

"You do?"

"Yeah. Before Santa came to us needing help, I'd been studying geology." He shrugged, an almost shy smile dancing across his lips. "I like rocks."

I grinned, biting it back as best I could. "I like rocks, too."

"Yeah?"

"Yeah. I collect crystals and things. Shiny stuff, rocks with colors that appeal to me, ones that feel good in my hand."

"Worry stones. Are you worried, my little one?"

Such a loaded question. "Not at the moment."

It was his turn to smile. "Good. Now, what is this place?"

I glanced up, not realizing we'd made it to the shopping district of elf village. "You've never been here?"

"No, ma'am. Can't say that I have."

"This is Tinsel Trail—it's our shopping district." My thoughts tumbled, the differences between us bubbling to the surface. "Do you have something like this on the reindeer side?"

He grunted, his eyes dancing from one building to the next as he took in the sights.

"We do but not nearly this charming. Ours is more...functional."

I took another look at the alley, taking it in with fresh eyes. The boughs of pine decorating the buildings, the colorful awnings, the rounded-top doors, the golden lights glowing all along the rooflines and draping across the alley. It looked like a winter wonderland for sure... and I hadn't given thought to how lucky I was to see it every day in more years than I could count.

"We like things cozy."

"I can see that." He placed his hand on my back again, letting me lead us through the small crowd of elves running errands and enjoying their time out. We received a few looks—okay, more than a few—but I kept a smile on my face and focused on the warmth of the man beside me.

We were halfway through the alley, moving closer and closer to my little apartment over the pharmacy, when an elf child raced out of the bookshop and nearly slammed into Prancer. He chuckled as he caught the tiny boy, crouching down to address him at his level.

"Where are you going in such a rush, young one?"

The little boy looked up at the man with huge eyes, his shock obvious. "You're a reindeer."

Prancer cocked his head. "Not at the moment, but yes."

"My mommy says the reindeer are like royalty."

A booming laugh exploded out of Prancer, his head tipping back with the force of it before he refocused on the child. "We're not royalty at all, just men and women with a different sort of job is all." He leaned closer, shooting me a wink before he drew his face into a serious expression. "I think the royalty are here in the elf community. You know why?"

The boy shook his head, enthralled.

Prancer nodded toward me. "Because right there is a woman so pretty, she could only be a princess. Don't you agree?"

The boy looked me over, so very serious. Really giving the idea some thought. Finally, he nodded once. "She is very pretty."

My face heated and my ears tingled. "Thank you, kind sir."

A harried-looking woman raced out of the bookstore, visibly calming when she saw the boy. "There you are." She nearly stumbled when Prancer rose to his feet, looking up at him with eyes almost as wide as her son's. "Is everything okay here?"

"Of course," Prancer said, returning to my side. "The young squire was just talking about princesses with me."

Her brows pinched, her confusion evident, but she rolled with the moment and didn't question things. "Thank you, sir, for entertaining him."

"It was my pleasure."

She nodded once, reaching for the hand of the little elf. "Come, Timmy. We have to get home."

Prancer and I watched them leave, neither of us moving. At least not until I turned toward the bookshop, not willing to end the evening just yet. "There's a nice coffee shop inside there. Would you care to join me for a warm beverage?"

Prancer's smile spread slow and wide, his eyes pinning me in place. "Are you asking me out on a date?"

More heat, more tingles. "I mean..."

"Because the answer is definitely yes if you are."

"Then, yes. I'm asking you out on a date."

He grabbed my hand, setting my fingers on fire with the energy between us. "I'd love to have a coffee with you."

I led him into my favorite store in the alley—Be Jolly Books. The space I'd spent hours and hours in as I perused various books and magazines. I'd always liked to read, and when I'd found my talent with baking, that fondness had turned into something closer to an obsession. I owned a lot of cookbooks. Likely too many.

If there were such a thing.

"What do you like here?" Prancer asked as he looked up at the minimal menu board.

"Gingerbread latte. With whipped cream. And an extra shot of espresso."

He smiled down at me. "Do you ever sleep?"

"Only when I have to."

Prancer laughed then redirected his smile to the girl behind the counter. He may not have noticed her apparent shock at seeing the man towering over her usual clientele of elves, but I did. I also noticed the way people were still trying to sneak looks at us. Some were even downright staring. It was...frustrating. Just because the man stood a solid foot over the tallest elf didn't mean he should be stared at. Just because his ears were rounded instead of pointy and he had a more muscular build than any elf ever would didn't mean he was that much different than we were. And really, so he pulled Santa's sleigh. That fact didn't make him *that* special, did it?

Ugh. It totally did.

"What's got you frowning, little one?"

"I'm not a child, you know," I snapped, unable to hold my emotions in check.

Prancer reared back, frowning himself. "I'm fully aware. Do you not like me calling you little one?"

"No, it's not that." I sighed, feeling horrible for my biting tone but unable to get over how uncomfortable the bold stares were making me. "I just...don't like drawing attention to our differences."

He paused, eyeing me. "Do you mean the differences like...I'm a shifter and you're an elf? Or are we talking solely appearances?"

I shrugged, growing more uncomfortable with all the eyes on us. Prancer must have noticed because he glanced around before grabbing the drinks and directing me toward a booth at the very back of the store. The lighting had been turned a little lower back there, and the higher walls leant an air of seclusion in an otherwise crowded space. The world disappeared once I slid into that booth, the outside influences gone. There was just Prancer and me left. We were alone. Sort of.

"Better?" Prancer asked once I'd sipped my coffee and sighed.

I nodded, returning the smile he gave me. "Yeah. Sorry—we don't get a lot of reindeer on this side of town. Or any, really. I know everyone is just curious as to why you're hanging out here, but being stared at like that made me uncomfortable."

"I understand. So long as I'm not the one making you uncomfortable."

"Not at all." I sat back, coffee in hand, and grinned as he obviously looked me over. "What?"

He took a sip of his coffee and shook his head, taking his time to answer me. "Just thinking how beautiful you are with your cheeks all flushed from the heat."

Pretty sure my cheeks flushed even more if the temperature of my neck and face were any indication. "I'm an elf—we flush. A lot. Especially when it's too hot. That's why most of our stores are colder than average—we need it. What about you?"

"What about me?"

"Do you prefer the heat or the cold?"

"Shockingly, the cold."

"Not surprising, what with all that fur."

He laughed. "I'm not furry all the time."

True. Very, very true. Though I had a feeling parts of him were fu—

"But honestly," he said, yanking my attention back to the moment and away from thoughts of where he might be furry even in his human form. "Give me cold winter weather, some snow, and the darkness that tends to come with this time of year, and I'm a happy man."

"I like the darkness, too," I said, knowing not everyone appreciated how little we saw the sun in the winter months this far north. "Forces everyone to turn on the lights and gives the world a bit of a golden glow."

"A perpetual gloaming."

"Very true."

"What else do you like?"

I shrugged, the question too vague for my mind to focus at first. "I like to bake, but you know that. I like to read. I collect cookbooks. I drink way too much coffee. I ice-skate whenever I get the chance. I have an unusual obsession with Halloween considering what I am and where I live. And I'd really like to know more about you, so I'm going to stop now."

Prancer bit back a grin, those dark eyes of his locked on mine. "You're adorable."

Oof, the word rankled. "Still not a child."

He grew serious, his smile dropping. "My apologies. How about beautiful, amazing, enthralling, or charming. Are those better?"

I swear, my cheeks felt as if they were on fire. "Much. Now, don't avoid the issue at hand. Tell me about yourself."

He sat a little deeper, his easy smile returning. "Well, let's see. I prefer sweet to savory, so your baking is going to be a joy, I assume. I like to read—horror, mainly, but also mysteries. I don't collect anything, but I have an interest in old radios and wouldn't mind buying a few more. I rarely drink coffee. I've never ice-skated, but skiing is my favorite sport.

I really like the idea of Valentine's Day but have never celebrated it. And I'd especially like to celebrate it with you."

"You barely know me."

He leaned forward, grabbing my hand that had been resting on the tabletop. "Maybe not, but I really like what I do know."

It was my turn to bite back a smile. "I like what I know about you too."

And so it began, the back-and-forth of getting to know each other. I discovered that Prancer liked a little solitude, that he was growing weary of the stress of being on Santa's team, but that tradition kept him there until a replacement became available. I told him all about the elf-run kitchens, the strive to provide the tastiest, most nourishing food possible, and the funny requests we sometimes received from the big man himself.

"You're joking."

I shook my head, grinning as widely as he was. "Nope. Every Christmas Eve, Mrs. Claus requests street tacos, guacamole, and a pitcher of margaritas for her and her friends. That's her girls' night."

"I had no idea." Prancer made to grab his coffee but bumped me, looking down in concern for just a moment before the closeness of our positions seemed to dawn on him. It had just dawned on me as well. Somehow, we'd closed the distance between us, inching nearer as time went on until we were side by side and practically touching.

I wanted to be actually touching.

So I shifted just that much closer.

Prancer never stopped staring, never looked away. Instead, he leaned in, the warmth of his breath brushing across my face and the heat of his body setting me on fire. He was just so...*hot.*

"Hey, Lolly."

"Yeah?"

He rubbed his nose against mine, and I closed my eyes. Unable to hold his stare. Unable to stop the trembling that had begun.

"I'd really like to kiss you right now."

"Then maybe you should."

So he did. He kissed me softly at first, quiet and sweet as if he worried I'd rebuke him. Not a chance of that—I ran my hands up his chest instead, gripping his neck and encouraging him to come closer, to kiss me deeper, to hold me tight.

The man took my silent direction well.

One second, his lips were barely a whisper against mine, and the next, he had me on his lap with one arm wrapped around my waist and the other hand holding me by the neck. And his kiss...lords a-leaping, it was a good kiss. Perfect pressure and wetness and his lips directing mine in a dance that had me writhing. It was a kiss to remember. A kiss to erase all previous kisses. It was a kiss of possession.

I was now Prancer's. Period.

"Oh, hey..." An elf I didn't know bumped into the table, his eyes going wide as Prancer and I broke apart to glare at him. "Sorry. Didn't realize someone was here."

With that, he rushed away, but the moment was already broken. I shifted my weight as if to leave his lap and reclaim my seat—twinkling tinsel, I was *on his lap*—but Prancer held me in place.

"Wait," he said, his voice a rough whisper. His hands firm but not harsh. "Please."

"We should probably go before people start talking even more than they already will be."

"I know," he said, his hands still clutching me to him. "Just give me one more minute holding you."

I chuckled and laid my head against his chest. "Are you greedy, Prancer?"

"For you? Yes. I'll admit that. But in my defense, I only just found you." He nudged me back, giving me that patented Prancer stare. "I've been looking for you for a long time, Lolly."

As had become routine, my cheeks heated and my ears tingled. "Sweet talker."

"Truth." He kissed the tip of my nose then patted my hip. "Okay, let's get out of here before I embarrass you any more than I already have."

"You don't embarrass me."

"Then perhaps I'll have to work a little harder." He grabbed my hand as we walked through the store toward the front. Made his claim known to all the elves who had gathered and were definitely watching us.

Every soul in North Pole likely already knew that Prancer and I had gotten coffee tonight.

Every. Single. One.

Tomorrow was going to be interesting.

# 3
# PRANCER

Lolly. The woman who had somehow broken through the walls around my heart and turned my head, was named Lolly. After a handful of centuries walking the earth alone—just me and my inner reindeer—I'd found someone who stirred my heart. Not just someone— the perfect someone. Or almost perfect. She wasn't a reindeer shifter— which complicated things, seeing as we only mated with our kind—but that didn't matter to me. I'd never felt a draw to a person the way I did to Lolly, so I wasn't walking away from our connection.

"No way, no how." I wiped the steam from the mirror before wrapping the towel around my hips and tucking the top into itself to hold it in place. I'd fallen asleep thinking of Lolly, of that sweet, sweet kiss. I'd dreamed of her. I'd woken up to her pretty face on my mind and the feel of her slight body in my lap. A shower had been necessary for more than one reason, but I had rushed through my solo session. I didn't want to take too long to get ready. Lolly would be at the dining hall for breakfast, and I missed her. I wanted to see her.

I was positively smitten.

Face washed but not shaved, hair product run through but my ridiculous curls not completely in place, I moved on to throwing on my clothes for the day so I could get out the door. It was going to be a light workout day—more training for the new O'Rudolph team member than the rest of us—so joggers, a gym tee, and a light jacket would do. Hopefully Lolly would like the forest green and black color combo I picked out. A woman had once said forest made my eyes look greener. Would Lolly like me in green?

"Whipped, Prancer. You are whipped," I reminded myself as I raced out the front door of my house and headed through Tarandus, the little village of reindeer shifters in North Pole, Alaska. Home to Santa Claus, flying reindeer, and Lolly. The elf with the biggest blue eyes I'd ever seen and the sweetest kiss known to man or reindeer. Not that I had kissed an exceptional number of women—I wasn't a serial kisser. I'd simply done my fair share of...stuff. I knew a good kiss from a mediocre one, and Lolly had given me *good* kisses. I wanted more of them. Lots more. And to maybe get my hands on her—

"What's up, Prance?"

On any other day, that voice would have soured my mood. Cupid—the only other first-generation Santa reindeer still on active duty—sat across and three spots over from me at our communal dining table. There was plenty of room between us, but I could still feel him invading my space. My headspace. My Lolly-thought space.

I grunted in response, the reindeer inside me sharpening his gaze on the man he saw as competition.

"Wow, you wake up on the wrong side of the bed? Or was waking up alone as always enough to put you in such a bad mood?"

Remember how I said I was not a serial kisser? The same could not be said for Cupid. There were a lot of female reindeer in North Pole who constantly vied for his attention, and he was more than happy to let them.

"I'm not in a bad mood." I kept my eyes locked on the door to the kitchen, only breaking my stare when an elf—one who was certainly not Lolly—came to bring me coffee. She was a bit older, with long, graying hair and a charming smile. I made sure to say my thanks and focus on her before returning my gaze to the door. *Open-open-open.*

"Isn't it time for you to retire, old man?"

106

That, unfortunately, stole my attention away from Lolly's door. "Couldn't the same thing be said about you, Cupid?"

"I'm still fit. You're growing a little haggard in your old age. Maybe you should give up the yearly run and start knitting or something instead."

As if that was an insult. "I already knit, you jackass. And there's no heir to take my space, so leaving isn't an option."

"There won't be an heir if you sit home and knit instead of using those fingers for other things."

*Like digging into the flesh of Lolly's hip again.* Which was not a thought I should be having right then and there. "You're a class act, Cupid."

"I'm honest is what I am. In my opinion, you need to..."

But his words evaporated the second the door opened and Lolly—beautiful, petite Lolly—came walking through it with a tray of mugs on her shoulder. Even the beast inside me stood up and took notice of her. I wanted to jump up and rush to her, to take that tray and help her, but an older male elf was following along behind her, holding another tray. I had to let them do their jobs.

Still, I angled my body toward her just in case she needed me.

"So, it's true," Cupid said from slightly behind me, barely scratching the surface of my mind as I stayed focused on Lolly. "I heard a rumor that you were hanging with an elf. I hadn't given it much weight, but I guess I was wrong."

Yeah, he was.

"Good morning, Lolly," I said the second she set down her tray on a nearby stand and turned toward me.

Lolly smiled shyly, her cheeks flushing. Swans a-swimming, I loved the way I could make her blush.

"Good morning, Prancer. Did you sleep well?"

"He slept alone is what he did!" Cupid yelled, laughing as if he were some sort of comedian. "Why don't you fix that, little elf?"

"Shut it, Cupid." I reached for Lolly's hand, wanting to bash Cupid's face in for dampening her smile. "I did sleep well, thanks. And, you? Well rested and ready for the day?"

Her smile returned. "Not really. But it's sticky toffee pudding day, so

I need to be on my toes. It's a tough bake."

"I'm sure you'll do amazing, and I can't wait to try it."

One more smile, then she glanced around the room. "Well, I should deliver these beignets so you all can get to practice. I'll see you at lunch."

Too long. "Yeah, of course."

She turned to leave before spinning around and placing her hand on my shoulder so she could lean close to whisper, "I made your beignets special. They've got chocolate and a little peppermint essence. You seemed to like those flavors last night."

This woman was the best. "I did. Thank you."

"You're welcome." She dragged her hand over my shoulder and down my arm before walking away, her touch sending a shiver up my spine and the sight of her swaying hips making my mood rush south. There was no way I was making it through the day without a kiss from those pink lips. No way.

A snort from behind me pulled me up short, though.

"You're really sinking low for that one, friend. You know, we've got plenty of women on our side of town who'd drop to their knees for you if you just asked. No need to go hitting on the short ones."

I clenched my fists, fighting hard not to swing at him for that comment. "Shut up, Cupid. You have no idea what you're talking about."

At that point, Clark Donderson joined his buddy Cupid, the two dropping their voices to talk about...well, who the fuck cared? So long as they left me alone, I was fine. Lolly had disappeared into the kitchen once more, so I drank the rest of my cocoa and took a huge bite of one of my beignets—which really did have a lovely peppermint flavor to it— before rising to my feet. The sooner this day started, the sooner it would end and I could spend time alone with Lolly. Hopefully.

Crap, I would need to ask her out. Like, on a date.

Totally doing *that* the next time I saw her.

But first, work.

I grabbed the rest of my beignets and headed for the door. "I'll see you guys on the training field."

Cupid was an asshole.

Not that this came as any sort of surprise for me—he'd been that way for a number of years. Sure, he'd started off kind enough—we'd *all* started off kind—but over the years, as more and more of our brothers had left the sleigh team to start families with their mates, he'd changed. Grown harsher. More arrogant. More...asshole-ish.

Today, he was proving that fact in spades.

"Think I can get your little elf to bring me some beer? This water ain't cutting it."

I gritted my teeth and ignored the 800th comment about Lolly. Specifically about Lolly being a waitress—a job that was not only nothing to sneer at and totally respectable but also not what she did. If it wouldn't have disappointed Santa, I would have punched him.

The big man still had power over me.

"Okay, team!" the lead elf who worked as our trainer yelled as he stood beside the man in red. "It's time to head inside for some lunch. You've all put in a good day's workout, so I'm going to release most of you from this afternoon's session."

I stood a little straighter, knowing this was a total gift. The lead-up to the Christmas run never offered us breaks. A night off—a night I could spend with Lolly—would be an amazing opportunity. I wanted it. And thankfully, I'd worked hard at the morning practice. Had totally focused on the reps and hitting my goals. I had earned this night off. I just hoped the trainer and Santa agreed with my thoughts on the matter.

The elf looked over his clipboard while he and Santa whispered back and forth, both men animated. I threw up one final prayer that they wouldn't call my name to stay. *One night—I just need one night off.*

"Donderson, Vixenni, Dasherwicz, and..." A bigger frown, more animated hand gestures. Santa leaned a little closer and whispered again before the elf nodded. "Cupid. That's it—those are who need to come back after lunch for more conditioning. The rest of you—"

I was running toward the mess hall before he finished his sentence. A whole evening to myself? Hours and hours of time away from work and stress and Cupid's cranky ass? I wanted it. I could only hope Lolly was allowed to have a little time off, too.

Speaking of which, I immediately started scanning the room for her blond hair the second I turned the corner. She stood close to the kitchen door, arranging something on a tray another elf was holding. She looked so beautiful—completely focused and in charge. I couldn't wait to tell her, to ask her, to...just *see* more of her.

Unfortunately, the announcement on the field had not turned everyone's mood as bright as mine.

"What are you doing here, old man?" Dasherwicz—Dasher's grandson, who had only spent a handful of Christmas Eves pulling with us and definitely needed the extra work. "Shouldn't you be home relaxing already?"

I shrugged, refusing to rise to the bait of his verbal jab. "I'm hungry."

Cupid took his seat across and down from me, snorting a sarcastic laugh. "He's whipped, is what he is."

At that moment, Lolly looked up and caught my eye, her smile widening and her cheeks flushing the way I was beginning to absolutely love. Whipped? Sure. Whatever. *No lies detected.*

Lolly hurried my way, the man with the tray right behind her. She was ten feet away when things started sliding a little sideways. Not on her tray—with my so-called brothers.

"Hold up," Dasherwicz said, leaning over the table and talking far too loudly. "I heard some shit, but you mean it's true? Old Prancer here is hooking up with a kitchen elf?"

Cupid laughed, the sound positively booming. "Yup. He's banging the help."

The room went silent, every elf and reindeer turning to look over at the two loudmouths. And then they all focused on me. I only had eyes for Lolly, though. She'd gone stark white, those big eyes extra-wide and looking awfully wet. And then she took a step back as if to retreat from me.

Not happening.

No fucking way.

*No.* Those bastards were not going to make her cry and run away.

Without a moment's pause, I rose to my feet and reached for my girl, pulling her toward me and directly onto my lap. She came willingly enough, though her body seemed awfully limp. That was fine—I could work with limp so long as she still allowed me to touch her. If she tugged away, it was over. I'd never try to force her hand.

Santa walked in right as Lolly's weight fully settled, catching my eye with a furrowed brow. I'd need to apologize for making a scene later—I had a point to get across.

Lolly obviously didn't understand my plan. "Prancer, I should—"

I squeezed her thigh and reached for my cocoa, every ounce of determination in my body running strong. "It's okay," I whispered, and then I stopped being so quiet.

"Dasherwicz, Cupid. We're teammates, but that doesn't mean there are no boundaries between us." I took a sip of my cocoa and clutched Lolly a little closer to me. Making sure everyone heard me. "Yes, I'm dating an elf—if she'll still go out with me after that display of classism. It's not your fucking business, but you decided to butt your nose in where it doesn't belong, so here's the scoop. Her name is Lolly, she's the one baking those amazing fucking pastries you two scarf down every morning, and she's mine. You ever say anything hurtful about her again —do anything to dull the smile from her beautiful face—and I'll cut your fucking antlers off."

Cupid stared, his face red, his eyes hard. "You wouldn't dare."

"Try me." Because cutting off another reindeer's antlers was a sign of complete domination, something only done in the absolute worst of times when a reindeer had crossed too many lines to remain in the herd. It had only happened in North Pole twice that I was aware of—once because of an adulterous affair, and once after a certain reindeer was caught stealing from the children's toy stash. I'd taken care of the latter of those, defending our herd and our legacy. And I would do it again if they forgot who the fuck I was.

Cupid broke the stare-off first, dropping his eyes to his cup with a piss-ass scowl on his face. "Fine. Sorry, Lolly."

My girl lifted her shoulder in a little shrug, still not looking happy. "It's fine."

"It's not anywhere near fine, but apologizing is a start." With that, I did the only thing I could think of to smooth things over. I squeezed my

Lolly closer, giving myself a little time to calm down before saying the words that I most wanted to. "So, I've got the night off tonight. I'd love to spend it with you, if you're available. Would you like to go on a date with me?"

Lolly nodded, still silent, still looking slightly uncomfortable, but that flush had begun its return to her cheeks. I couldn't ask for much more, considering.

"Good," I said, leaning closer and lowering my voice so only she could hear me. "And don't worry—those two won't ever disrespect you that way again. I'll make damn sure of it."

Because I hadn't exaggerated or stuttered—if they came for my girl, they would get my full wrath. Period.

"It's fine," Lolly whispered back. I was about to argue the whole *fine* thing when she lifted her head, her eyes hard as steel when they met mine. "But he does *not* get the sticky toffee pudding for dessert. I'll make sure Arthur serves him graham crackers instead."

And that, my friends, was definitely something my girl would do.

"Sounds like a fitting punishment."

She nodded, gave me a quick kiss on the cheek, and hopped off my lap. "Time to get back to work."

And work she did, laying down plate after plate with a gooey pudding that smelled absolutely amazing. At least until she made it to Cupid. The male elf with her—who must have been Arthur—placed the plate in front of him.

Three squares of graham crackers.

"What the fuck is this?" Cupid yelled, glaring at the elf.

It was Santa who answered, though. Sneaking up behind the cranky reindeer and missing his usually jovial expression.

"I would call that your punishment for being naughty, Cupid. Eat up...you're going to need your energy for tonight's workout."

And with that, the big man strolled off, and Lolly—my sweet Lolly—continued on her way, happily delivering delicious puddings to all the other reindeer.

And setting a second helping in front of me.

# 4

# LOLLY

The afternoon of *the incident* ended up being quite uncomfortable. Why? Because everyone kept staring at me. Reindeer and elf alike simply couldn't take their eyes off me, all because Prancer had confirmed we were... Dating? That's what Prancer had said in the dining room, but I could hardly believe it. Was I really dating one of the original sleigh-pullers on Santa's team? One of the premier reindeer in North Pole?

I had to stop thinking about such things. If my heart beat any faster, I was going to be sick.

"Lolly!" Miss Cici yelled, her eyes on her clipboard. "You're needed."

That sounded a bit ominous and brought even more attention my way, but I kept my chin up and rushed over. Ready to work.

"Yes, ma'am?"

She gave me a laser-focused once-over, the weight of her gaze making me want to take a step back. "Your presence has been requested by the staff of the Queen. Are you prepared to stand before her?"

I had to blink a few times, give my brain a moment to make sense of her words, before I could even think of opening my mouth.

"The...Queen?"

Miss Cici nodded, still staring at me hard. I gulped.

*Look what you've done.*

"I suppose I am," I said, my voice weak, even to my own ears.

Miss Cici nodded, looking pointedly toward the back door where two of the royal staff elves stood. "They'll escort you." She leaned a little closer, those eagle eyes softening, her voice dropping so others couldn't hear. "Don't worry, child. If this were a bad visit, they'd have sent guards."

That didn't quite make me feel better. The Queen was known to be a kind, benevolent ruler, and most elves looked upon her fondly. That didn't mean I wanted to be in a meeting with her. In the world of North Pole, she had the same hierarchy level as Santa himself, but hers was focused over the elfdom. See, no matter what legends were spun in the human world, Santa didn't tell us what to do—the Queen did. And she worked closely with Santa. There was no more powerful elf.

And she wanted to see *me*.

The walk to the royal house took very little time, and I soon found myself wringing my hands in what could only be called a sitting room. So I sat. And I waited.

Not for very long, though.

"Ah, you must be the little elf making all my handmaids twitter." The Queen swept into the room with a guard at her side, her smile wide and the scent of cloves wafting around her. Her deep blue dress hung to the floor, the skirt full and flowing. She was quite the sight, to be honest—a graceful, gorgeous elf who lived up to her title.

Meanwhile, I was stumbling to find my feet so I could bow. "Your Majesty."

"Oh, let's not," she said, coming to place a delicate hand on my shoulder. "I've been watching people bow to me for centuries, and though I do like it when there's business to be done, today is not about that."

"It's not?"

"No. Sit, Lolly. Your name is Lolly, yes?" She grinned when I nodded. "Oh good. I had a moment of anxiety, thinking I'd gotten it wrong. Callon, please bring Lolly and me a tea service."

"Of course, Your Highness."

And then the guard was gone, and I was left alone with the Queen.

"So..." I said, trying so hard not to sound like...well, me. "You wanted to see me."

"I did," she said, her eyes positively glittering. "You've created quite the buzz around here."

"Me?"

"Yes, you. The elf who caught the eye of one of Santa's original reindeer."

"Oh." I deflated a little, afraid of what was coming. "Am I in trouble for...crossing a line or something?"

"Leaping lollipops, no. You're not in trouble at all. In fact, I quite envy you right now."

That sounded...so very wrong. "You do?"

The guard—Callon—slipped back into the room, rolling a cart covered in treats and pastries, with a full teapot and cups on saucers within the display. The Queen smiled up at him, waiting as he poured her a cup and added three sugars.

"And for you, ma'am?" he asked, indicating the empty cup nearest me.

"Oh, uh...one sugar and a little cream, please."

"Of course." He poured my tea, added the extras, then headed to the doorway, leaving me alone with the Queen once more.

"As I was saying," she started, apparently not one to let subjects sit idle. "You've been the talk of North Pole. When I heard that you had begun spending time with Prancer, I knew I had to meet you."

"But...why?"

"Because for the first time in centuries, we'll have a cross-species mating, and I wanted to make sure you were ready."

My headshake came automatically, requiring no thought. "We're not mated."

The woman—the darn *Queen*—rolled her royal eyes. "Of course you are."

"Reindeer only find their mates within their own species." Everyone knew that.

She leaned forward, practically vibrating with excitement. "Not true, dear Lolly. Not at all true."

Breathing had become difficult, and the entire room seemed to be spinning. "But...wouldn't we know if we were...we were..." My mouth went dry, words hard to make sense of in the tornado of my thoughts. "We realize...would know that...the...thing."

Nope. My brain was not about to work right.

Thankfully, the Queen just laughed softly and sipped her tea, resting the cup in the saucer when she was finished. "For many centuries, it has certainly appeared as if reindeer only found their fated mates in their own species, but there could be reasons for that."

"Reasons?"

"Availability—they tend to keep to themselves, and it's not like there are a lot of options up here. Right?"

Nodding seemed appropriate, especially since words were hard.

"So, they stick together, spend all their time with one another, and the fates work a little harder to find them a fated mate within their circle because there are simply no other options." She leaned forward, her blue eyes practically burning into me. "But there *are* others here. There are us elves, and sometimes the fates toss us into the reindeer paths."

"I've never heard of an elf who—"

"Or have you?" She sat back into her chair, her face a little paler. Her eyes a little less focused on me. "I was once thrown into the reindeer world and found my true love. I gave my heart to him, and the fates rewarded us with a true mating."

"What happened?" I asked as I leaned all the way forward in my chair. Because *this* was not known. No one talked about the Queen and a reindeer. Not ever. The question of why we lived in North Pole had many different legends tied to it, but not that.

The Queen certainly didn't seem all that willing to share, though.

"Things ended badly," she said, looking to the side with eyes that were suspiciously red for a long moment, taking time to collect herself, it seemed. "But that's all in the past. You are the present, young Lolly. You are the one with the fates in her corner now."

I took another sip of my tea, letting the sweet, hot liquid recenter me in the moment. In the now. In the feelings I'd been dealing with all afternoon. "People stare, and the other reindeer—"

"Don't ever let those ignorant fools get in your way."

I jerked back, the furious tone of her voice and the harshness of her words taking me by surprise. "I didn't mean to—"

"Listen to me, Lolly. People will stare, they will say things that are hurtful, they will make fun of you and him. They mock and ridicule what they can't understand. Their ignorance is not something you can fix. Be careful—but follow your heart. It won't lead you astray." She sat deeper in her seat, taking a big breath before pasting on a very royal smile. "Would you like another cup of tea?"

Five minutes and no more tea later, I was released from the Queen's presence and running across town. She'd given me so many things to think about, had filled my brain with opportunities and fears. I didn't know what to do, but I knew where to go. Who I wanted to see. Needed to be in the presence of.

"Patrick!" I yelled, waving at an elf friend who worked on the Tarandus side of North Pole.

Patrick looked up and gave me a confused smile. "Lolly? What are you doing over here? Are you lost?"

"Not really, but I am looking for someone. Do you know where Prancer lives?"

His face went stiff, and for a moment, I thought he was going to tell me to go back to where I belonged or something. Instead, he eventually nodded. "I'd heard you two were dating. Best of luck to you, girl."

And then he gave me the directions and a full description of Prancer's house so I could find it. I practically ran the rest of the way, needing to find him. To see if the pull I felt to him made sense as a mating pull. To feel the energy connecting us. Maybe the Queen was wrong. Maybe this wasn't the fates and was instead just attraction. Chemistry. All that stuff. Maybe I'd see him and realize he wasn't the one for me.

Prancer's house came into view, and I took off at a full sprint. Racing down the street and then up his little pathway to his porch. I hit the buzzer multiple times, desperate to know. To figure this out. I hadn't thought being mated to a reindeer was possible, so the draw to him had seemed strong but not mating strong. I needed to look at him with new eyes, to experience his presence with this knowledge. I needed to—

Prancer opened the door, his hair wet, his chest bare, and wearing nothing but a gray towel wrapped around his hips. He had a toothbrush in the corner of his mouth and a confused—but happy—expression on his face.

And I *knew.*

"Oh my cinnamon stars."

One corner of his lips turned up in a crooked sort of smile as he pulled the toothbrush from the other. "It's about time you showed up here."

It was. Because that man was my fated mate.

And I had no idea if he knew that yet or not.

# 5

# PRANCER

S tupid, stupid reindeer." I finished shaving and set my supplies back where they belonged, muttering insults to myself the entire time. I had asked Lolly out, had wanted to take her on a date. I had just forgotten to acquire two key pieces of info: how to get in touch with her after work and where we were going. I was apparently too stupid to have asked for the woman's phone number.

"You're an idiot." I shook my head, flexing my shoulders in an attempt to relieve the tension I'd been experiencing since the moment I had realized tonight may not happen. Tension that only continued to grow as the day had passed by. Tension that was far outside the norm of a man wanting to spend time with a woman. My interest in Lolly was growing stronger every day, but the animal inside me had it worse. His interest was bordering on obsession, and being unable to reach her was causing him something close to panic. His anxiety fed mine, which wasn't good for either of us. I had to calm down. To calm us both down.

I truly *hated* not knowing exactly where Lolly was or when I would see her next.

"Let's brush our teeth," I said, as if the reindeer running laps inside my brain would listen to me whatsoever. "Then we can get dressed and go look for her." Good plan, even if the beast wasn't the biggest fan. He wanted to leave immediately, to scour the city until we found her. To sniff her out. I had no idea if he could even hunt her down by scent, but he was confident in his abilities. He was also irritated that I would doubt him.

"I've known you my entire life, and we've never hunted someone down using our sniffers. Don't blame me if I question the option."

He snorted audibly, the sound reverberating in my head. Which was about as close to an acceptance as I was going to get.

I had just started scrubbing with my toothbrush when someone pounded on my front door. Somehow, I knew it was Lolly. Knew it as if I could see her face. My reindeer immediately took over. Without thought—without any control—he put us in motion and raced for the door. Lolly, our sweet elf, was on the porch. I knew it, and the reindeer knew it. He could *smell* her.

"Fine, you win. Next time, we go a-sniffing." I took a deep breath just before I opened the door, the scent and flavor of mint overwhelming all my other senses. Not that it mattered. Lolly was there, on my porch, looking absolutely adorable and flushed. Smell not required.

"Oh my cinnamon stars."

That was the moment I realized what the poor woman was looking at. I'd showered and not gotten dressed yet, so I had a gray towel around my hips and a toothbrush in my mouth. That was it. I'd opened the door as close to naked as I could get without offending the neighbors.

And if the expression on her face was any indication, she liked what she saw.

Things were about to get a little steamy.

I pulled the toothbrush from the corner of my mouth, leaning into the doorframe a bit. "It's about time you showed up here."

Because I'd missed her. Because I'd wanted to see her. Because I'd been craving her in my home. And now I had her—I wasn't going to screw this up.

"Please, come inside." I stepped back so she could enter, catching another whiff of that scent my reindeer craved so much. Spun sugar. She always smelled like spun sugar. "Would you care for a drink?"

Lolly didn't speak, though. Didn't tear her eyes away from me either.

She just stood there, watching me, her cheeks pink and her hands twisted together.

"Are you okay?" I asked, taking a step toward her. She shook her head, still staring, still silent. "Lolly, baby. Tell me—"

I never got to finish my sentence because the woman launched herself at me. One second, I was concerned, and the next...well, ready. I was ready because I had my girl in my arms and her taste on my tongue. I heard the clunk of my toothbrush hitting the floor, but that didn't matter. I spun and pushed my elf against the wall, tugging her upward for a better connection. Kissing her hard and deep for the first time. Her body felt so warm under my hands. So soft. I wanted to touch her everywhere. To learn each individual curve and dip. To rip those clothes off her body so I could feel her heat with my skin. But that was likely too much, too fast. She'd need to be wooed. To be seduced. She'd need more time to get to know me. I couldn't rush this and mess it up.

Lolly broke away from the kiss, breathing hard. Her little body writhing against mine. "I swear on the sleigh runners, if you don't drop that towel and take me to your bedroom, I'm never going to make you another beignet again."

Okay. So...the only thing she needed was me. Naked. Got it.

*LOLLY*

I wasn't one to climb handsome men on a normal basis, but Prancer was just so warm and strong. He was also practically naked. No woman—elf or otherwise—could have resisted him. Heck, there were plenty of men who would have jumped at the chance to rub themselves all over him if they'd gotten the same view and feel that I had. I couldn't have blamed them—the man was the epitome of sexy.

And he was mine.

"Prancer," I moaned as he ground his hips into mine, his entire body pinning me against the wall in the best way. "Please."

"No begging." He hoisted me up higher and carried me to the stairs, running up them as if he weren't weighted down by my body wrapped around him. "Not for this—you can beg me not to stop later."

"Will I need to beg you not to stop?"

He chuckled. "No, baby. I'll make sure you're good and taken care of. Is that what you want?"

I nodded into his shoulder as he turned a corner. A simple bedroom with accents of blue and gold was all I could see before I was airborne. The man tossed me onto his mattress then followed, crawling up my body and using his weight to, once again, pin me in place. This time, horizontal.

I smiled up at him, reaching for his neck in a play for more kisses. "Nice bed."

"Better with you in it."

Oh, the man had skills. But I needed more than words. "Prove it."

With a very un-reindeer-like growl, he yanked my body upward, nearly tossing me once again onto the pillows. With speed and agility I was not prepared for, he gave me another sloppy kiss, using his entire body to rub against mine. His *entire* body.

"You lost your towel." I ran my hands down his back and over the curves of his butt, grabbing a solid handful of each cheek. "You're naked."

"And you're not." He kissed and licked down my neck, frowning as I continued to massage what was usually covered up with jeans. "Can I undress you?"

Oh, I liked being asked. "Definitely."

He rose up over me, his knees spread on either side of my hips, his dick thick and weighty as it lay against me. He really was *naked*. And without shame, it seemed.

"Nice view," I said as I reached for him, brushing the tip with my fingers just to get a reaction.

He growled again, his eyes fluttering as I made contact. "You're my favorite view."

Cheesy. "And I'm not even naked yet."

"Yeah. I should fix that." So, he did. Within seconds, the man had my sweater pulled over my head, had my bra unclasped and my breasts freed, and had his mouth firmly attached to my nipple as he fought to yank my skirt down my legs. Fought hard.

"Let me help," I said, arching up and using my feet to pull my skirt off the rest of the way, not wanting to interrupt the man from what he was doing because it felt so darn good. "There."

Prancer reared back again, dropping a hand to his dick and stroking slowly as he took me in. As he stared down at me in all my unclothed glory. "Yup, definitely my best view."

I had never felt more beautiful. "You're such a charmer."

"Nope. Prancer. Don't worry, though—you won't forget my name once I have you screaming it."

I laughed as he dropped back down over me, unable not to. But as his dick pressed into my stomach, as the evidence of his arousal became so much more obvious to both of us, the laughter faded. Prancer leaned in for a kiss, starting slow and shallow. Deepening it over time as his hands began traversing every inch of me they could reach. Legs, thighs, arms, breasts, tweaks to my nipples, tickles to my neck. The man liked to *feel*, which worked out perfectly for me because I loved to be touched.

Back muscles bunching under my hands, Prancer began a slow grind, working his hips with mine. Teasing me. Keeping our lips connected even as our bodies began that ancient dance. The one we all knew so well by instinct. The one that needed him to drop a little lower to get me off.

"Prancer—"

"I know," he panted, his voice clipped and his body taut. "Fuck, I know, baby. I want to be inside you so bad."

"Please."

He shook his head, his refusal nearly making me cry. At least until he gave me one last kiss before heading south. Very far south. All the way south. If I'd been a lady, I might have clamped my knees together and grabbed his shoulder, told him he didn't have to do that.

I was too far away from being a lady for all that.

"Oh, yes." I spread my knees wide as his shoulders dropped between them. Even tilted my hips up to present myself to him. If he was willing, I was ready. His little bump and grind had gotten me all worked up. I needed the release.

"You're so damn pretty. All over." He sighed and leaned closer, dropping a soft kiss to the seam between my thigh and pussy. "Every inch."

I wanted to tell him to hurry up—because, again, no lady—but I didn't have to. Prancer seemed to have read my mind or my body. He dove in without another bit of hesitation, licking me from one end to the other before focusing on my clit. Before hitting the exact spot that ignited the flame within me and sent my mind reeling. I nearly arched right off the bed when he began slashing his tongue against me in the most obscene way ever. Had to weave my fingers through his hair and hold on as he lifted my hips higher and closer to him so he could continue to torture my clit. Good torture, though. The kind that had me biting my lip and shaking all over. The kind that had me speaking in tongues and grunting in a very unladylike way.

The kind that would definitely make me come in an embarrassingly short amount of time.

"I'm gonna...I'm gonna..." I arched harder, pressing myself against his face and rocking my hips as the tightening inside me increased. "Don't you dare stop."

He didn't stop, no siree Bob. Instead, he doubled down on his efforts, sucking my clit between his lips and slipping a couple fingers inside me. Curling those digits as if he knew my anatomy already. As if he'd studied me. And maybe he had, because the pressure increased and the tightening grew stronger and the earth-shattering trembling started with nothing more than a few swipes.

Obviously, the man had magic fucking fingers.

I was almost completely off the bed, hanging with my backside to his chest with my legs thrown over his shoulders and his fingers inside me when my entire body finally clenched down. When I screamed—not his name, mind you—and arched and tugged his face against me even harder. Bliss. Darkness. A soothing sort of relief that pulsed through me, centered in that space between my legs. The most perfect moment in the history of moments. Snowball fights and candy canes and hot cocoa be damned—I'd take sex with Prancer over any one of them. And we hadn't technically had sex yet.

Which meant he was not feeling the relief I was.

Oh, balls.

"Come here," I said, my voice no longer my own. That orgasm had clawed its way into my throat and taken over, leaving me with a sound much huskier and deeper than my usual voice. This was the sound meant only for Prancer's ears. For my fated mate. He still didn't know that part, though. Unless he did and wasn't telling me. Unless he had figured it out and simply hadn't thought to share—

*Not the time, Lolly.*

"Did I do okay?" Prancer laid me down then moved up and over my body, settling right on top of me. His weight like a blanket to my physical and mental unrest. A sort of physical grounding.

"Okay is an understatement. Somehow, I doubt you've been just okay at anything in your life."

I reached between us, gripping him firmly. Holding his eyes as I moved him to line up with where we both wanted him to go. *Cock, meet pussy. Pussy, meet cock. Y'all will get along just fine.*

"You sure?" he asked, appearing almost in pain as his hips rocked forward in a short, stuttered movement. As if he was holding back. As if he was right on the edge of not being able to control himself.

An edge I was happy to push him off of.

I tilted my hips up, making sure he slipped inside where I was so darn wet for and from him. Rocking my own hips to take him just a little deeper.

"I'm definitely sure."

"Thank fuck," he said, and then he thrust inside. *All* the way inside. Buried himself deep. Thank the snowflakes he'd already gotten me off because the wetness he'd caused smoothed his way. Destroyed any sort of resistance that might have happened in other circumstances. My pussy was warm and welcoming, and he took full advantage—making himself right at home. Then he rocked those hips backward and pulled out a little, just enough to get some leverage so he could pound his way back inside. And that, my friends, was the moment I knew I was in trouble. Big trouble, because he was hitting spots that had never been hit, and my body had begun singing a song just for him. The man had skills I didn't know what to do with.

125

Prancer was going to sex me to death, but at least I'd die a happy elf.

Had he succeeded in his plan to kill me with his cock, I would have died in a state of pure bliss because the man seemed to know exactly what to do to make me scream. He plunged, he thrust, he slipped and slid and picked me up and tossed me around and flipped us from one end of the bed to the other. He kept up a relentless pace within me that should have been honored for the sheer longevity of the action. He also never forgot the best part—he kept a hand between us, kept his flattened thumb against my clit, and made me see stars at least three times. Maybe four. I figured counting wasn't a requirement of the evening. Still, I was drenched by the time he grunted and said my name in the most exhausted, sweetest voice I'd ever heard. When he dropped his head to my shoulder and shook from one end to the other. When he held back his own pleasure for the sake of mine.

"Lolly."

The torture in his tone gutted me.

"I want you to come." I gripped him with my legs, tugging him closer. Feeling the tension under his skin as he seemed to continue holding back. "Come on, my love. It's your turn."

"One more. One more," he said, shaking his head.

The man was far too stubborn. "No. I won't come again."

That was wording I quickly regretted.

Prancer popped up without warning, holding his weight on his arms and looking down at me with a fierce expression. "Fuck, Lolly. I can't resist a challenge."

And that, friends, was how I ended up on top, riding my reindeer shifter to my fourth—or maybe fifth because counting was hard— orgasm of the night. As soon as I crashed, the second my body bowed and I dug my fingers into his chest with his name on my lips, he thrust his hips upward, pushing me into the air once more. Groaning long and loud and deep as he came. As he finally finished. As we came together in an unbelievable moment of something like fireworks. Something bright and fun and unique. Something forever.

As he collapsed, tugging me down to snuggle with him, I knew that conversation was going to need to happen. Soon. But not tonight.

Tonight was for comfort and newness and...well, more sex. Eventually. Because I really needed a nap after that.

"You good?" Prancer asked, sounding just as exhausted as I felt.

"I'm far more than good—I'm ready to crash. You should rest, too. You put on quite the performance there."

He tugged me with him as he rolled, stopping once we were on the other side of the bed. Once I was completely secured within his arms. "I can do better. I'll show you. I just need a few minutes to catch my breath."

I ran my fingers through his hair, staring up at his closing eyes. Smiling back at his lifted lips. "I'm sure you will."

# 6

# PRANCER

Did you ever wake up with someone and couldn't remember how you got there or who they were?

That didn't happen with Lolly. At all. It was totally the opposite, really.

I woke up to her scent, to the feel of her skin against mine, to the energy of her body. And in that very first instance of consciousness, I *knew* it was her. Not for a second did I question or doubt. My sweet elf had stayed the night with me—which I came to realize was potentially a problem as she may have been needed in the kitchens. That thought woke me up quick.

I raised my head to check the clock—it was still early. Likely before dawn. I could wake her up and send her to work, take a shower, then get myself to practice. Plenty of time.

Without preamble, I slipped beneath the covers and spread her legs, using my thumbs to massage her pussy from one end to the other. To expose that little ball of flesh that had made her tremble and scream last night. My end goal...reached.

"Prancer?" Her voice came out soft and husky, her hands gentle as they found the top of my head. Good. I wanted her awake for this.

"I just need ten minutes, baby. Promise." And with that, I dove in, licking, sucking, biting a little. Doing whatever I could to get her good and wet. To push her from sleepy dreams to orgasmic bliss the fastest. Fingers buried deep within her, clit between my lips, tongue rubbing and whipping against her...I put on a damn show. A successful one, too —it took her about two minutes to come with me feasting on her. I could feel her body pulsing around my digits, the wetness that came from her letting go. One down, but that wouldn't be the only.

I lunged up the bed, directing my cock straight to her pussy. Sliding inside her wet heat without hesitation. I was careful, though. I paid attention to the way she breathed and arched and accepted me. I focused on her until I was balls deep, and then I let myself *feel*. Oh, jingle my bells, she was so tight. So wet and warm and snug—perfect. Absolutely perfect for me.

Those thighs of Lolly's rose so she could wrap her legs around me, those arms I'd slept in dropping over my shoulders. My girl was surrounding me in her warmth. We were one—connected in so many ways. Not the least of which was at the heart.

"You're my girl, Lolly," I said, wanting so badly to say more. To claim her in another way. To make this official and permanent and...real. "All mine."

"Yours," she said, and my heart leaped in my chest. Mine. Always. Forever.

*Mate!* my reindeer roared within my head. *Our mate.*

And that was the thought I finally came to, bringing Lolly with me as I gave her clit a little attention from my thumb. Both of us quaking as we held on to each other as if our connection truly mattered.

*Mate.*

I practically skipped along the streets of North Pole on my way to drop off my girl for work. Almost. Or at least my reindeer and I wanted to, but we both knew doing so would attract far too much attention. That was okay, though—I had my Lolly holding my hand and walking beside me. Skipping was not a necessity.

We'd showered and gotten dressed quickly, then headed out so we could stop by her apartment. The place was cute—small and comfy, but very her. I could see hanging out there with her. Or her at my house. Whatever worked so long as we were together because the back-and-forth was going to end as soon as I finished the Christmas run.

Yes, I'd decided. No, I hadn't mentioned it yet.

Once we were both in clean clothes and ready for our days, I walked her to work. The timing was off—I was about to be super early to training camp—but it didn't matter. I had no interest in leaving her side. Ever. My reindeer was pretty much set on that idea too.

"You're early," Lolly said as we approached the rear entrance to the training hall where the kitchen was. She sounded sad, which wouldn't do.

I tugged her to a stop and picked her up, hugging her to my chest. "So?"

"I just..." She bit her lip, looking away. "What are you going to do? I feel bad that you—"

I kissed her to shut her up. I loved hearing her voice and knowing what was going on inside that head, but this wasn't okay with me. So I kissed her until I felt her body relax and the negative energy subside.

Time to reassure my girl. "We're not going to think that way, you hear me? There's no feeling bad for me. Period. I got a night with you, a morning spent together, to see your place, and am more than happy to sit and think about all the things that've happened in the last ten hours." I nuzzled her neck, biting once before whispering, "Or maybe just all the ones that won't make me hard as a rock for you."

She giggled, tightening her arms around me. "Fine. But I don't want you just hanging around out here like a creeper."

I laughed out loud. *This woman.* "I promise not to be a creeper if you promise not to worry about me. I'm a big boy. I can take care of myself."

She looked up at me from under her lashes, a saucy smile beginning. "I know exactly how big you are, boy."

*Reindeer shifter murdered by elf. Death by sass. News at eleven.*

"All right, smartass," I said, placing her back on her feet and taking a moment to lay a solid smack on that smart ass. "You go to work. I'll try my hardest to *not* be a creeper before practice. Let's meet up afterward for some dinner together."

"Yeah? You want to spend more time with me?"

"Yeah. I do." One last kiss—just a quick one—before I nodded for her to go. "Get to cooking, woman. Your man needs sustenance after that performance last night."

Her grin was contagious, her eyes practically sparkling. "Don't worry. I'll take care of you."

And I knew she would.

I watched her skip into the training center then started on my own path toward my entrance at the front. She'd been right—I was awfully early. But I could head to the gym to get in a quick workout. Not that I needed one. In fact, I had a feeling my muscles would be sore later from all the activity last night. I bit back my own grin, trying valiantly not to get hard as I remembered my girl in all her glory riding me. Fuck, I needed that again. Immediately.

Sadly, we both had work to do, so sex was going to have to wait.

As was working out. A sauna sounded way better.

After a good thirty-minute sauna to loosen up my muscles—and some alone time to ease the tension in my balls—I showered again and got redressed, heading for the dining room. I was still early, but not obscenely so. I could get away with being there at this time. Besides, it wasn't like anyone would know why I was there so early. It would be fine.

"Yo, Prancer!" Cupid yelled the second I walked through the doors from the gym. "You fucking that elf yet?"

Change of plans. Today was in no way going to be fine.

Cupid may have been the biggest asshole on the team, but he wasn't the only one. I spent the day on runs and in the gym, dodging questions and ignoring comments. Even in reindeer form, the other guys chortled and mocked me. Had we been children, they wouldn't have let me play in their reindeer games. But we weren't children. We were grown-ass adults. And their behavior was nothing more than annoying.

As soon as practice was over, we were sent inside for dinner. I rushed like never before, having had to deal with a picnic lunch and no Lolly. It had been too long since I'd seen her, and I needed to bask in her presence. Needed to see those gorgeous eyes land on mine and that smile light up her face. I needed her.

*Mate. Mine.*

"Yeah, dude. I know," I whispered under my breath. And we'd deal with that after the Christmas run, the second I got her alone. And naked. Because that seemed like something to talk about while naked.

I hadn't even made it to my table when I spotted her. Lolly stood in the corner with another elf, the two chatting in a casual sort of way. But she must have heard us or something because her head whipped around, and that gaze locked in on me. I was so enthralled with the way her eyes lit up, with the slow spread of that smile I loved so much, that I forgot how to put one foot in front of the other. In other words, I tripped, stumbling my way toward a table in an attempt to stay on my feet. It was neither graceful nor suave, but it made Lolly's smile grow wider, so I considered it worth the embarrassment.

"He can't even walk around her. Talk about whipped." Cupid pushed past me, his jealousy coloring every syllable. I grinned—unable not to. I was whipped, all right. And proud as fuck about it.

It took Lolly just seconds to meet me at my spot and me an even shorter amount of time to grab her and pull her into my lap. I buried my nose in her neck to inhale her scent the second I had her where I wanted her to be.

"Beautiful," I said, unable not to. Unable to keep my hands from gripping her tight. "You're so damn beautiful."

She chuckled, those fingers massaging my head and making me want to purr. "Good practice?"

"No, but it's over now, and that's all that matters." I leaned back, kissing her quickly. "Come over tonight. Stay with me again. I need more time with you."

Before Lolly could answer, Cupid had to prove himself an asshole of epic proportions.

"Hey, Coach. Prancer here is scheduling sleepovers with an elf. I thought any sort of extracurriculars the week before our big day were not allowed."

Lolly pulled back, her cheeks reddening. I let her go. Let her crawl off my lap as my coach approached. I kept a hand on hers, though. Kept my head up. And I made damn sure Coach—an elf I both trusted and respected—didn't come between us.

"What's going on here, Prancer?" His eyes—pale from age and surrounded by wrinkles—darted from me to Lolly then back to me, an understanding there. A curiosity as well. Coach had never been an ass to me, but he rode some of the less professional among us pretty hard. I knew he had it in him to make my life miserable, but I also knew that I could walk away at any time. There were other reindeer right there in the room waiting for their shot at the main team. I could quit...and I would, for Lolly.

I was really hoping it didn't have to come to that just yet, though.

"Sir, this is Lolly. She and I are together." Not saying mate stung, but I held that word in and dealt with the disappointment. It wasn't the time.

Coach's eyebrows darted up just a bit, his lips tightening as it appeared he tried not to smile. The man had a mean poker face, but I'd been around him for centuries. I knew happy Coach from grumpy Coach.

"Nice to meet you, Lolly. It's been a long day for our boy here, and tomorrow is the eve of Christmas Eve. I'm asking you to head back to the kitchen so he can eat his dinner after a hard day of training. You two can have dessert together, though." He gave her a bright smile. "If your boss doesn't mind."

My temper flared, the beast in me wanting to tell him to fuck off. But Lolly—sweet Lolly—placed a hand on my elbow and rose onto the balls of her feet to kiss my cheek before whispering, "I need to clean up my station anyway. I'll be back with your dessert, then we can leave together. Okay?"

"Fine," I grumbled, keeping my glare firmly on Coach. Even as she walked away, I didn't stop the staredown. Neither did he, actually.

At least not until Lolly was well out of earshot. "Prancer—"

"Look at him pouting," Cupid said, interrupting Coach and making me dislike him even more.

Before I could reply, O'Rudolph slid over to Cupid's side of the table, smacking him upside the head as he took the seat between us.

"Dude, shut the fuck up," he said, giving me a head nod. "The man has found his mate. He will kill you if you keep riding him about her."

The entire room went silent, Coach and Cupid and...well, everyone...looking completely dumbfounded. I understood that— reindeer mated to their own. Except this time.

Cupid broke the silence first. "She's your *mate*?"

I didn't get a chance to answer him.

"Prancer," Coach said, his head tilted and his brow furrowed. "Is this true?"

I laid my napkin over my lap and grabbed my fork, ready to eat. To get this night over with. Because I was about to have to admit something that I should have told Lolly first. She deserved to be the one to know about our connection before anyone else. I'd wanted to wait just a couple days so I could focus everything on her, but Cupid had just shot that plan all to hell with his big mouth.

"Yeah, it is," I said, the words cutting into my throat. I pointed my knife at Cupid. "So you'd better show her the respect she fucking deserves."

Cupid—still looking completely dumbfounded—nodded. "Understood."

"Matter closed!" Coach yelled, the hardness to his voice making sure everyone knew there would be no more discussion. "Now, let's eat. We've all got better things to do tonight than hang out here."

My stomach sank, the very thought of the conversation that needed to be had—of making Lolly panic at the thought of being tied to me forever—stealing my appetite.

"And by better things," the coach yelled again, looking right at me, "I mean sleep. No extracurriculars allowed tonight." He patted me on the shoulder. "For anyone."

Fuck, I had just messed up. Big-time.

# 7

# LOLLY

The eve of Christmas Eve dawned bright and quiet. I woke up alone in my apartment, having been sent off without Prancer by his coach after last night's dinner. At least we'd gotten to say goodbye. Prancer had looked so upset, but I couldn't argue with his coach. Tomorrow was an important day for the reindeer—he needed his rest and to stay focused on the job. Tonight, Prancer and the rest of the team would head out with Santa to begin delivering presents to the children of the world through an amazing amount of magic and more than a little might. I refused to be a distraction that caused him to mess up at this important job. Even if I missed him.

"You barely know him," I said, frowning at myself in the mirror. But I knew I was telling my reflection what I was supposed to say. Truth was, I'd known from the start he was mine. Talking with the Queen and finding out we were fated mates had only sealed that deal. And once Prancer was back from his Christmas run, I'd tell him about that. Until then, my lips were sealed.

No distractions, remember?

But apparently, Prancer and I were not on the same page in terms of what he needed to have a successful toy run.

"What are you doing here?" I practically screeched as I opened the door of my building leading to the street. Prancer stood on the sidewalk outside, flowers in hand, looking adorable and sweet and…slightly tired. Shoot. "Did you sleep okay?"

He shrugged, his smile falling. "I think I might have slept better with you."

"You would have kept both of us up all night." I rose onto the balls of my feet, grateful when he leaned down so I could give him a soft, sweet kiss. "You can't keep your hands off me."

He grinned. "Who could blame me? You're beautiful."

Such a wonderful way to start my day, even if I did have a bit of worry scratching at the back of my head. The man was so kind and thoughtful, but he had other things that required his attention. He needed to focus on the job—not me. I had to figure out how to get him to do that.

"How many hours until you take off?" I asked, leading him toward the training facility. I still had to work a bit this morning—the main team would have breakfast and lunch delivered to their houses so they could stay rested. The backups would be fed in the dining room. Prancer had apparently chosen not to remain home.

Because of me.

"We're leaving at around one in the afternoon for Samoa, then we'll start dropping into relative clouds for the time jumps as we work our way west." He gripped my hand a little tighter. "I'll be gone for almost two days."

Ouch. "Okay. Almost two days."

"Will you be all right without me?"

I bit back a smile, his vulnerability obvious and not something I would ever make fun of. "I will. Though I'll miss you, of course."

He nodded, quiet for a moment before his energy picked up. "But once I'm back, I can focus on you. On us. Building an us."

I cuddled closer to him, clinging to his arm as if to hug him while still walking along. "I would like that."

"Good. Good." He tugged me to a stop as other reindeer came into

138

view. Reindeer who should have been home and resting. Reindeer who seemed oddly focused on us.

My heartbeat picked up as they moved closer. "Isn't that the main team?"

"Most of them."

"What are they doing here?"

He shrugged, seeming almost distracted all of a sudden. "I think they just came to say hi."

That seemed...off. "Why?"

"Hold up." He gave a head nod to the reindeer who was closest to us. "Lolly, this is my teammate, Dasherwicz. He's Dasher's grandson."

"Good morning, Miss Lolly." One of the reindeer—Dasherwicz, as Prancer had said—gave me a slight bow and shook Prancer's hand. "See you this afternoon, brother."

With that, he walked off. But that didn't mean the oddness stopped. Oh no. Because the next closest reindeer took his turn and walked up, giving us the same treatment. And then the next. And the next. Every time, Prancer would take a second to tell me which family that reindeer belonged to. O'Rudolph, or Rudolph's son, McDancer, or Dancer's daughter, Vixenni, Cometes, Donderson, Barblitzen. Until finally, there was only one left. The man who seemed to push Prancer's buttons. The one who had said some pretty foul things about Prancer and me.

Cupid.

"Prancer," the reindeer said, shaking hands like all the rest.

Prancer stood tall, his arm around me as if in protection. His muscles hard and tense. Ready for a fight, it seemed.

"Cupid. This is Lolly."

Cupid gazed down at me, his brow furrowed and his eyes wide, something in his expression making me feel oddly...important. "Welcome to the family, Lolly."

Before I could ask him what he meant by that statement, he was gone. Rushing off through the foggy morning air with his long coat trailing behind him like in some sort of movie.

Weird.

"That was a little strange," I finally said, unable to hold in my surprise.

Prancer grunted then spun me around, planting a big kiss on my lips as he tugged me off my feet to hold me tightly. His touch, his affection—even his manhandling of me—soothed everything inside of me. Made me forget the weirdness. Almost.

"You need to get to work," he said when he broke the kiss. My brain was a little scrambled, so it took a few seconds for those words to make sense. But when they did...

"Oh!" I wiggled out of Prancer's hold and took off running. I *hated* to be late. "I have to get to work. I'll see you—"

I came to an abrupt stop because it was the eve of Christmas Eve. I wouldn't be seeing him. "Oh...right."

Prancer shrugged, one side of his mouth lifting. "I'll come by later today before we tack up. Then...like, two days."

Why two days sounded so long, I had no idea. Or maybe I did, because that man was my mate. He just didn't know it yet. But he would the second he made it back from his run.

*Not long now, Lolly.* "So, I'll see you in a few hours, then."

His smile was present but sad. "Yeah, baby. In a few hours."

"Okay." I gave him a smile of my own, one I tried my hardest to make as bright and happy as possible. "See you in a few hours."

And with that, I waved at him then headed inside the kitchen to finish up my baking for the day. I'd be making quick breads instead of yeast ones because when Prancer showed up in a few hours, I wanted to be able to give him my full attention.

*Just two days.*

Four hours, about two hundred mini loaves of various sweet quick breads, and some cheesy-garlic dinner rolls the Queen requested, and I was ready for my workday to be over. Or at least ready to see Prancer one more time. My stomach had been twisting all day, worry and anxiety stealing my appetite. The man was about to fly off around the world. Yes, I knew the reindeer and Santa were magically protected by the elf Queen. Yes, I knew that for hundreds of years, they had all managed to come home with only the smallest of injuries—scrapes, pulled muscles, and bruises being the most common. But that didn't mean—

"Poultices," I said into the empty kitchen, heading for the pantry once more. "I should make a few poultices for when they get back."

But before I could reach the pantry door, Prancer swept into the room, and all thoughts of sore muscles or bruises fled. That man—that man *right there*—was my sole focus. My entire body zeroed in on him, my soul screaming to make contact with his. The rest of the world had disappeared completely.

This mate stuff was hard-core.

"Hi," he said, slowly stepping toward me. If he had been a predator shifter, I'd have said he was stalking me. He might still have been—and I wouldn't mind being his prey.

"Hey. Are you—"

"Yeah, in like ten minutes."

I nodded, nearly shaking with the need to grab him, hold him, and keep him with me. His pained expression told me he was likely feeling the same, and yet we stood so many feet apart. Waiting on something to release us.

That something was Prancer himself.

"Baby," he said, lifting a hand as if to summon me. "I really need to feel you right now."

That was all the permission I needed. I rushed across the kitchen, so grateful that the rest of the staff had left early so they didn't see me slip and slide my way to him. That they missed out on the pure desperation of that trek across what felt like an endless space. But it wasn't endless after all. Once close enough, I leaped, jumping right into his arms. Unable to resist the instinctual need to cling to him as his warmth and scent surrounded me. In that moment, I felt the shift in the universe around me.

I was finally *home*.

"I know this sounds strange, but I really missed you," I whispered, burying my head in his chest. "I'm going to miss you more once you leave North Pole."

Prancer growled, turning and pressing me against a stainless-steel counter, using his body to pin mine in place. "I know, baby. I feel the same way. I don't want to leave you."

And then he was kissing me—lips on mine, tongues tangling, his hands cupping my ass as he adjusted our position. I wove my fingers into his hair and gripped tight, twisting my hips. Knowing what was coming. There'd be no getting naked, no true joining of our bodies, but there would be this. A dry hump of desperation and longing in the elf kitchen before he had to say goodbye. Of course there would be. Who could blame us?

No one, that's who.

"Baby," Prancer warned, pressing against me, his hands rougher than usual. His grip clinging.

"I know." I leaned back, rocking my hips against his. Supporting my weight on one hand while hanging on to his hip with the other. "I know, Prancer. Just go. No one will see us."

And go, he did. With a hard thrust that would have knocked me over had I not been braced for it, he growled and twisted and rutted against me like an animal out of control. Covering my body with his to steal kisses and nibbles of my lips as he chanted my name. There was no holding him back, no slowing him down. He was on a mission to come, and I was more than happy to help him get there.

But Prancer was nothing if not a gentleman. Without direction from me, he bit my lip and tweaked my nipple through my clothes, spouting some pretty impressive dirty talk so that I would come first. Talking about all the naughty things he was going to do to me once Christmas was over.

Dirty, dirty things.

I couldn't wait.

"More," I moaned as he continued to move and I grew close to that crest. "I need more."

Prancer picked me up and turned us, placing me on the short edge of the counter. Pushing the front half of me back so I was more exposed.

One hand slid up my shirt, giving attention to my breast, while the other...

Well, it slid far, far lower.

"Oh, fiddling fruitcakes." I pulled my legs up, bracing my feet on the edge of the counter as he slid two fingers inside. As his thumb found my clit and began a maddening pattern of pressure and release. As I arched my back and opened my mouth to scream, even though no sound would come out. My release came quickly and silently, my body clamping down on his. My brain scrambling.

"Fuck, so beautiful," Prancer said, continuing to tease me and send aftershocks up my spine. At least until I grabbed him and tugged myself up to sitting, needing his taste on my lips. Wanting so badly to feel the real him inside me. Something I didn't think I could get away with. But that didn't mean I couldn't make sure he finished.

"Move." I shoved his shoulder, hopping off the counter once he obeyed, giving him a saucy smirk when I wobbled a bit on the landing. "Yes, you made me come until my balance is shot."

His grin was immediate and sexy as hell. "Good to know. Next time, I'll try for full-out falling."

"Sure you will." I knelt before him, tugging at the waistband of his pants. Opening the flaps so I could reach inside and pull him out. Prancer didn't argue—he simply leaned against the counter and groaned, watching me with hooded eyes. Knowing what was coming.

"We've only got a couple minutes," he said as I gripped his girth in my hand.

"I won't need more than that." I gave him a kiss to the tip, then a lick, then dragged him inside my mouth. He was right—we did only have a few minutes. Someone could come into the kitchen at any moment, looking for either one of us. I needed to make him come, and quickly.

I sucked and I licked and I made sure to keep a hand wrapped around the base to give attention to what wouldn't fit in my mouth. I even reached into his clothes and gave his balls a tug, knowing how much he liked that. And Prancer helped. He rocked and groaned and held on to me, whispering words like *more* and *so wet* and *gonna come* until he finally exploded. Until he went stiff and released inside my mouth.

Until he finished, standing right there in an elf kitchen, completely disheveled and sexy as hell.

Until it was time for him to get ready for his trip.

The next two days were going to be so difficult.

For the both of us.

# 8

# PRANCER

The afternoon that the team and Santa left had always been a bit of a celebration. All the reindeer shifters in town came to see us off along with hundreds of elves. There had always been food and entertainment and festivities that could not be beat, but on this eve of Christmas Eve, the party held no interest for me. All I cared about, all I wanted to see, was my girl. Sadly, because I still hadn't told her she was my mate, I stood alone while she waited in a crowd somewhere outside my line of sight.

"Idiot," I whispered under my breath. Or at least I thought I had.

"Always have been, but you don't need to call me out like that." Cupid gave me an elbow, his head up and an arrogant sort of smile on his face. "Where's your girl, Prance?"

Fuck, this was not what I needed. "Out there...somewhere."

He jerked his head in my direction, that smile faltering. "Your mate isn't coming to see you off?"

"No, she is. She's just..." *Not where I want her to be.* "Out there."

"Trouble in paradise already?"

"No."

"Then why—"

"Because I haven't told her she's my mate yet."

He froze, staring. Speechless for what was likely the first time in his very long life. "Why the hell not?"

And of course, I didn't have an answer for him. Now that the big night was here, now that I was leaving her for two solid days as I traversed the globe with my team and delivered presents with the big man, any sort of reasoning I'd held seemed trivial. Of course, I wanted her to know. Of course, I wanted to stand on the stage with my mate beside me, showing her off, and giving her that final kiss before I shifted and prepped for work. I wanted it...

And there was no good fucking reason why I couldn't have it.

"Where is she?" I said, rising up on the balls of my feet and looking over the crowd. "I can't see her."

"Maybe she left," Cupid replied, though he began seeking her out as well. "Yo, Dasherwicz. See Prancer's mate out there?"

Dasherwicz—long known for his abilities to find his way through any sort of soup the skies threw at us—turned toward the crowd, his eyes panning, his gaze sharp. He seemed to struggle as much as I did, though how could I blame him? Lolly was a tad...short. In a crowd the size of the one in front of us, spotting her would be near impossible. Even if I could, how I would get her up on the stage was—

"There," Dasherwicz said, pointing. "She's next to that elf dressed as a candy cane."

It took me three seconds to lock eyes with her, but when I did, I felt that pull deep in my belly that had been driving me in her direction for days. My mate, my woman, my world. I needed her by me.

"Hey, Coach," Cupid hollered, catching the attention of the older elf who stood close to our feet. "Prancer's mate is out in the crowd. Let's get her up here with the rest of them."

Coach looked to me, surprise on his face. "You forget how things go tonight, Prance?"

I shrugged, still watching Lolly. "It's new."

"Understood." Coach headed to the fence line and spoke to the security there, hollering into the crowd. Lolly broke my gaze, obviously hearing her name, and frowned before walking closer to the fences that kept the mass of people back. A few words spoken, some arm movements I couldn't explain, and Coach reached across the barrier and picked up my girl, hauling her toward the stage before lifting her as if she were a lion cub being presented to its pride.

"This is new," Dasherwicz said as he helped Cupid and me lift my elf onto the stage. "Did we get the right Lolly?"

She nodded, looking cautiously between the three of us as the crowd roared. "What's going on?"

Dasherwicz gently led his own mate—a lovely, sweet reindeer who had been mated to him for decades—so she stood in front of him. "This is Vena, my mate. How about she comes to pick you up for our return ceremony and shows you where to go to be on the stage? That way, no one gets lost in the crowds."

Vena waved at Lolly, who smiled and nodded back. Meanwhile, I stood stock-still, wanting her in my arms. Needing it but afraid of breaking the moment. Of her figuring out what I still needed to tell her. Of somehow losing her even though she stood just a few feet away.

I was an idiot.

"Come here, baby," I finally said, my voice rough and low. Lolly didn't hesitate. She ran and jumped at me, curling herself against my chest and wrapping her arms around me. And in that instant, all was right with the world. Mostly.

"When I get back tomorrow night," I started, holding her tight. Keeping my voice low so it was just her and me in the moment. "The second my hooves hit cobblestone, we're going to have a conversation about how you're mine. You hear me?"

She nodded against me, her arms tightening.

Mine for sure.

Forever.


*LOLLY*

Standing onstage with the other reindeer and their mates was absolutely surreal. As was watching as Prancer shifted in front of my eyes from human form to animal. He stood at least two feet taller than me as a reindeer, his cloven hooves bigger than my own feet and his chest at my eye level. He was massive.

And oddly...arousing. A feeling that felt so very wrong.

"It's the power," Vena said, slipping in beside me. "I assume this is your first time seeing him as a reindeer."

"Yeah. It is."

She nodded, her eyes locked on her own mate. "The power of them in this form is almost an aphrodisiac for us. Don't worry—totally normal."

"So I'm not...attracted..." I couldn't even finish my sentence. Luckily, Vena didn't make me. Instead, she laughed.

"Of course not. I promise, this is just a draw through the mating bond to the power they exude. Once they land and shift human, the real fun begins."

Mating bond. As if she knew. But I hadn't even told Prancer yet, so that wasn't possible. Was it?

*Damage control.* "Oh, we're not...you know. That."

She leaned in closer, lowering her voice. Her eyes practically sparkling. "If you're not mates, I'll eat those reins they're putting on your man right now."

I spun, meeting the eyes of Prancer in his reindeer form. Something about the deep brown surrounded by fur, about the way he had to look so far down to see me. Something about the way he carried himself in that form. Yeah, Vena was right. It had to be the power making me crave him so much.

"Fine," I said, still whispering. "But I haven't told him yet."

She laughed again, patting me on the shoulder as she said, "I think he already knows."

And with that, she walked off to where Dasherwicz stood, his traces and collar in place. His eyes locked on the willowy woman approaching him. She leaned in once she reached him, burrowing into his fur and speaking soft, quiet words only for him. He arched his neck and wrapped it around her—the reindeer equivalent of a hug. All things I'd seen hundreds of times. All things I'd never been this close to.

All things I was about to experience for myself.

"He's all yours for a few minutes," the elf who'd been preparing Prancer for the flight said, moving out of my way. I approached my mate the same way Vena had, looking up into those deep brown eyes in wonder. Reaching to weave my fingers through his fur once I could.

Soft but wiry. And so very thick.

"You're fuzzy." I chuckled as his hoof slammed down. "Don't worry —I like it."

He snorted, dropping his head and groaning softly in that way reindeer did. Speaking a language I couldn't understand but getting his meaning across just fine.

"I'll miss you too. But you'll be back in two days." I looked up at him, locking our gazes. Holding him the only way I could. "And then, I'm all yours."

His hug was nowhere near as gentle as Dasherwicz's had been for his mate. In fact, Prancer nearly knocked me off my feet as he bent his neck to hold me to him. Not that I minded. My first reindeer hug was strong and warm, the fur soft against me. It was perfect.

And I couldn't wait for more.

# 9

# PRANCER

I *love my job. I love my job. I love my job.*

"There's a bit of a blizzard up ahead, but I know you all will be able to handle it," Santa said as he logged our current location on his tablet. "It may slow us down a bit, though. Thankfully, we have a few hours built into the schedule, so we can take an easy pace through the worst of it."

*I love my job...but want it to be over.*

I stood in line as I'd done hundreds of times, all dressed up in collars and traces and a bridle to help pull the sleigh with the magical being sitting in it. This position had always been an honor—a responsibility we did not take lightly. But the years had worn on me, the loneliness dragging me down a path I had barely even acknowledged. Until Lolly.

Now, all I wanted was to be back home with my girl. To love on her, to spoil her, to bring her happiness so I could see her smile every day. I'd only just found her, and already, I was being pulled away to work for two entire days. A blink of an eye in my long life, but an agonizing length of time for a newly mated pair.

I was miserable, and a run through a blizzard wasn't going to help that.

"I'm off to deliver," Santa said, pulling me from my depressing thoughts as he stepped out of the sleigh. "Stay warm."

With that, he disappeared into the night, bouncing magically to houses all across the region we'd posted up in. It would take him about ten minutes to complete the run for this stop, covering more miles in that time than humanly possible via time warps and relativity clouds. It was a tough job, but the man seemed to love it. Me, on the other hand...

"You hanging in there, Prance?" Cupid asked, his human form taking me by surprise. We didn't shift once the run started. Ever.

I grunted, staring at him. Noticing the others looking as well. Though they all seemed far more focused on...me.

*What the...?*

"Look," Cupid started, still human. Still racked up in his pulling harness. "We're all thrilled that you found your mate, but we're worried about you."

I glanced around at my team as much as I could. They'd never needed to be worried before.

"The other guys and I had a talk, and we're down to get you back to North Pole as fast as possible so you can spend time with your Lolly. So, this blizzard? Run. Hell-for-leather, no matter what...just run. You're going to be the pacesetter on this one." He gave me a look that held more understanding and respect than I'd seen from him in decades. Centuries, maybe. It was as if he understood the chaos on my head on a personal level.

The other reindeer stomped their hooves, all of them apparently in agreement. Cupid gave them all a glance, nodding to each segment before leaving me with one final statement.

"We've got your back, Prancer."

And with that, he shifted to his reindeer form again, shaking himself into his harness saddle and standing on four legs as he should have been. He even stomped his hooves to rid the snow of his human footprints. Meanwhile, I could only stare, unable to believe the brotherhood I'd just experienced. The support.

I was going to have to make sure Lolly baked them beignets every morning for the rest of their lives.

When Santa returned, he eyed Cupid hard. The man had such a sense of what was going on around him, was so intuitive, there was no way he didn't know what had happened. But Cupid stared straight ahead, looking completely ready to take off and do his job. As did the rest of the team.

Me? I pawed at the ground, wanting to fly. Needing to get in the air. I had a girl to get back to and a team ready to help me. The old man needed to *move*.

"Prancer," Santa said as he headed toward the sleigh, stopping right beside me. "Forgive me, son. I was remiss in not wishing you the best on your mating. My overlook is more a sign of my busy mind than of any negative feelings. I hope you can forgive me."

I nodded, still impatient. Still wanting him to load up into the sleigh so we could move.

He, unfortunately, had other plans. "It's funny that you mated to an elf. There hasn't been a pairing outside the reindeer breed for your kind in..." He looked up at the sky, a slight smile on his face, his cheeks rosier than usual and more of a twinkle in his eye than I'd ever seen before. "Well, since my own parents came together in a mated bond, I suppose."

I jerked in the reins, the other reindeer doing the same. All staring at the man who'd been our leader for lifetimes. The one we apparently knew nothing about. Santa was half reindeer?

And Santa—true to form as ever—just laughed at being the subject of a nine-team stare. His belly even jiggled like a bowl full of jelly. "You all look so surprised."

I snorted, trying hard to find a way to say *we are surprised* while in a form that couldn't speak. Santa just chuckled again and headed to the sleigh, finally climbing inside.

"So I assume my slow pace through the blizzard has been overruled. I'm okay with that but hope you can all keep the sleigh steady enough not to lose me along the way. Now, brothers and cousins and friends, let's be on our way so our newest couple can be reunited."

I glanced over at Cupid, whose eyes were as wide as I had to imagine mine to be. Santa was part reindeer. We'd had no idea. There was going to be so much to learn once we made it back to North Pole.

153

But first, we had to finish our run and give Santa the opportunity to deliver all the presents he'd promised.

And then, I had a mate to woo.

"Lead the way, O'Rudolph. Lead the way."

With that, we were off again. Heading lightning fast into a blizzard. Working together to shorten our trip so I could make it home faster. The team definitely kept their word, letting me set a blazing pace through the night sky and working hard to keep up. All so Lolly and I could be reunited a few hours earlier than planned.

*I love my job...but especially my team.*


*LOLLY*

Two days. Two very, very long days all alone. Well, not *all* alone—my fellow elves couldn't seem to leave me be. Everyone had seen me snuggling Prancer onstage, and they all wanted to know what was going on. Not that I knew. Not really. Okay, I knew—we were fated mates— but I truly felt as if I should talk to him about that before I started blabbing to every elf on this side of North Pole. Even if I did want to shout it from the top of the highest building to make sure *everyone* knew.

Thankfully, Vena kept me busy while we waited for our reindeer to return. I only worked a couple hours a day, making treats for the remaining reindeer of Santa's vast team, and my nights would have been horribly lonely had she not shown up in the kitchen that first day and dragged me out for coffee. Coffee became dinner which became movies at her place. The next morning, after I'd finished baking the Christmas Eve treats, she'd said we needed to do some retail therapy, which led to six hours of shopping in stores I hadn't even known existed, as they were in Tarandus, the reindeer side of town.

Two days of talking, waiting, and being impatient...that ended quite a bit sooner than I'd been prepared for.

"Hurry up, Lolly!" Vena yelled, reaching back for my hand as the crowds pressed in around us. The sleigh was due back any minute, the announcement having been broadcast through North Pole only moments before. Vena and I had rushed from another coffee date and raced toward the stage, both of us giggling and giddy.

*They're back!*

With the stage still barely in sight, I began to worry about getting lost in the sea of people ready to celebrate another successful Christmas run. There were just so many bodies all heading in the same direction we needed to go. Vena didn't let that happen, though. She grabbed my hand and pulled me along with her, both of us slipping through the people as best we could until a security guard from Santa's brigade finally spotted us. He cleared a path so we could reach the stairs, not even batting an eyelash at my presence.

Guess everyone knew I was with Prancer after all. Screaming from buildings not required.

We weren't onstage and in position more than two minutes before the sleigh appeared on the horizon. The crowd grew louder with every passing moment, getting downright raucous when the sleigh was finally close enough to see each individual reindeer. I barely noticed the other eight of them, though—my eyes were locked on Prancer's heavy form, his long legs pumping hard as he raced across the sky toward me. Toward us. This was it. The first day of our forever. No more secrets or excuses.

"I think I'm going to be sick."

Vena laughed and rested a hand on my shoulder. "Wait until they land. The mating bond is strong on an average day. Seeing our boys all sweaty and worked up from two solid days of dangerous, physical work?" She shook her head, her eyes going unfocused as she watched the approaching sleigh. "In case you've never noticed, these welcome home ceremonies don't last long. That's all I'm going to say."

She didn't need to elaborate—I could already feel the tug inside me. The deep, swirling warming happening. My man was close, and the fates were fully prepared to torture us for the next few minutes as we waited to be released to our own devices.

Santa had better hurry up.

I hadn't even finished that thought before the leader of the team—O'Rudolph, of course—set his first hoof on the stage floor. The entire structure shook under the force of nine husky reindeer and a huge sleigh along with a rather large man landing on it, but no one seemed worried, so I stood tall and waited. Held my position as the reindeer and sleigh came to a sliding stop on the wood floor. Once still, it only took a few seconds for Santa to hop out of the sleigh and grab a microphone from one of his elves

"Ho ho ho, another successful year in the books," he said, waving and smiling as the crowd roared in celebration. I clapped along, but my eyes were locked on my Prancer, all sweaty and riled and...fuzzy. *So much fur.*

"I don't want to take any more time than necessary," Santa said, walking along the length of his team and toward where all the mates were standing. "But I do want to thank my team for always making sure we get to where we need to be when we need to be there."

I glanced up just as Santa stopped in front of me, the man blocking my view of Prancer. "And I'd like to thank the family, friends, and mates of my team who make everything so much easier on them. It is time for all of us to rest for a few weeks before we begin working on the next trip around the world." He handed the microphone to an elf and leaned down to speak directly to me. "It is customary for the reindeer to have their harness and bridle removed by their mates. Since this is your first time, the equipment manager will come assist you."

*Mates.* Oh. He knew. And I certainly wasn't about to deny it. "Thank you, sir."

His smile grew, those eyes truly twinkling. "No sirs allowed. Welcome to the family, Lolly."

And with that, he disappeared into the crowd to greet the elves and reindeer who supported him, while those of us on the stage approached our reindeer. As promised, the equipment manager met me at Prancer's side, giving me a smile and a single head nod.

"It's not hard, you see," he said, pointing to a buckle that sat just above my own head. "You just unfasten this right here, then..."

156

And so it went, him pointing out what needed to be done and me following his instructions. To his credit, he never jumped in to do the work himself—instead, guiding me through what would apparently be my yearly task. A task I was definitely going to master—if the other mates could handle this, so could I.

Eventually, I ended up at Prancer's head, his bridle in my hands and his body completely removed of all the leather accoutrements he'd been wearing. He stood tall and strong, almost vibrating with an energy I, too, could feel.

"You're sweaty," I whispered as I wove my fingers into his fur. "I think a long shower is the first thing we should do once we get home."

He huffed and groaned that reindeer groan, nudging me with his head.

"What? What do you want?"

He nudged me again, pushing me backward and yet following me as well. I had no clue what he wanted, but apparently the equipment manager did.

"Hold still, miss," he said before dropping down to one knee. "Hop up."

I blinked. "Pardon?"

It was Vena who answered me, though. "He won't shift human with this crowd watching, Lolly. You'll know why later. Besides, this is the fastest way home."

Without another word, she hopped onto Dasherwicz's back and swung her leg over him. Once she was settled astride her mate, he took off, his feet pounding and her laugh echoing off the buildings around us.

"Oh." I glanced back at the elf still waiting on me. "So...I guess he's my transportation."

He patted his knee. "Your mate is ready to go home. He's had a long couple days—it would be rude to make him wait."

How very right he was. Without another moment to waste, I stepped onto his knee and reached up, thankful when the elf pushed me onto Prancer's back. I wasn't graceful in the least, but I made it to where I needed to be. Sitting astride Prancer's warm, fuzzy back.

My life had gotten so weird. Wonderfully so.

"Okay, mate," I said, leaning forward a little to make sure he heard me. Loving how he tensed at my first use of that term. "Take me home so I can get you all cleaned up before making you dirty again."

The man didn't hesitate. He took off at a full gallop with me on his back, running faster the more I laughed.

And I laughed a lot. Every second on the way to Prancer's house, I giggled and chortled and truly let my enjoyment be heard.

Prancer barely paused once he arrived home, simply kicking the door open and racing inside to shift while pulling me from his back. It was the most acrobatic thing I'd ever done—trying hard to hang on to him and not fall to the floor. Not that I would have. Prancer's grip was rock solid. As were the muscles pressing against me now that his fur had once again become skin.

"Mine," he growled once he was fully human again. "All fucking mine."

"Yours." I reached up and bit his earlobe, loving the way he shivered at the sting. "Your mate."

With a deep rumble from within him, Prancer turned and shoved me against the wall, pressing his hips to mine. Showing me how hard he really was. "Again."

Greedy boy. "You like that, don't you?"

"I like everything you do, but hearing you call me mate is pretty fucking amazing."

"Prove it."

He froze, staring into my eyes for a moment before his lips turned up just enough to make my heart stutter. "You're my mate, Lolly. My fated forever. And if you'll have me, I'll make sure that forever is as happy and filled with love as possible."

I nodded, clinging to his shoulders even harder as I fought back tears. "Okay, yeah. That *is* pretty fucking amazing."

"Told you." He turned and headed for the stairs, carrying me the entire way. "Now, how about that shower?"

"And a massage."

"For me or for you?"

"For you, my hardworking reindeer mate."

"I'll definitely take it, my sweet elf mate. But first, I need a taste of you, so let's get naked. I can spend a few minutes worshiping that pussy before we hop in the shower. Sound like a plan?"

What it sounded like was heaven. "Whatever you say, my mate."

# EPILOGUE

## LOLLY

Summer in North Pole was a busy time of year. Not because of vacations and traveling, but because toy manufacturing and reindeer training were in full swing. I'd left the kitchen for the season, the heat making it difficult to want to bake. Instead, I made frozen treats for all the reindeer and elves who wanted them—popsicles, lassies, fudge bars, ice cream cookie sandwiches—all of them. Prancer particularly liked my snow cones because I made my own syrups to flavor them.

Which was why it didn't surprise me at all when he walked up behind me while I was making said snow cones.

"Hungry, mate?" I asked, grinning when he growled that reindeer sound I loved so much. Yup, I was never going to get tired of calling him my mate.

"Definitely, but I really only came over to see how you're feeling."

Tired. I'd been tired for weeks—more than just the normal "my mate is a sex fiend who keeps me up all night" tired. I'd been suffering from a soul-heavy exhaustion that had taken me to the local doctor's office.

The doctor who looked so darn surprised when the routine pregnancy test he had run turned out positive.

The doctor who had looked at Prancer and said, "I hadn't thought it possible, seeing as how usually reindeer only mate with their own kind, but you're going to be a dad."

I placed my hand over Prancer's as he rubbed my still nonexistent belly, so excited to experience a pregnancy with this sweet, caring man. "I'm fine."

Prancer's hand stilled, his fingers tapping a small rhythm against my belly instead. "And our little stowaway?"

"They seem to be fine as well."

"Good. Now, how about you call it a day and come take a nap with me?"

Shimmering stockings, that sounded divine. "Are you sure you can take a break?"

He shrugged, bringing my hand to his lips to kiss the back of it. "My mate needs a nap. Nothing is more important than that. Now, come on —I want to take care of my girls."

Girls. He was so certain the baby was going to be a little girl that he simply referred to us in the plural. I wasn't as sure yet, but I looked forward to finding out. Just as I looked forward to every step in this journey of life, mating, and parenthood I was taking with Prancer by my side. Boy or girl, elf or reindeer or some magical combination of the two—those things didn't matter so long as we had each other. And our little gift from the fates.

And since I was due at the end of December, I wouldn't refuse a little Christmas magic either.

# CINNAMON CLAUS

## KINSHIP COVE: HEARTTHROBS & HOLIDAYS

**No one ever said working with Santa was all reindeer games, and North Pole isn't a place of wonder and amazement...until it is. It may not be the holidays, but magic is definitely in the air.**

Working in Santa's post office wasn't an easy job. Each letter had to be read—even the ones that dug a hole in your heart and left shadows of the pain they imparted. But every elf needed a job if they were going to afford things like food and heat and a place to read a good book.

Every elf except Santa's brother. He's wild, charming, and totally unrestrained by the monotony of life...or so go the rumors. He's totally not the type of man I would take a second look at. At least, not until an accident he causes forces me to and my world heads down a path I hadn't thought possible.

. . .

What should a good elf do when the bad-boy brother of the big man himself comes to town and burns down the rumor mill with his smile, his kindness, and his heart? The spare may just be more vital to the Claus name than anyone expected. And I might be falling in love with him.

# 1

# ZIRA

Being the illegitimate child of one of Santa's most trusted elves was definitely not something I would recommend. Like, ever.

Neither was working at the postal office for the big man himself.

"Another one." I sighed and set the letter to the side, running my fingers over the loopy, messy script some child had worked hard to put down on ruled notebook paper likely torn out of a school pad. "These are the worst."

Dahnearys, the older elf who helped me keep Santa's wish list up-to-date, sighed. "Was it socks or a coat?"

"Socks. It's always the socks that get me."

Because how bad must a child's life be for them to use their one shot at toys and fun to ask instead for something as basic as socks? It gutted me to read those requests, especially knowing Santa was going to disappoint them.

"I wish he'd actually bring them a pair of socks. Just once."

Dahnearys sighed. "I know, child. Those letters are hard."

She stared off for a second at another, much smaller pile. The one that grew every year and forever would. The one there was no way for us to help with. The "please bring back my..." pile. The older elf had once said those were the letters that kept her up at night. I couldn't even begin to fathom them, so my focus remained on the ones asking for socks. We actually could have actually done something about socks.

A sudden alarm broke the stillness of the mail room, a light in the corner flashing green.

"Oh, come on," I said. Whined, really. I wasn't in the mood for *this*.

"You know he has to push out content this time of year. Otherwise, the kids might forget about him and move on to some other mythical creature just waiting in the wings to take over." Dahnearys rose to her feet and straightened her work area, hurrying off to the little cubby at the front of the mail room that actually looked like an antiquated post office. I did the same, but at a much slower pace—tucking away my cell phone, tidying the stacks of mail, closing the lid on the computer I used to receive the emails from more modern children. Once finished, I also headed into the old-fashioned postal room. I grabbed my bonnet from the hook by the door and stood next to Dahnearys, ready for our yearly visit from the man himself.

"This is such a waste of time," I said, keeping my voice low and my plastic smile in place. "He knows we're super busy."

"He does, but there's nothing we can do. Smile, be pleasant, and hopefully he'll leave us alone in a few minutes. You do remember what to say if he calls you out, right?"

I would have answered her, but at that moment, the door flew open and Santa himself came walking through. He had a handful of elves following him, one with a big camera on his shoulder. All of them practically tripping over themselves to keep up with the man in red.

"Ho, ho, ho. And here we have our post office, where all your letters come in to be prepared for me to read."

The urge to roll my eyes was a tough one to resist, but I managed. That man hadn't read a letter in years. He had us to do that for him.

Santa said a few more things into the camera, putting on a good show, before moving across the room to where the huge sacks of mail sat, all filled with letters in hundreds of languages. All waiting to be read.

"Looks like my postal elves are falling a little behind. Don't worry, kiddos. I'll make sure to read every letter before I take off on Christmas Eve. No one will slow me down."

Dahnearys looked ready to spit nails but stood stock-still, glaring at the old man. The one who both made us so proud *and* drove us absolutely bananas.

Thankfully, at that moment, the elf Queen walked into the postal room. Her clove scent wafted around her, and her soft smile for each elf in her vicinity eased the tension. Especially for Dahnearys and me.

"Good morning, ladies," she said, her voice practically filled with magic. "How goes the letter-reading this year?"

Dahnearys and I both nodded, whispering words like *Well, ma'am* and *Fine, Your Majesty.* The Queen's smile grew, and she glanced over her shoulder to where Santa seemed to be speaking loudly directly into the camera. About what, I had no idea because I had the Queen's attention.

"Miss Zira," she said, dragging her eyes away from Santa and keeping a smile on her face even as her eyes seemed to darken. "Are there any letters to be discarded? Any...basics-only requests?"

My heart jumped in my chest. This was why I loved the woman so much. See, when children only asked for basics—socks, a winter coat, new gloves—and no toys, the letters were discarded and the list updated to state, "generic toy." The Queen knew this, and she also knew our giving her those letters was strictly forbidden. Not that I had any intention of following Santa's rules.

I glanced at the scene across the room before slipping back to my work area and grabbing the stack, the letter on torn, ruled paper right on top.

"Here you are, Your Majesty," I said once I made it back to the little room. "Lots of need for socks this year."

She sighed, her smile dimming before her eyes darted to Santa's group once more. Keeping her gaze on him, she took the letters from me and slipped them to her guard, a tall elf named Carron.

"Take care of these, please," she said. Carron nodded before stepping between the Queen and me, the motion blocking my view for just a split second. The letters suddenly gone. The handoff had been completed right in front of me, and yet I hadn't seen a thing. That was the magic of Carron. He made everything so easy and looked so smooth doing it. I had no idea how he managed to defuse the moment the way he did, but even the Queen herself seemed to relax a little.

"Thank you both for all the hard work you do. I know this job isn't always easy and some of those words stay with you." She reached for Dahnearys's hand, squeezing it as if she knew the wishes of the children who had lost loved ones haunted the other elf. "Please know we're here for you if you need someone to talk to or a break from the strain. For all the positivity and light Santa brings, there is darkness in this process. You do not need to brave it alone."

She released Dahnearys's hand, taking the time to grab mine and look me in the eye. "And if you find more of the things that pique my interest, please ring Carron. He'll make sure I'm made aware."

"Thank you, Your Majesty," I said, certain the little human child who had written to Santa for socks would see a pair or ten show up at their house soon enough. The Queen would not fail us. She couldn't take care of all the children asking for basics, but she tried her best. Which was more than I could say for Mr. Bowl-Full-of-Jelly over there.

Speaking of the cookie collector, Santa and his crew left soon after, not bothering to come back and give us thanks or apologize for the interruption. The Queen and Carron left as well, both exhibiting far better manners. Dahnearys went immediately back to her work area to continue opening and reading the letters, but it took me another minute or two to regain my focus. The Queen herself had come to say hello. No matter how often she did that—and she was known to pop in and check on her elves regularly—it still always surprised me and made me a little giddy. And distracted.

"I need to get back to work," I finally said, more to myself than anything.

"Yeah, you do, child. Let's go."

Dahnearys and I worked the rest of the day as we always did— mostly quiet, sometimes chatting about our fellow elves or upcoming events in town, sometimes bemoaning a particularly difficult letter we had to read. Eventually, though, the time came for us to shut down for the evening. With a quick goodbye and a *have a good evening*, I rushed out the door and down the staff halls. I wanted out of the castle, out of the work rooms. I wanted a break from the drudgery of my life, even if it would only last for the few hours I had to eat, relax, and sleep before returning to the bags of letters.

I shoved my way into the evening air, breathing deeply before heading to Tinsel Trail, the elf shopping district. The street was packed with elves rushing about, most likely grabbing food with friends or family. It was dinnertime, after all. I myself had been looking forward to popping into my favorite little diner and grabbing a big bowl of soup and some crusty bread. Unfortunately, my day decided to go from bad to worse in the blink of an eye.

"Pooping peppermint sticks," I whispered as I came to an abrupt stop right outside the diner. There, at a table directly in front of the window as if being featured in some sort of advertisement for the place, were two of my cousins. The women looked to be having a wonderful time with their animated chatter and multitude of empty wineglasses around them. Had I come from a normal family, I would likely have rushed inside, said hello, perhaps joined them for one last drink. Normal cousins would have been happy to see one another.

Our family wasn't normal, and I'd never actually met those women.

"You coming inside?"

I looked away from my cousins to find an older male elf holding the door open for me, smiling my way.

"Oh, no. I've changed my mind."

He nodded, allowing the door to fall closed behind him as he stepped onto the sidewalk. "Well, get yourself something hearty. I recognize the uniform—" he tapped the lapel of my postal worker shirt "—you have important work to do."

I stood a little straighter, knowing others saw my job as valuable instead of torment. "I do. Thank you."

I spun and hurried away, not even giving my cousins a single glance more. Between them and the letter from the kid who wanted socks for Christmas, my day was shot. Torpedoed. Crushed. I might as well have just gone home and pulled something horrible and not all that good for me out of the freezer to warm up for dinner.

But before I could do that, I had to walk past the candy shoppe, a store I usually avoided. Something tugged me inside this time, refusing to allow me to ignore the craving. And there, right on top of the counter, was exactly what I always looked for in the place—peanut brittle.

"What can I get you, love?" The lady behind the counter gave me a smile, looking so very happy and engaged.

I shook off my envy and plastered on a weak smile of my own, hoping she didn't notice how fake it was. "Can I please have a small box of peanut brittle?"

"Of course. Anything else for you?"

"No, just the brittle." I watched as she filled a small box practically to bursting with the hard, sticky stuff. Peanut brittle had been one of my mother's favorite treats. She had made it every Christmas season, along with honeycomb. But it had always been the brittle that had reminded me of her. And in that moment, with such a horrible day pressing on my shoulders, I needed a little bit of my mother to pull me through.

"Here you go, love." The lady handed me the box, waving me off when I reached into my bag to grab my wallet. "On the house. You look like you've had a hard day."

"Are you sure? I can—"

She shook her head and took a step back, her body language screaming that she wouldn't take my money. "My husband used to work in the postal room. There was many a night when he came home with the same expression on his face as what was just on yours. Go on now. You need to recharge."

She was right. So very right. I gave her a nod and a soft thanks before slipping back outside, my faith in elfdom restored. My mind ready to go home and find a way to unwind.

Sadly, the rest of the North Pole decided not to cooperate with my plan.

A huge motorcycle came roaring around a corner, and the crowd on the street practically gasped in unison, the excitement rising as the loud machine rolled closer. I had no idea what was going on, too busy pulling a piece of brittle from the box to suck on. I had just turned to walk the rest of the way home when a group of elves started screaming in some sort of high-pitched, joyful chorus and rushed toward the street.

"It's Santa's brother," a woman yelled with a giggle, which didn't make me any more interested. The Not-Santa had been seen as a rock star around these parts my entire life. I had no interest in the man.

Unfortunately, I got caught up in the wave as the crowd surged closer to the street, shoved and pushed and crushed in the press. At some point, I must have made it over the curb because the ground no longer met my foot when I stepped, and my entire body went down. I had this moment of fear, this thought of dying right there on the street in front of the candy shoppe surrounded by fallen brittle that went flying the moment my knees hit concrete.

Candy...destroyed.

"Oh, come on," I wailed, ready to surrender to the dark cloud obviously following me around. Ready to give up and let the elves around me crush me under their overexcited steps. My eyes burned with unshed tears, and my empty hand curled into a fist at the loss of the one good thing I had been given during the length of my crappy day. Done. I was done. Every good thing inside of me destroyed like the brittle being crushed to grit. There was no point in trying anymore.

As if denying my desire to be trampled to death on the street, a hand reached through the crowd, appearing right before my tired eyes. I grabbed it out of pure instinct, not fighting the pull as whoever it was picked me up and lifted me out of the chaos. Empty brittle box in hand.

"Thanks," I said as soon as my feet once again hit the cobblestones. I stared at the crushed candy box, unable to tear my eyes away from it. "Guess my knees and my brittle are victims of an overrated elf."

"I'm sorry?"

That was the moment I actually looked up. The moment I realized the overrated elf had been the one to reach into the crowd and yank me back to my feet. The moment I knew exactly why so many elves practically fainted when Santa's brother was around.

The bluest eyes I'd ever seen locked me in their gaze, and my entire world went sideways. Not in a bad way—I stayed on my feet—but the physical tug between us sent ten lords a-leaping right through my solar plexus. I knew that feeling—had been told about it a thousand times. While elves didn't usually have the same fated matings as the reindeer on the other side of town, there had been instances. I had heard one or two stories about the feeling of wanting to crawl inside the person your soul was tied to. One of our bakers had met her mate in an OG sleigh-puller just a few seasons before. This almost instinctual desire to burrow into the man's arms and stay there sounded an awful lot like the stories she had told of what she'd felt the moment she'd met Prancer.

I had just found my fated mate…in Santa's brother.

I let out the breath I'd been holding and shook my head. "Not today."

# 2

## ZIRA

E xcuse me?"

The brother looked confused. Of course he did. He had likely just felt the same pull I had, had likely gotten his hopes up that fate had gifted him something precious, and there I was, backing away from him.

"This is nuts." I spun and hurried away, too boggled to even contemplate sticking around. My steps pounded on the cobblestone streets, the sound of Santa's brother following making me walk faster than usual. I might as well have been jogging at that point.

"Wait, little elf."

But I didn't wait. "No. I need to go home."

The man was persistent; I could give him that. He continued to follow me, silent but there. Not forcing me to make small talk but refusing to give me my space. I couldn't decide if that was more of a positive or negative trait. Tenacity had its appeal, but I was not in the mood for such a thing to be turned on me. I needed a bath, a peppermint tea, and my bed. I could deal with the mess my life had become in the morning.

"So, we're just going to ignore the fact that we're mated, then?"

Ooooorrrrrrrrr...not.

I froze, practically wobbling as I went from striding to standing in a breath. My spin to face the man behind me went slower than usual, the fear of what I'd see when I faced him swirling deep in my gut.

Yup. He was handsome. Almost painfully so. Especially when he smiled at me. The jerk.

"You figured that out?"

He cocked his head, that smile tugging harder at his fun pink lips. "I'm not an idiot."

"I didn't say you were. I just assumed you were lacking self-awareness like your brother."

"You're not that lucky."

I sighed, fighting the urge to smack—or kiss—that cheeky grin off his too-handsome face. "Well, shoot."

He rolled his eyes in an exaggerated sort of way. "Quit running away and come with me."

That was when he reached for my arm. I'd like to say he grabbed me, yanked me off my feet, did something to make my sudden unease around him worthwhile. I would have liked to, but then I'd have been a liar. The man grasped my arm carefully, strong but not demanding. Leading but not pulling. He even kept his eyes locked on mine, obviously seeking approval. Why did he have to be so attentive? So not what I thought he'd be? If he had been willing to live up to the image of him in my head, he would have been a jerk.

Heck, he was a jerk for not being a jerk. The jerk.

I really needed to get some dinner before my brain circled around itself so much that it got tangled.

I followed Santa's brother back into the crowds, not really wanting to but super curious. What could possibly be so important that he braved the throngs of people on Tinsel Trail? The ones staring at both of us. Especially me. If he thought—

"Here," he said, then stepped back to guide me inside the candy shoppe. "Let's fix what I messed up for you."

Agog. I had never used the word in my life, but there I was, agog. Agogging? Feeling agog? Whatever. I was stunned.

"You want to buy me candy?"

Those blue eyes met mine, twinkling in the bright lights. "I want to replace what my presence cost you."

With that, he led the way to the counter, killer smile in place. "Good evening, miss. I was hoping you could help me."

The woman looked about ready to cough up a frog or something. Her skin had turned an unhealthy shade of red, and her eyes were as round as the lollipops standing up in a display on the counter.

"Of course, Mr. Claus. Whatever you need."

"I'd like a box of peanut brittle, please." He leaned closer, murmuring, "That was peanut brittle you dropped, yes?"

I nodded, unable to speak. The woman behind the counter grabbed the large box, and I moved to raise my hand. Santa's brother squeezed my bicep and stepped behind me, looming over me. Bending down so he could whisper in my ear.

"What's the problem?"

"I dropped a small box. She's packing a large one."

"Do you like peanut brittle?"

"I do."

"How much?"

I stared at the woman taking the hardened golden-brown chunks of sweet and salty delight from the display, thinking of my mother in the kitchen making the same.

"It's my favorite."

"Then we go with the large box."

I watched as the woman behind the counter made a big show of stuffing the large box full of brittle, smiling at Santa's brother the entire time. She even wrapped a red ribbon around the box and tied it into a beautiful bow.

"Is that all you need?" She handed the box across the counter, practically shaking as he took it from her. She may have even whimpered—I couldn't tell if that sound was real or something I made up in my head. We'd go with made up just to save the woman a little dignity.

"Yes, thank you," Santa's brother said, either oblivious or simply ignoring her obsession with him. "I appreciate you making this look so lovely for me."

That red color deepened, her cheeks practically on fire. "Oh, it was no problem. *Anything* for Santa's brother."

The stress on the word anything was what did me in. I changed my mind immediately. She *had* whimpered when she handed him the box—it wasn't some auditory hallucination on my part. She whimpered. All dignity lost at that point.

Once he had paid for the box of brittle, he turned and placed it in my hands. Giving me a private sort of smile.

"I cost you your treat. I couldn't live with myself if I didn't replace it."

My quiet *thank you* was likely only heard by him, made obvious by the way the woman behind the counter spoke over me.

"I thought the treat was for you."

Santa's brother shot her a little smirk, glancing at her from the corner of his eye. "It is, in a way. I'm giving it to my friend…"

And there we were. Two people tied together by fate who didn't even know each other's names. He'd always just been Santa's brother, no name needed. And I…well, I was nobody. Yet that man wanted to know my name.

"Help me out here," he whispered, his expression turning a bit softer.

I couldn't leave him helpless. "I'm Zira."

"Zira." His smile widened once more, that twinkle back in his eyes. "That's a beautiful name."

"Thank you." And then I stood there. Silent. Unsure what to do next. Wanting to shrink into the floor as both he and the lady behind the counter stared at me. Finally, my brain clicked into place. "Oh, right. I guess I should ask—"

"Jericho," he said, all calm and…normal. "I'm Jericho."

His saying the word pinged a memory of learning about Santa and how he came to be in his position. How he'd given up his name to fill the role of Santa Claus. How he had a brother who would step in if needed to keep the legend alive. That brother being named Jericho.

"Right. Jericho. Now I remember."

"You knew?"

"Everyone knows who you are."

"Then why did you ask?"

"It had totally slipped my mind." I shrugged. "Plus, it seemed the polite thing to do."

His brow furrowed, his twinkle lessening. "You know what? Let's throw politeness out the window. I'd rather you be real with me than do things because you think you're supposed to."

Real was good. Real was easier. "Fine."

"So," he said, leading me toward the door. "Where were you going when you fell to the ground at my feet?"

Someday I would learn how not to roll my eyes like a spoiled teenager. Today was not that day. "Trust me, that fall had more to do with the crowd and nothing to do with you in particular."

"The crowd formed because of me."

"True."

"So, my presence made you fall to the ground. And you just so happened to land at my feet. I see nothing wrong with my statement."

"Oh, there's so much wrong with it."

"You haven't answered my question," he said, allowing me to pick whether we turned right or left on Tinsel Trail. "Where were you going?"

I took the right. "Home."

"May I join you?" Jericho asked, keeping step with me. Also nearly making me fall again with that question.

"You want to come inside my home?"

"I mean...eventually," he said, that brow once again furrowed, those blue eyes suddenly avoiding mine. "At some point, I hope we will be comfortable enough for that. Tonight, my only intention is to walk with you so we can chat and I can make sure you arrive safely to your home."

"Oh." I glanced his way again, catching him watching me. Nearly melting as those bright blue eyes met mine. How could anyone turn him down? "Okay. I'm fine with company on the way home."

"Excellent." He spun and moved in front of me, walking backward for a few steps. "So, where do you live?"

"You'll find out."

"A mystery. I like it." He moved back into his spot beside me, inching closer than before. "Tell me about yourself, Zira."

"Like what?"

"I don't care—what do you do? What was your childhood like? What's your favorite color? Why peanut brittle?"

"That's a lot."

"I'm a curious man."

"Some might call it nosy."

"I've been called worse."

I sighed, because he was right—he had. I'd heard all those rumors. I knew more about him than he had any way of knowing stuff about me. So I capitulated.

"Let's see...I'm Zira. I work in the post office for Santa—"

"Hard job but so very vital."

"Very. My childhood was not the easiest, but my mother tried her hardest to make the best for me. My favorite color is silver, and peanut brittle is my sugary treat of choice because it reminds me of my mother. And you?"

"My childhood wasn't too rough, but it also wasn't *Santa Claus is my brother* extravagant. Being a child of an elf/reindeer coupling certainly made things interesting at times. My favorite color used to be blue but has suddenly shifted to green—" he shot me a smile, staring into my eyes. That just so happened to be green. I would have blushed, but he continued on "—and I'm not a fan of peanut brittle, though I can't stop myself from eating an entire tray of those peanut butter, chocolate, and oatmeal no-bake cookies they sometimes have at the coffee shop."

"Oh, I love those. I wonder why they aren't more readily available."

"Because my brother hates them."

My teeth snapped together as I froze, staring at him. "Are you serious?"

"Yup. He can't stand them, so no one makes them." Jericho shrugged. "That's the power he has."

"Well, that's ridiculous."

"I won't argue that." Jericho grabbed my hand and tugged, forcing me to begin walking again. He didn't let go once I started, though. And I didn't mind.

"So," he said after a while, still holding my hand, his steps slowing.

"What else do you know about me?"

Seven swans a-swimming, this was about to get awkward. "I don't think I should—"

"You should. That way, I know what I'm up against."

"In terms of what?"

"In terms of deprogramming." He shot me another smile, this one not as bright as the ones before, and squeezed my hand. "Go ahead. Let me have it."

"Fine," I said with a sigh. "You're Santa's younger brother. The spare, if you will. Since you didn't have the stress of growing up to be the big man, you've had it easy."

"Easy, I have?"

"That's what the elves say—everything comes easy to you, and you get to have no responsibilities, while Santa toils away in the toy shop. You're practically a rock star around here, though. All the elves want to get with you because you're handsome—"

"You think I'm handsome?"

My neck burst into flames. At least, it felt that way. "Again, it's what I've heard. You're also quite the party boy."

"Am I?"

"That's—"

"What you've heard. Yeah." He looked down, breaking eye contact and seeming almost...sad. Which made absolutely no sense. Of course, nothing about this evening or the fact that I had somehow found a fated mate—something elves usually weren't party to—in the man at my side, Santa's brother. It was all ridiculous.

And whether I was prepared for it to end or not, over.

"We're here."

Jericho nodded, still not looking at me. Definitely avoiding eye contact.

"I'm glad we got you home safe. May I have your number or something? I'd love to be able to chat with my mate."

"So, we're admitting that?"

He looked up, stabbing me in place with that piercing blue stare. "Absolutely."

Well, then. "Fine. But don't get needy and start calling me at all hours."

I held out my hand, grabbing the phone he offered me.

"I will do my best to only need you when the timing is convenient." He took his phone back once I finished entering my info and sending myself a text so I would have his, tucking his hands into his pockets and once again looking like the confident man who could have had any woman in town warming his bed. "Good night, sweet Zira. It was nice to meet you."

I nodded and headed for the door, quiet. Unsure what to say. Feeling as if the night shouldn't have been over but having absolutely no clue how to extend it. Should I have invited him up? Asked him out to dinner? Why hadn't he asked me out to dinner? Was I not date-worthy? Was I—

"And hey, Zira," he called right as I opened the door to my building.

I turned, cocking my head at him. Ready to hear whatever he had to say. "Yeah?"

"People aren't right about me."

That took me by surprise. "Then why don't you fight against the lies?"

"Never had a reason to. Until now." His smile grew, practically lighting up the street. Like a tractor beam or something, I felt drawn to it and to him. Wanting to hug him, to feel those lips on mine, to make sure he was okay. He didn't give me the chance to overcome my hesitation, though. "Get some rest."

And with that, he turned and jogged back toward town, leaving me standing on my doorstep with so many unspoken words and unclear feelings. Was I... Had he just... Why had that smile made my heart beat so fast? Did I already care about him?

Inside, my brain screamed yes, which had me shaking my head in surrender.

I was smitten. Within just minutes of meeting Jericho, I had fallen headfirst into a tub of smittenness. He had me right where he wanted me.

Crap.

# 3
# JERICHO

Being the brother of the current Santa usually meant my days could be spent in more of a leisurely fashion, especially when visiting North Pole. Something that had always made me feel slightly worthless and unnecessary. Thankfully, meeting Zira—my one and only fated mate—meant I had a lot of work to do. Work that I was looking forward to.

I rushed back down Tinsel Trail to my motorcycle, smiling and nodding as people recognized me and called my name but not stopping to chat. Zira had been right about a few things, one being that I had been showing off a bit. I hadn't needed to be on Tinsel Trail that night, but I'd come down on my motorcycle to feel the energy of the crowd I knew would assemble when I rolled in. I usually liked the attention such ridiculous actions brought me because my life was mostly lived in the shadows. I no longer wanted the attention of strangers, though. I only wanted one elf to notice me.

Roaring through the streets, I made my way to the Claus compound. The outside stood quiet and still, lit up in reds and greens and whites as usual, though there were no actual signs of life. I was thrilled with that —the last thing I needed was to have to deal with my brother at that moment. I parked my bike in the garage stall on my side of the building and headed inside. The Claus compound connected to the elf castle through a long and twisting corridor that I had traversed many times over the years. I followed the same route that night, expertly maneuvering through the shadowy spaces and avoiding any rooms or areas where my brother might be. I had no need for him, but the elf Queen... Yeah, it was her I was after.

I knew I'd found her when I spotted her guard, Callon, standing outside the entry to one of the sitting rooms.

"Mr. Claus," he said with a nod. "She's waiting for you."

I slipped inside, grinning, having no idea how she always knew when I was looking for her but so very glad that gift had stood the test of time.

"Jericho," the Queen said, smiling up at me from a comfy chair by the fire. "Come. I feel as if you need to talk to me."

"Your intuition never fails, does it?" I swept into the seat beside her, giving her a respectful head nod. "How are you, my Queen?"

"I am well, but I am far more interested in how you are doing." She leaned forward, eyes practically glittering in the firelight. "Tell me about her."

"How do you know?"

"Quit wasting time asking questions I will never answer. Tell me."

I leaned forward, my elbow going to my knee as a smile came to my face completely unbidden. "She's...beautiful."

The Queen scoffed in a good-natured sort of way. "Of course she is. What else?"

"She's...spunky. She gives not one care about who I am or how that could benefit her. She seems kind and thoughtful. She hasn't had an easy life, but it looks as if she's making the best of things. And she likes peanut brittle."

This time, the scoff she released sounded very un-Queen-like. "No one actually likes peanut brittle."

"She says her mom always made it."

"See? She doesn't like it—she likes the memories attached to it."

I chuckled. "Perhaps. Either way, I have this urge to keep her well stocked in the stuff."

"Good plan. What's her name? What does she do?"

"Her name is Zira, and she—"

"Works in the postal room." The Queen squealed, looking far more excited than I had expected her to be.

"How did you know?"

The Queen laughed again, sitting deeper in her chair. "Oh, my dear Jericho. Zira and I work together to make sure the children get what they need."

"Are you two conspiring against my brother?"

Her eyes went purposefully wide. Exaggerating a look of surprise I knew she didn't feel. "Against? Oh no, I would never. Let's just say he neglects the needs for the wants. Zira and I address the needs while he prattles on with the wants."

My sweet, caring mate. Knowing she and the Queen had a secret process to help children only made me more thrilled to know she was mine.

And I needed her to stay that way.

"I need a favor, Your Highness."

The Queen cocked her head, her bright eyes sly and her smile slick. "What might that favor be, Jericho Claus?"

"I hate to ask, but I need to keep this a secret from my brother."

Her smile fell, a look of concern slipping into its place before she was able to place her regal mask back on. "That could be quite difficult."

"Just for a few days. Give me the chance to show her the real me and not the Jericho the elves in town think they know."

She sighed, glancing directly at the fire for a prolonged moment. "I will give you my silence for as long as you need it. I can attempt to control the staff for a day or two as well. After that..."

"I know—they'll talk. But I'll take your help. Thank you so much." I reached across and grabbed her hand, so very grateful for the kind, loving ruler she had grown into. We'd known each other since we'd been children, had been friends all that time. The fact that she would stick to my side for the next few days was a gift I knew was a lot to ask of her. I had never felt more grateful than in that moment.

But then a shadow crossed across us, and my gratefulness turned bitter.

"Well, ho ho ho. My little brother *is* in town. I thought perhaps the elf gossip mill had been wrong, seeing as how I hadn't been informed directly." Santa Claus stared at the two of us, forcing us to break apart with just a look. "You came to see the Queen before your own brother?"

"I was apparently easier to find, Santa," the Queen said, sounding slightly aloof and disinterested. The character she played when she wanted to keep things at more of a business level. "I apologize. I had sent Callon to find you, but—"

"It is my error, sir." Callon slipped in behind the Queen, bowing slightly. "The Queen asked me to retrieve you on behalf of Mr. Jericho, but I was unable to locate you."

Santa didn't look thrilled, but I definitely enjoyed the show. Callon would have died for the Queen, and we all knew it. Lying was likely one of his easiest tasks.

"See?" the Queen said, that joy back in her tone. "All settled. Now, isn't it wonderful to see Jericho?"

I grinned up at my brother, not at all surprised to see the corners of his mouth twitch downward.

"Of course," he said, nodding once so that his thick white beard practically bounced on his chin. "What brings you to town, Jericho?"

I shrugged, trying hard to keep my body language casual. "Just thought I'd pop in before the season got a little too busy for you."

"It's always busy here."

"Yes," the Queen said. "Which is why you're so lucky to have all my elves supporting you."

I grinned up at my brother, knowing a needle from the Queen when I heard one. "Absolutely. You're so lucky."

"Of course." Santa sighed, shaking his head. "I apologize. It's been a long week."

"Same." I rose to my feet and motioned to the chair. "Why don't you have a seat, Santa? I need to get up to my room anyway."

"Are you sure?"

"Sit," the Queen demanded, still grinning. "Let's have a cup of tea. Callon, be a dear."

"Of course, ma'am."

I snuck out the door with the guard, catching the wink the Queen shot me as we disappeared around the corner.

"Please tell the Queen I said thanks," I whispered once we were in the hall, patting the man on the back. "I appreciate the escape."

"She is intuitive beyond measure. I will tell her, but I'm sure she already knows."

With that, Callon strode toward the kitchens, while I hightailed it back down the winding hall toward the Claus side of the castle. I eventually made it, turning sharply in the direction of my wing of the residence. Not every previous Santa had had siblings, but luckily someone along the way must have because they had built an amazing apartment for the Not-Santa of the generation. That was me, and the rooms I stormed into had somehow become my home.

"Mr. Jericho." A small, old elf came hobbling around the corner with a bright smile on her face. "It's so good to see you."

"Charisma!" I rushed to the elf who had always been my personal assistant for a quick hug. "What are you doing here?"

"I came to make sure your rooms were ready."

"You don't have to do that."

She patted my arm as we both stepped away from each other. "I know that, child. But it's what I've always done. It would break my heart if I couldn't take care of you in some way."

"You are a dream of a friend, you know that?"

"And you are a charmer. Now, your bed is made, pillows and blankets are on the couch, and everything is dusted. I have the kitchen bringing up some food for you to fill your cabinets. Anything in particular you would like?"

I paused for just a moment, my memory spinning to life. The opportunities of what may come over the next few days giving me ideas.

"Peanut brittle."

Charisma froze, staring at me. "You want peanut brittle?"

"Yes. I have a friend—"

"Say no more," she said with a laugh. "I hope this one appreciates the gesture."

Because she had seen me with more women who definitely hadn't appreciated anything other than my name. And while I had never felt a need to brag about a conquest, this time, I seemed to want to tell everyone except my brother.

"I met my mate."

Charisma spun, a watery grin lifting her wrinkled cheeks. "Oh, dear boy. Are you sure? We elves usually don't mate like the shifters, but with your being half-reindeer shifter, I always thought there was a chance."

"I'm sure. She felt it, too."

"Who is she?" Charisma grabbed my hands, looking ready to explode with excitement, which only made my own smile broaden.

"Her name is Zira, and she works in the postal room."

"I know Miss Zira. Beautiful girl." She frowned, almost seeming lost in her thoughts for a moment. "Her mother was a bit of a mess, if I remember correctly, but the girl has done well for herself and is as solid as they come. She's a good match for you."

"She likes peanut brittle."

"Then I will make sure there is plenty in case your lady comes over for a visit."

"Thank you, Charisma. I appreciate you so much."

She patted my cheek as she had since I'd been a wee little boy sitting before her. "You're a good man, Jericho Claus. I'm thrilled that you have found a good partner as well. Now, I need to go. I don't think the kitchen staff has made peanut brittle in an age. I'll need to oversee their work."

I laughed, following her toward the door. "You'll keep them in line, I'm sure."

"It's my gift. Goodnight."

I closed the door behind her, still feeling light and happy. Still wanting to run around and...I didn't know. Maybe find Zira and talk to her some more. Maybe risk a little hug or a soft kiss. What I didn't want to do was be without her for a whole night.

I rushed through the hall and into my living room, practically jumping and sprawling on my couch. Once settled, I reached into my pocket for my phone. There, in lights and pixels, was my way to contact my Zira. The only way, because showing up at her house unannounced would be a little...

"Stalkerish, yes. Better to text."

I sent her a quick message, simply asking how her night was going. Casual. Hopeful. Not at all desperate and lonely. I hoped, at least.

Thankfully, she replied almost immediately.

*I have peanut brittle, a fire in the fireplace, and a good book. My night is amazing. How is yours?*

*I have none of that, but I got to see the Queen and my brother, as well as my favorite staff elf. It's not too bad.*

*You saw the Queen?*

*Yes. She's an old family friend.*

*Did you see her guard, Callon?*

*Of course. Why?*

*I've just always thought he was handsome.*

She sent that one with a winky-face emoji, as if knowing she would need to soften the blow.

"You're in so much trouble," I muttered, tapping on the screen faster than before.

*You think he's handsome?*

*The whole town does.*

*I'm not worried about the town. I'm only worried about you.*

A long pause followed, and I worried I had somehow pushed her too far. Thankfully, she eventually answered.

*That's sweet.*

*Thank you. I noticed you didn't answer my question, though. You think he's handsome?*

Another pause. This time when my phone lit up, I groaned and rolled over. The words making me long for her even more.

*Not nearly as handsome as you.*

I had an urge to invite her over. To drag her underneath me and make her scream my name. To taste her all over and prove I was more than just a pretty face. I suddenly felt like a teenager again, all twitterpated and immediately in love. I wasn't a child, though. I was a man. One who understood what love was and how fragile it could be. This woman was my mate, my fated one and only, and I needed to do everything in my power to take things at her pace so I didn't make her life uncomfortable.

But she was all I was going to think about. I could already tell.

*I am nothing in comparison to you, beautiful. I miss your smile already.*

*Perhaps you'll be able to see it tomorrow.*

*That would be ideal.*

*Hey…can you shift?*

It took me a long moment to focus enough to understand what she meant.

*Not at all.*
*My reindeer half is a shadow of my elf half.*

*Pity. That would have been fun to see.*

*You like the idea of me covered in fur and sporting antlers?*

*Maybe.*

*I am sorry to disappoint you.*

*I'm not at all disappointed. More curious about you than anything.*

I rolled over, sighing. Clutching my phone like a lifeline.

*What else do you want to know?*

*I would much rather talk in person to learn about each other than over text.*

I had a moment of wanting to invite her over, of being ready to just send that message and let the chips fall where they may. Thankfully, common sense overruled the impulse.

*Tomorrow, then. We can get together and have a long chat.*

*Perfect. I'm going to bed since I have to be up early for work. Text me tomorrow, and we'll set something up.*

*Sounds like a plan. Goodnight, sweet Zira.*

*Goodnight, handsome.*

"She's going to kill me," I murmured to the empty room. Without thought, I tossed the phone onto the coffee table and slipped a hand into my pants. Groaning into my pillow and already beginning to writhe.

189

My mate thought I was handsome and wanted to see me tomorrow. That was a better reaction than I could have hoped for.

Though it still left me alone in this huge apartment.

If we kept things slow, the next few days were going to be hard.

As was I.

# 4

# ZIRA

I woke up the next morning with a message from Jericho already received. It was an offer to take me to dinner after work. I didn't reply, knowing I would have time as I walked to work, so I jumped in the shower instead. Thirty minutes later—freshly washed, dinner attire in my bag since there was no way I would refuse him, and ready for my workday—my phone pinged again. Another message from Jericho "just checking in." I was ready to punch him...and kiss whatever I hit better. I wasn't used to the attention, but I liked it. A lot. Still, I had a routine and a job to get to, so I grabbed my bag and headed for the door. Still not having replied. Apparently, that was too much for the man.

"Jericho?" I froze on the doorstep, hand still on the handle, absolutely stunned to see him on the sidewalk where he'd dropped me off the night before. "Have you been here all night?"

He grinned. "Of course not. Though that would definitely gain the attention of your neighbors—Santa's brother sleeping on your doorstep."

"They would certainly talk." I closed and locked the door, fighting hard not to smile at him even though I was actually so excited to see him. "So if you haven't been here all night, what are you doing here? It's awfully early for a visit."

He shrugged, falling into step beside me as I headed toward work. "I missed you."

"You just saw me last night."

"I know, but then you wouldn't answer my texts this morning—"

"I was getting ready for work."

"You should call off."

I stumbled and whipped my head around to stare at him. "Excuse me?"

"You should call off. Skip work. Spend the day with me."

Such arrogance. I walked faster. "No."

"No?" he asked, sounding truly shocked. As if all the other women he had dated would just...do as he said. Regardless of the consequences on their own lives and those around them. Those they helped. I was not one of those women.

"No. Your brother ignores—" I clenched my jaw and took a deep breath, redirecting my thoughts so as not to insult his brother. "My job is important to me, and I feel the need to be there."

He followed beside me, quiet and calm. Not saying anything at first. I had a moment of worry, like I had pushed him too hard. Like he would see my need to be at work as a rejection, but then he sighed.

"I apologize. I shouldn't be so selfish. Of course you have responsibilities—it's honorable that you take what you do so seriously." He nodded, inching closer. Bumping shoulders with me. "May I walk you to work, though?"

This man was going to ruin my heart. Destroy it. Set it on fire and rebuild it to recognize only him. I could already tell, and there would be no denying him.

"Sure."

So we walked, chatting like friends. Discussing the changes on Tinsel Trail since the last time he'd been there, as well as what we would like to see in the few empty buildings along the way. Casual, friendly conversation with no pressure or undertones. I liked it.

He came to a stop in front of the coffee shop on the corner, grabbing my arm to make me pause as well.

"Got time for breakfast?"

I glanced over his shoulder. "Not to sit, but I can wait if you want to grab some coffee for yourself."

"I'd love to buy you one as well. Maybe even a pastry. Something to give you a sweet start to the day."

"You don't have to—"

"I insist."

He insisted, and I was not fool enough to turn down coffee twice. I nodded, and we headed inside, ordering lattes and croissants before returning to our trek to my work. We were only a block away when he coughed and asked the question I did not want to answer.

"So...what had you been about to say about my brother earlier?"

"You caught that, huh?"

"Yup."

I took a sip of my coffee, wishing I hadn't opened my mouth. Knowing this could be a delicate conversation and not sure I had the mental energy to handle it as such.

"I... Look, I don't want to speak ill of him. I know he's family."

Jericho chuckled in a very un-funny sort of way. "There are relatives, and then there is family. My brother is a relative. The Queen is more family to me."

"She seems really nice."

"She's the nicest. The absolute best and very excited about us."

I gasped. "You told her?"

"To be honest, I think she already knew. At least, that something good had happened to me." He smiled down at me, looking ridiculously charming. "She always seems to know when I'm truly happy."

Neck—on fire. Cheeks, too. I took a sip of my coffee, suddenly off-balance because the man was just so darn charming. What was I supposed to do with him?

Finally, I brought my cup down. "She helps me help the needy."

"She mentioned something about that. Tell me more."

I took a deep breath, the sadness I felt every day at work rising within me. "Sometimes, children don't ask Santa for a toy or a game. We get requests for basics—a winter coat, new boots, socks. I tend to think a child who is taking their one shot at reaching Santa Claus to ask for socks must truly be in need. Your brother ignores those letters and sends them a generic toy. The Queen helps me by taking the letters and making sure those children also get the necessities they're asking for. Especially the sock ones."

"Socks are definitely a need," he said, his voice growing harder. Colder. "And Santa doesn't help with that? Not even something as simple as a stocking stuffer for them?"

"I asked him once about the letters, and he said everything in life can be cured with a toy."

"Not frostbite."

"Exactly. Not frostbite." We reached the employee entrance to the castle. I stepped to the side to allow the other elves—all who seemed to be side-eyeing Jericho and me—room to enter. "This is me."

He sighed, crowding close. "I assume you won't be able to text once you're at work."

"Probably not."

He nodded, his frown deepening. Looking about as lost as I suddenly felt.

"Jericho—"

"Lunch. Can I take you to lunch?"

"I only get half an hour."

He leaned down, resting his forehead against mine as he murmured, "My brother is a cockblocker."

I laughed, unable not to. "How is not being able to take me to lunch a...that?"

"I don't know, but it sounded like a good insult in my head."

"It made me laugh." I inched closer, wanting so much to be wrapped up in him. "Are we still on for dinner?"

He grabbed my arm, keeping us together. "Yes, absolutely. I probably should have been the one to confirm that."

"You were too busy worrying about what your brother was doing to your cock."

He laughed, tossing his head back and garnering way too much attention. I couldn't help but smile, though. His laugh was infectious and bright. Filled with joy. I wanted to hear it every day.

"Oh, my sweet Zira. You are a handful."

"And yet, not wrong."

"Not wrong." He tugged me into his arms, finally hugging me. Wrapping me in his scent and filling me with a comfort and joy I had never experienced before. "You'd better get inside."

I snuggled into his coat, my heart breaking. Needing just one more moment of the happiness he somehow infused me with. Just one. "Yeah. I need to."

But I didn't let go...and neither did he.

"Have a wonderful day at work," he whispered, finally relaxing his hold on me. Not letting go, just...softening his touch.

"What will you be doing?" I asked, suddenly cold without him against me.

He took a step back, fully letting me go, before giving me a sad sort of smile. "Picking up my brother's slack. As usual."

"What does that—" The shift horn blew, interrupting me. I was about to be late to work, which had never happened. "I have to go."

Jericho seemed to understand my dilemma. "Hurry. We can talk about everything over dinner."

I nodded and rushed through the gate, practically running toward the postal room. I had a geyser of excitement bubbling up inside of me, an unstoppable sense of anticipation building. Jericho was going to take me to dinner tonight. My new mate and I would have a meal together. Alone.

This was going to be the longest day *ever*.

# 5

# ZIRA

I had been correct in my assumption—that had been the absolute longest day in the history of my adult working life.

I walked out of the castle—having changed out of my uniform into the outfit I'd brought for out date—and headed for the staff entrance, already looking for Jericho's auburn hair. Looking and looking and finally realizing he wasn't there. Beginning to feel the heavy weight of disappointment, I reached into my bag and pulled out my phone. No texts. No missed calls. Nothing. He just...wasn't there. I would have cried, but the idea of all the other elves who had seen Jericho dropping me off now seeing me sobbing alone in the same spot wearing my nicest dress was horrifying. More so than all the times coworkers had mentioned knowing my cousins and having to explain to them that they were strangers to me. More so than anything I had ever experienced.

Falling apart would have to wait until I was home alone and in the bath.

Once through the castle gate, I turned and strode for home. I kept my chin up and expression neutral, determined not to show any emotion until I was safely locked inside. Until I had some privacy. Jericho not showing up after he had promised was worse than a punch in the gut. It was painful and upsetting and deeply jarring. He had said he would be there. Why—

A motorcycle roared to a stop beside me, a grinning Jericho sitting astride. Ooh, he was so darn handsome. That didn't erase the sick feeling in my stomach, though.

"You're late."

"If I tell you what I was up to, you'll be thrilled and totally forgive me being—" he glanced at his phone "—thirty seconds late."

When he said it like that, my ire seemed misplaced. Sort of. Perhaps. "Maybe. Maybe not."

He reached for my hand, tugging me closer. "Please, Zira. I didn't mean to be late, and I will tell you exactly why. But first, I want you to come with me."

"On that?"

He nodded. "Yes."

I scrunched my nose, looking over the big, loud machine between his legs. "But is it safe?"

"I'm safe." He leaned closer, pulling me in. Practically bringing me so I stood nose-to-nose with him. "I will never let anything happen to you. You can trust me."

I shivered, unable not to. Something in the tone of his voice sent a bolt of excitement up my spine. His words were both a promise and a warning, and I liked them. "Sounds dangerous."

"Oh, what we're going to do is a bit dangerous, but I think you'll love it." His lips turned up in a small yet almost worried sort of smile as he looked me up and down. "You look so pretty in your little dress."

The man was pure charm. "Thank you. I'm still upset that you were late."

"Understandable. I will make sure to never again be even a second late if you just forgive me this one slip. I promise, you will be thrilled once you know what I was doing." He tugged me again, drawing me almost close enough for a kiss. "Please, angel."

It was the angel that did me in. That and the breathy, needy sound of his whisper. I would have said yes to just about anything in that moment. Thankfully, all he was asking for was that I ride on his motorcycle. Way less dangerous than other things. "Fine. But if we crash, I'm not speaking to you again."

"There will be no crashing. I promise." He sat back, rocking the bike a little and making my stomach swirl. I had to ride that beast with him. Something I had never done. Who rode motorcycles in North Pole? Just him...my mate. Of course.

Jericho did the gentlemanly thing—I had to assume—and reached for my hand to lead me to where I needed to mount up. He helped me throw a leg over the bike and settle on the seat. He even tugged me up close to him, showing me how I should wrap my arms around his waist and lean into his body.

"You want me this close?"

He nodded. "Absolutely. For safety, of course."

Of course.

I did as he directed, clinging to him with all I had as he started the engine. Ready to move. He smelled so good and felt so solid under my touch. Felt like he fit in my arms as if made to be there. I took full advantage and clung to him, hugging him from behind, as I waited for us to move. And waited some more. And some more.

Eventually, I had to speak up.

"Jericho?"

He jerked, grabbing my hand at his stomach and clinging to it. "Yeah. Sorry. I was just..."

He didn't need to say anything because I knew. "Enjoying the hug?"

"I...yeah. I was thinking about how I don't get hugged very often and how nice it is."

I squeezed him harder, breathing him in one more time. "Glad I could scramble your brain a little bit. I think that puts us on a more even footing."

"Oh, sweet Zira. We will never be on equal footing. I will forever be tap-dancing to keep up with you." He lifted my hand to his mouth to kiss the back before placing it on his waist once more. "Now, hold on."

I did just that, clinging to his hard body as he took off toward town. We circled Tinsel Trail but didn't head down the busy street, riding around the edges of North Pole instead. Jericho would reach and squeeze my thigh when he didn't need both hands on the handlebars, something that both terrified and excited me. The drive was nice, though. I enjoyed every second, especially being pressed up against Jericho as we rode through the streets. The roar of the engine couldn't be ignored, though. People stared and pointed, obviously talking about Santa's brother spending time with me. I couldn't find the energy to care, for once not minding the attention. I didn't feel the need to be invisible when I was with Jericho. An odd realization, for sure.

Eventually, Jericho took us back toward where he'd picked me up, bypassing the worker entrance and heading instead toward the resident drive. He rolled right past the staffed gate, giving the guard a salute as he passed. I had never been in this part of the castle, never had a reason to know what the entrance looked like. Apparently, I now did.

Jericho pulled to one side of the wide drive and drove into a garage, stopping in the darkened space and cutting the engine. I couldn't stay quiet even though I had a feeling I already knew the answer to my question.

"Where are we?"

"I have something I want you to see."

I laughed. "I can't see anything right now."

He chuckled softly, lifting me off the bike then dismounting himself. "Sorry—I don't want to draw attention to us right now." He grabbed my hand, tugging me forward through the dark. "Do you trust me?"

I wanted to say no just to be sassy with him, but I couldn't lie like that. Not to Jericho. Not after such a fun start to our evening together.

"Yes."

"Good. Come with me."

I followed behind him through the dark garage and up a set of stairs only marginally more well lit. He led me down a hall and through a huge, thick wooden door that seemed as if it could stop an entire army from busting through. The room we ended up in was large and open, with windows looking out over the town and beyond. Dark furniture that appeared soft and like the perfect place to curl up sat on bright, plush rugs. Definitely an apartment of sorts.

"What is this place?" I asked as I crossed toward the windows, drawn to the lights of the city below.

Jericho slipped in behind me, wrapping me in his arms this time. Snuggling me close as he nuzzled my neck and whispered, "My place. My living quarters."

I shivered, his breath tickling me. The tone in his voice enticing. "Jericho—"

"Come on. I want to show you something." He tugged me through the space, past many rooms and hallways, and out another ornately carved door. Everything in his space and the long hallway we ended up in looked so fancy, very fitting of a royal palace and the home of Santa Claus. Very fitting of him. Me? I felt dirty. As if I didn't belong in the stone hallways with the dark metal fixtures lighting the path along deep-red patterned rugs. As if I shouldn't have been there.

And really, I shouldn't have.

"I think I should—"

"Three minutes," he said, giving me a smile that held more apology than words would have. "Just give me three minutes, then we can get out of here."

I was never going to be able to say no to the man. He could have been leading me to my death, and I would have just kept holding his hand and walking behind him. Thankfully, he didn't seem to be on a path to kill me. Though I was definitely lost.

"Is this all your quarters?"

Jericho's jaw ticked. "No. We're on my brother's side now."

My stomach dropped. Santa's private quarters. He had taken me to Santa's private quarters?

"I shouldn't be here."

He squeezed my hand. "It's fine. This is the working level and where all the maintenance stuff is for the entire castle. He never comes down to this end."

"But where are we going?"

"Right here." He stopped in front of a door, looking like an excited toddler with a huge smile on his face and an energy I could feel. "What you said this morning about the children in need, that hit me right in the heart. It's a problem I've been working on away from North Pole, which left the Queen to deal with it here. The Queen and you, of course."

He opened the door and guided me through it, turning on a light as we entered. What I saw before me made no sense for about two solid minutes. The room looked so much like the postal room, I thought maybe we'd gotten lost. But then I noticed things beyond the letters. Stacks and stacks of things. Not toys like were sometimes placed in the list room when production was high. Oh no. There were no toys to be found. Only clothes.

"Jericho," I whispered, moving farther into the room. Touching things along the way just to make sure they were real. Coats and hats, gloves and mittens. Boots, shoes, dresses, pants, and so many pairs of socks. All colors, all sizes, stacked from the floor to the ceiling. "What did you do?"

Jericho snuck in behind me, wrapping his arms around my waist and pulling me against him. "I used what little power I have to collect all this stuff. Figured children who ask Santa for socks should maybe get a toy *and* the socks they need."

"Are you kidding me with this?"

"Not in the least. Truth is, I like helping people. I work with charities around the world to make sure children have access to clean water and nutritious food. That they get the best start to a good life, no matter what that means in their culture. It's been a passion project of mine for a long time, though on a smaller scale. I figured it was time to bring my love for philanthropy home. where there is a bit more magic in the logistical support."

My brain refused to accept everything before my eyes. Jericho Claus —younger brother of Santa, party boy, wild child—had collected clothes and blankets for children trapped in poverty. Had worked to give them a gift they both needed and deserved. Nothing made sense.

"I never thought you were the type to do...*this*."

"Because you thought I was a dolt? A manwhore?"

I spun in his arms, staring up at him. Wishing I could take back what

I'd said, even if his tone had sounded more matter-of-fact than hurt. "No. Jericho, I would never—"

"It's okay. I know how the elves talk about me." He tugged me closer, calming visibly. Growing more serious. "Because I do all my work away from here, rumors about me are inevitable. Everyone assumes they know what I'm like and how I live my life, and I've played into their fantasy world because it always seemed easier. I've put on a show to fit their perceptions." He pressed a soft kiss to my forehead, breathing me in. "I don't want to play a role with you, though. And I couldn't see a better way to let you get to know the real me than to show you this."

I stared up at him, seeing his seriousness. His honesty. His heart. "I'm just so...stunned. You *help* people."

"It's been my passion for a long time. And now I'm going to help the children whose letters keep you up at night."

That was it. The moment my heart exploded and came back together with Jericho Claus in the center of it. I jumped into his arms, grabbing him around the neck as he lifted me up, diving into a kiss my entire life in the making. Deep and soulful, the sort of kiss that sent your world spinning off its axis. The kind that left you gasping for air as you ripped at each other's clothes. Needing contact. Needing more.

"Zira," Jericho whispered, my name almost like a prayer on his lips. "Can I—" He groaned, sliding his hands up the backs of my bare thighs to squeeze me tighter. I wasn't sure exactly what he was asking for, but I had a good idea that I would want it too.

"Yes." I rocked against him, pinning his hardened length between us. "Anything. Yes."

Jericho had us in motion within a heartbeat, striding across the room and past the socks without so much as a sound escaping his lips. He kissed me instead, tangling his tongue with mine. Holding me close as we moved. When he finally stopped, his kiss slowed. His fingers still gripping me tight.

"We can go upstairs."

I shook my head, clutching at him. "It'll take too long."

"I agree. I just want you to be sure."

I stared into his eyes, grasping his shoulders tight. Holding us together as I spoke in a firm voice. "I am absolutely sure about this."

His smile exploded, lighting up the room, and then he was kissing me again, groaning softly as he moved to lay us down. I landed on something soft and velvety, something that made my entire body feel alive and ready to explode. Something...

"Oh." I gasped and arched as a feeling of pure and utter arousal practically wrapped itself around me. "What is this?"

"It's magic. The bag gives the user whatever it is they need." Jericho settled on top of me, his hips notching between my legs as he dropped to kiss and bite up the length of my neck before murmuring. "What is it you need right now, sweet Zira?"

"You." I arched against him, tugging at his shirt. "Me. Naked."

Jericho chuckled then rose onto his knees. "We don't need magic for that."

He wasn't kidding. My mate had his clothes off within seconds, even before I could tug my dress up. Thankfully, Jericho decided undressing me was a priority. He leaned over me, dropping a kiss to my lips as he began lifting my skirt. Allowing me time to rock from one hip to the other so he could rescue the fabric underneath me. The dress came off with ease, my undergarments also seeming to practically disappear. We went from fully clothed to naked in a matter of seconds. Went from layers of fabric in the way to nothing between us but the magic of the velvet.

"Come here," I said, reaching for him. Pulling him down with me into the silky-soft pile of fabric. "I want to feel you."

But Jericho didn't come down with me. Instead, he stayed on his knees with one hand holding up his upper body, leaning over me. Kissing me until I finally fell back. He stared down at me with something that looked like reverence before rising onto his knees and grabbing mine.

"You are so beautiful." He spread my knees and lifted, bringing my ankles to his shoulders. Exposing me in ways that should have made me feel awkward or insecure. The magic, though. That tingle of something more than us in the air. That made everything feel so right in the moment.

At least, that's what I would forever tell myself.

Still, I reached for him. "Jericho."

"Let me make you come," he said, his voice low and rough. His eyes trailing over my body before stopping right at the junction of my thighs. "Give me your pussy. I'll take such good care of you."

I couldn't speak, could hardly breathe, so I nodded my consent. Jericho shot me a soft smile, kissed one of my knees, then settled between my legs. The first touch of his lips to my pussy had me arching and reaching for his hair. Feeling the need to hang on to something. The second had me whispering his name. By the time his tongue joined the party, I was using his shoulders as a brace to push my hips toward his mouth and gripping the velvet bag tightly in my hands.

I would have loved to say the moment lasted forever, that I held off as he worked me over with his mouth. I would have loved to say I was able to hang on and enjoy long minutes of his attention. I would have loved to, but the fact of the matter was, I came within about two minutes. Jerking against him, riding his face, and eventually pushing him away from my sensitive flesh. I'd never come so fast in my life, but this was my mate. And there was magic in the air around us. There would be no holding back tonight.

"Come," I said, chuckling softly as Jericho wiped his mouth and kissed my thigh from my hip to my knee. "Get up here and fill me up."

He slid over top of me, groaning as our naked flesh came together. "Is that your Christmas wish?"

Forever the brother to Santa Claus. Of course. "That's my *every* day wish."

He froze, his smile growing, his shoulders seeming to relax a little. As if he'd needed to hear that for some reason.

"Come," I said again, tugging him down. "Kiss your mate. I want to feel you."

Jericho did as I asked, laying his entire weight on me as he kissed me slowly, deeply. I could taste myself on him, but that only ramped up my own arousal. I was again a writhing mess beneath him, needing him to fill me. To bring us both the completion we deserved. To quench the ache building within me.

"Sweet angel," he whispered as he once again moved to suck on my neck. "I would do anything for you."

I shifted my hips, aligning him with where I wanted him to be. Groaning as the tip of his cock nudged against me. "Then make me come. Like this."

"Anything." He kissed my neck again—once, twice—as he began to move his hips. As we finally started to come together. I was not prepared for him to bite me hard, though. Not at all prepared for him to take the moment of my gasping misdirection and thrust inside me. I felt a second of pure pleasure-pain, when my body locked down on his as he entered it. When I nearly came from the conflicting sensations setting my skin on fire. But then that feeling ebbed, and I grabbed for him. Wanting to feel him along every inch of me. Needing his warmth to cover me.

Jericho groaned and pulled almost all the way out, thrusting back in with a speed that had me calling out his name. That had me digging my nails into his back. We found our rhythm quickly enough, both of us breathing hard and working together toward a completion we needed. I, of course, came first, head thrown back and body arching into his as pleasure overtook me. Jericho continued thrusting, gripping my hips and driving up into me. Chanting "Angel" in my ear until he finally thrust hard and remained still for a long moment as he groaned and tightened his hold. As he likely left bruises that I would treasure on my hips.

As the magic swirled and made the moment absolutely perfect in a very imperfect place.

# 6

# JERICHO

I had never felt so fulfilled in my entire life. Had never experienced such a level of satisfaction and calm. My Zira lay beside me in the velvet, sleeping lightly in my arms. Making me the happiest man I could have possibly been. Sure, the magic of the bag helped. That fabric brought peace and joy to those who made contact with it, granted wishes and made sure needs were met. Santa used the bags—of which there were a handful—to be able to have an endless supply of toys for the big run every year. I used it to deepen my connection with my mate.

Slightly selfish, perhaps. But worth it.

As I ran a hand over Zira's bare arm, she rolled toward me, whispering my name. Home. There was no other way to describe the feeling of complete and utter belonging that filled me. It was as if I had been lost my entire life and meeting Zira had brought me home. My heart—hers. Life as I knew it—over. I would do anything for her, no matter what that anything happened to be. Would support her in any decision. Hell, she could tell me she wanted to keep working her shitty job for my brother, and I'd...well, I wouldn't be happy about it. I'd accept it, though. Even if she no longer needed to work.

Not that she knew that.

Crap, I had so much to tell her.

"We have so much to learn about each other, still," I whispered, letting my hands wander a little. Unable to stop touching her. She murmured my name again—a sound I could totally get used to hearing every day—and rolled right into me. Pressing her lips against my chest as her fingers dug a little deeper into my arms.

Those were not the actions of a sleeping elf.

"Are you awake, angel?"

She mumbled something in response, though I couldn't understand any of the words. What I did understand was the way she grabbed me and tugged, as if trying to pull me closer. I didn't resist her, allowing my body to fall forward. Her bright smile greeted me as I rolled her underneath me, our bodies once again entwined. Swans a-swimming, but she was beautiful.

And wet. I could feel her heat against me as she spread her legs and let me settle between them. My girl was soaking wet.

"Were you dreaming of me, mate?"

That naughty grin grew, her hands holding tight to my shoulders. "Yes."

My cock jerked, ready to go to work. Ready to make that woman come six ways from Sunday. But first, I had a little more playing to do. I leaned in close and kissed her neck before biting it good and hard. Making her jump.

"Good dreams?"

"The best."

"I can tell." I ground against her, already soaking myself in her. Groaning as I fought the urge to plunge right in and fill her the way I wanted to. "You're so wet, angel."

"Because I've been dreaming of you." She tugged me closer, bringing her knees up to my chest and lining us up so I slipped just inside. I held my breath and locked my body in place, knowing if I gave in for even a second, this would be over. I'd be inside her. I wanted more for her, though. Wanted to make sure she came at least twice this time, which meant slowing down my pleasure so she could get hers. That was my job as her man—to take care of her every need. That was the work I would forever be proud to do.

Once I had my wits about me, I rolled to the side and dropped a hand to where my cock so desperately wanted to be. I started with my thumb on her clit then slid two fingers inside, making sure to curl them so I could find the spot that would bring her the most sensation. Working my hand in tandem to tease her until she groaned and grabbed my wrist.

Gotcha.

"So wet and ready, aren't you?"

"Jericho. I want—"

"I know what you want, but we're going to do this first." I added a third finger, sliding deeper and staring at her beauty as she arched her back and her mouth fell open. "This pussy was all primed and ready for me, wasn't it? How close do you think you are?"

"So close. So, so close."

"Good. I want you to come on my fingers."

"Want you...so bad."

"Then come for me."

Zira groaned again, tugging at my wrist as if trying to pull my fingers deeper inside her. And then she moaned my name as her body began to tighten. As the muscles tensed around my fingers and started their pulsing. That sound, the one of my name on her lips as she came with me, had my balls tucking in tight. My orgasm right there at the precipice. She had me wrapped around her little pinkie and didn't even know it yet. I would do anything to hear my name in that voice again, including making her wait longer for what she thought she wanted.

I was not above teasing her.

I shifted my thumb over her clit as she came, knowing it was probably really sensitive but pushing anyway. Ignoring her tugs on my wrist as I covered her clit and pushing inward while my fingers began to curl in rhythm with it. She cried and wriggled beneath me, definitely trying to both get more and move away at the same time. My angel was so hot and wet that the noises my hand made filled the space around us. I relished every sound, wanted to dive down and taste that wetness. Wanted to have her come on my tongue next, but that wasn't the plan. I had her on the brink, and I needed to finish her. I could lick her until she begged me to stop next time, could fuck her endlessly another night. This was my fated mate, and we would have plenty of time to come together in a variety of ways. Tonight, I needed to feel her come on my fingers again.

"Jericho," Zira gasped as she pulled on my shoulders.

I resisted the tug, holding my position and working my fingers faster. "Come for me, angel. Then I'll fuck you. I'll fill you up over and over again. Make that pussy all mine. Just come once more for me."

"I can't...I can—"

She moaned long and loud, her body tensing and arching away from me. That *can't* turned into a *can* real quick, every muscle of hers locking into place. Sucking my fingers deeper before quivering all over me. Soaking my hand. I couldn't resist another second, couldn't put off my own pleasure even to find the time to say something to my beautiful mate. Instead, I slipped my hand from between her thighs, rolled her back underneath me, and thrust inside. One push and I was balls deep exactly where I had wanted to be. Where I belonged. Zira gripped my shoulders and chanted my name, still coming as I filled her. Squeezing my cock with her wet pussy in a way that had me grunting and bunny fucking her like a teenager on one of Santa's magic sacks.

I was likely going to pay for that, but it didn't matter. I had found my bliss, and nothing would stop me from chasing after it.

Nothing.

# 7

# ZIRA

I can't say I had ever expected to be running through the halls of Santa's compound in the middle of the night—half naked and postcoital—with Santa's own brother leading me back to his place by the hand. Never expected to, never wanted to, and yet quite enjoyed the reality of it. Who would have thought?

"Oh," I yelped as I slipped, tugging Jericho in the process. He grabbed me by the waist and held me up, refusing to let me fall.

"Are you okay?" He placed a soft kiss to my forehead once I nodded. "The rock floors can get slippery. Come on, we're almost there."

With that, we continued running, him keeping firm hold of my hand and slowing us down to make sure the coast was clear at every hall we crossed and me giggling behind him. This was crazy. Everything about this night had been crazy. It had been our first date, but we'd had sex on one of Santa's magical sacks in a room filled with necessities Jericho was somehow going to distribute to children in need around the world. We had also run through the halls of the castle only partially clothed to get back to Jericho's quarters. None of that beyond the first date part seemed to make sense, yet there I was. What was I doing with my life?

"Made it," Jericho said, yanking me inside a door then spinning me around to press me against it. The hall we had entered sat bathed in darkness, the only light the soft glow of the moonlight creeping inside. I had one moment to gasp, to feel a single jolt of fear, and then Jericho was on me. His body pressed against mine, his lips owning mine. He kissed me deeply, groaning as our tongues tangled and his hands wandered over my flesh. Who needed their life to make sense when they had a man like him kissing them as if he would die without their taste? Sense could take a back seat to passion, for sure.

I moaned and tugged him closer, wanting to wrap myself around him and see what happened. I would have taken him again right there, would have switched positions and pinned *him* to the wall so I could drop to my knees before him, but Jericho had other ideas.

"Mmm, you taste good," he said when we broke apart, his voice a rough-and-tumble mess. "But I need food. Are you hungry?"

He didn't wait for me to answer, even though I would have given him a resounding yes. He simply grabbed my hand and dragged me down the hall, both of us laughing this time. He led me into the kitchen and pulled out a stool at the counter for me to sit on, making sure to kiss my neck before walking to the refrigerator and yanking the door open.

"I never heard an answer," he said while shuffling through the contents. "Are you hungry?"

"Starving."

He peeked around the door. "Too starving to wait for real food?"

Tough call, but I nodded eventually. "Yes."

He dove back into the appliance, eventually reappearing with a stack of various waxed paper-wrapped blocks, a container of what looked like mayonnaise, some sort of thin sliced meat, a tomato, and butter.

"Grilled cheese, it is."

My mouth watered. "I love grilled cheese sandwiches."

"Good thing it's what I make best, then." He set all the supplies on the counter before me then turned to bang around in the cabinets for a bit, setting a cast iron skillet on the stove then returning with a cutting board and knife. "There's actual food in there, you know. I had been planning on bringing you over and cooking you a real dinner."

"Instead of dragging me through the castle to have sex with me on one of Santa's bags?"

He froze, staring at the block of cheese he had just unwrapped, his jaw ticking.

"Jericho?"

"That really was hot," he said, then shook off his distraction and began cutting thin slices of cheese.

"It was." I bit my lip as he glanced up, that wicked smile of his making my body heat up. "But now, we need food."

"Right. Food." He got to work, continuing to slice cheese then tomatoes, setting up a little station with all the parts and pieces before moving to slather the bread with mayo. He melted some butter in the pan—*for the flavor. The mayo will give you the good, toasted feel*—then began assembling the sandwiches.

"Any cheese you don't like?" he asked.

"Is that a thing?" I laughed. "I grew up eating grilled cheese with processed cheese product slices. I now like any sort of real cheese I can get my hands on."

"A woman after my own heart," he said, shooting me a wink. "So, fake cheese. Did you put prosciutto on yours? Tomato?"

"You're really making a lot of assumptions about the working class in North Pole. No, we didn't put prosciutto on our sandwiches. I had never even heard of it until I was an adult and had moved out on my own. Tomatoes, yes. My mom grew them in a little greenhouse at the apartment."

"I always wanted to grow my own vegetables."

"The castle doesn't have a garden?"

He huffed. "Oh, it does. I wasn't allowed to be down there, though."

"Why not?"

"Even though I was just the spare behind my brother, there were expectations made of me. Digging in the dirt was not something Santa's brother was allowed to do."

Oh. *Ohhh.*

"So...the whole idyllic childhood of the Claus brothers?"

"Pre-selection as the next Santa? Truth. Post? Myth." He flipped the sandwiches onto two plates and came to the counter, setting one down before me. "Though I can't complain too much. I got to spend my teenage years here."

"Here isn't too bad, I guess." I took a bite of the sandwich, groaning when the deliciousness of salty cheese, crunchy bread, and soft tomato hit my tongue. "Lords a-leaping, this is good."

Jericho chuckled. "Better than processed cheese product?"

I shook my head, grinning. "Nothing is better than processed cheese product grilled cheese, but this is delicious."

"I'll have to remember that for next time."

Next time. There would be a next time. Oh, the butterflies *that* thought stirred up in my belly.

We ate in a companionable sort of silence, occasionally commenting or laughing about something, but mostly just enjoying our food. The sandwich was amazing and super filling, leaving me unable to finish it. Jericho ate the rest of mine, leaning in to kiss my cheek when I offered it to him. A quiet meal in the middle of the night—something I considered at a level of intimacy I'd never experienced before. I loved that I got to share it with Jericho.

"This is nice," I said as I got up to wash the dishes. Jericho tried to wave me off, but I simply hip checked him out of the way and walked to the sink. "Thank you for dinner."

He grabbed a towel, obviously not allowing me to handle cleanup on my own. "It was just a grilled cheese."

"The best grilled cheese."

"Second only to fake cheese on plain bread."

I shrugged. "True."

"So...your mom..." He paused, the words not coming, yet somehow I knew what he wanted to ask me. What he felt he needed to know.

"She's a good woman—strong and independent—which didn't sit well with the men in town. She raised me on her own, and while it was a struggle, we were really quite happy."

"Has she passed?"

"Nope," I said with a laugh. "She moved to Boca when she retired."

"Boca...the elf retirement community. My parents are in Flagstaff—

my mom prefers the desert." Jericho laughed for a moment before growing more serious, drying a plate for far too long as his brow furrowed. "And your dad?"

"A nonentity in my life. He worked closely with the Santa before your brother and then through the transition, so he had status in the community. He didn't want to *marry down*, as he once told her, so he walked."

"He sounds horrible," Jericho said. "Did you ever meet him?"

"Once. He wasn't kind to me, so I just tucked away the knowledge of who he was and went about my life. It's hard when I see his family in town and know I don't have that, but those moments are few and far between."

"You have me as family now," he said, leaning close to drop a kiss on my forehead. "Though I'm going to hate the people you're related to on sight for not caring about you. Is that okay?"

"Of course." And it was because I would feel the same if anyone had ever hurt his feelings along the way. We were mated, tied to each other. Anyone who hurt one of us hurt us both.

Subject closed, we got back to work. I washed and he dried, both of us finishing the dishes in just a few minutes. When we were done, Jericho grabbed my hand, tugging me into his arms with a sigh.

"Would you like to watch a movie with me?"

I glanced at the clock on the stove. "Now? It's really late."

He shrugged, pulling me closer. "I usually fall asleep to the TV. You know…since I'm always alone here."

My heart broke for him, for his loneliness. I lived by myself as well, but it had never really bothered me. I liked being alone. He obviously struggled with it.

I dropped a kiss to his collarbone and nuzzled into his neck. "Sure. Let's watch a movie."

He led me to the couch, settling us both on one end so we could snuggle close. I couldn't tell you what movie he put on—something magical and slightly dark—but I could tell you that he fell asleep approximately two minutes into it. I chuckled quietly when I realized, smiling up at his sleeping face. Taking a moment to really look at him.

He was undeniably handsome, but also so youthful-looking. A feat for a man as old as him. Elves hid their age easier, but he was only half elf. His reindeer side seemed to handle age the same way his elf side did.

But his long-lasting youth wasn't the only thing to admire about him. The reddish hair, the sharp jaw, the cheekbones—they made up a man who could have been on magazine covers. Could have been an international celebrity, charming women and men alike all over the world. Instead, he had been fated to me. He slept at Santa's castle, entertaining me. Making me food. Making my dreams of helping children in need come true. I was the luckiest elf in the elfdom.

Feeling way too sappy to sit still, I ran a finger over his cheek before rising up to kiss the corner of his mouth. I simply couldn't help myself. Jericho woke up suddenly, looking down at me with blue eyes that seemed to pierce my soul. I had been planning to say I should go home, but that wasn't happening. No way, no how.

"We should go to bed," I whispered, running my hand into his hair. "I'm tired."

He didn't respond, simply rose to his feet, turned off the television, grabbed my hand, and led the way to a room at the end of the hall. He swung the door open and followed me over the threshold, looking around as if he wasn't sure what to do next.

"It's huge," I said, speaking of both the bed and the room. Trying hard to break the awkwardness that had fallen over us. "Jericho?"

He took a deep breath and grabbed my hand again. "I've never slept in here."

"Never?"

His frown deepened, his body stiffening a bit. "It's a really large and quiet space to be alone all the time."

My heart broke. Shattered right there in the doorway to his enormous bedroom. I did the only thing I could think of—pulled him by the hand, keeping eye contact, until we reached the bed. I crawled onto it first, kneeling on the mattress and not letting go of him. Thankfully, he followed, both of us working our way into the middle. Falling together once we were ready. He yanked the covers over us, pulling me right back into his arms. Both of us still dressed. Neither of us caring.

"Thank you," he whispered.

"For what?"

"Staying."

I cuddled closer, holding him tight. "You're not alone now."

"No, I am not. And neither are you."

My stomach twisted, my independence not thrilled with that statement even as my heart soared because of it. It was fine for him to need me—I could handle that. Me needing him? Not as comfortable.

But I had a feeling I did. I needed.

And that scared me.

# 8

# ZIRA

I woke up to a loud banging on the door and a brain foggy enough to take a few seconds to realize that I was not where I should have been. I sat straight up in bed, mouth falling open as I gasped. Someone was banging on the door, all right—the *bedroom* door—and I was not at home. What threw me off even further was the fact that Jericho wasn't in the bed with me.

Recap as my brain caught up with the situation: someone was banging on the bedroom door in Jericho's quarters, and yet he wasn't there. Totally normal.

The door suddenly swung open, making me pull the blanket around my shoulders and cover up as if I were naked—which I was. *Good work, brain.* An older female elf walked in, pushing a trolley and looking completely frazzled.

"Sorry I'm late with your coffee service, sir. I thought perhaps I had missed you when you weren't on the couch like normal, but then—" She looked up, her eyes going wide. "Oh. You're not Mr. Jericho."

"No," I said, shaking my head. "I am not."

"Well…where is he?"

*If only I knew the answer to that one.*

It was at that moment another door in the room—one obviously leading to the bathroom—swung open, and Jericho appeared. All of Jericho, sans the parts covered by a shortish white towel. He looked clean and flushed, as if he had just showered. Which meant he was wet. Jericho stood wet across the room from me with almost nothing covering him. I would have liked to have said that my body was smart enough not to react to such a sight when there was a strange elf in the room. I would have liked to, but that would have made me a liar.

So much wet skin.

*Focus, Zira.*

"Sir," the other elf said, sounding exceptionally happy. "Good morning."

"Good morning, Charisma. I wasn't expecting you." Jericho shot me a wink, his smile solid and sure. "You know I usually make my own coffee, right?"

"Of course, sir. I came because I have a message for you." The elf—Charisma—glanced my way before lowering her voice. "Mr. Santa has requested a visit."

Jericho's smile fell. "This morning?"

"Yes. With you and—" she snuck a look my way "—your guest."

"He knows I have a guest?"

Charisma chuckled. "The entire castle does. It's all any elf can talk about."

Whether Charisma caught the look of anger that flashed across Jericho's face or not didn't matter because I did. He was definitely not happy about these developments, even though he kept an even tone and a relaxed expression with the older elf.

"When does he want us?"

Charisma nodded. "Fifteen minutes, sir."

"Fine." He glanced my way, his eyes giving away nothing. "We'll be there."

"Very good." Charisma turned for the door, leaving the cart of coffee behind. "Nice to meet you, ma'am."

With that, she was gone, and I was left a little stunned and a whole lot awake.

But really stunned. "We didn't actually meet."

Jericho chuckled and came to the bed, taking a seat beside me and reaching for my hand. "That's Charisma, and she's been my favorite staff elf forever."

"I see."

He remained quiet for a long time, playing with my hand in his. Finally, he sighed. "We're going to have to see my brother."

"Are we in trouble?"

"No," he said, shaking his head slightly. "Of course not. We're adults, after all. I'm just concerned because...he may not be friendly."

I shrugged, forcing his attention to me. Giving him a gentle smile. "He never has been. I'm not worried about that."

Jericho took a deep breath, seeming to relax a little bit. That charming smile returning. "I am so sorry."

"For what?"

He pushed me back, hovering over me with one arm planted on the mattress as I giggled beneath him. Laying his body on mine slowly, purposefully.

"I'm sorry that I didn't get to wake you up in a much more pleasurable way."

I wrapped my arms around his neck and planted a kiss on his chin, loving the way he groaned. "It's okay."

"It's truly, *truly* not. I'll have a conversation with Charisma to make sure she understands the situation and ends her impromptu visits."

I groaned as he rolled us over, ending up sitting astride his hips, wrapped up in only the sheet. The man was so beautiful, but there was a darkness around his eyes. A shadow of something. I couldn't have that.

"Don't get her in trouble now. At least she brought coffee."

"That she did. And don't worry—I adore the elf. I just don't want anyone else to see you naked."

"Just you?"

"Forever."

I laughed and rolled off him, hurrying to my feet before he could grab me and pull me back into the bed with him. I would have let him, and then we wouldn't have met up with Santa. Who knew how much trouble *that* would have brought down on us?

"Come, my mate," Jericho said, rising to his feet. "Let's get dressed. We need to go see the Grinch."

"He's literally Santa Claus."

"He is. He's also an old, single man who really needs someone to soften up the heart inside him."

I slipped into his arms for the briefest of kisses. "Meanwhile, you're handsome and fun, and you have gone out of your way to truly help those in need. He's definitely the Grinch in our story."

"Told you so."

We broke apart with a laugh, both on a mission to get ready for the day. I hurriedly tugged on my dress from the night before while Jericho pulled on jeans and an old sweatshirt. He looked so casual and cool that I found myself stopping to stare more than once. Thankfully, he only chuckled and winked my way when he caught me. A quick sip of some coffee to clear away the cobwebs, a longer brush of my teeth to at least pretend to be presentable, and we were off through the castle, walking to our doom.

At least, that's how it felt.

"Do you have any idea how beautiful you are?" Jericho asked. I had been so distracted with my nerves that I had almost forgotten he was beside me. He tugged me close, wrapping an arm around my shoulder. "Don't panic. We're not children being called to the principal's office."

"Then why does it feel that way?"

He gave my hand a kiss, not answering me. A telling sign, for sure.

We made the final turn into what looked like a dining hall, Jericho holding my hand in a firm grip. Both of us walking with our heads up. I followed his lead, letting him set the tone and mood. Keeping a close eye on his energy so I could match it. This was his brother—my boss, technically—but his brother. Jericho had the best knowledge to be in control of the situation.

Santa sat at one end of the long table, but he wasn't alone. The Queen sat across from him, neither taking the head chair. A breakfast of equals. Her guard stood just behind her, giving us a nod as we approached.

"Ah, my little brother," Santa said, rising from his seat and waving us over. The smile on his face too wide, too fake. My stomach dropped—I never did like when people put on a show. It hid their true intentions. "Come, come. Join us."

Jericho clenched my hand a little tighter and led us deeper into the room, smiling at the Queen as we approached. "Your Highness."

I nodded as well, ready to full-on curtsy if need be. Thankfully, the Queen seemed awfully relaxed.

"Good morning, Jericho. Good to see you, Zira. So nice that you two could join us."

"I must say," Jericho started as he pulled out a chair two down from the Queen for me to sit in. "I'm surprised to see you here. I was not informed I would be having a meal with the Queen."

She grinned, shooting a glance at Santa before refocusing on the two of us. "I woke up with a huge desire to break my fast with others, so I hunted down your brother. And now look at this! All four of us get to enjoy a meal together. How lovely."

Santa did not seem to agree, if his expression was any indication. Or perhaps he wasn't thrilled that Jericho sat beside me instead of walking around the table to join him on the other side. Three against one, it seemed. Not that this was any sort of fight or war. Yet.

A door at the back of the room opened, and six elves appeared, each carrying trays loaded with covered plates and bowls. Four of the elves moved to what I assumed was their assigned person at the table, setting plates of food in front of us. I gave my elf a quiet thank you and nod, knowing this was someone like me. A nobody in North Pole just trying to make a living. Another elf brought a coffee urn with creams and sugars. She started with the Queen—obviously—then moved to Santa when Her Highness refused. After Santa, she moved to Jericho, but he gave her a smile and nodded my way, making sure my cup was filled before his. An oddly gentlemanly thing to do and something that made me relax.

"So," Santa said as the elves disappeared once again into what I had to imagine was a kitchen. "This is a bit of a first."

Jericho went stiff. "What's that?"

"Bringing one of my factory workers to the dining table."

"You sent an invitation—"

"Well, yes. Of course. When the entire castle was talking about the elf who had stayed the night with my brother, I had to. You understand, of course."

I had no idea if Jericho understood or not, but I didn't. By the look of concern on the Queen's face, neither did she. I wanted Jericho to turn and give me a smile or something—anything—so I knew where his head was, but he kept his gaze centered on his brother, which left me looking over his shoulder. Alone at his side.

"Santa," the Queen said, keeping her voice light but firm. "Perhaps this is a conversation you and your brother can have another time."

"Yes." Jericho finally shot me a glance, giving me a wink and a small smile just as I'd wanted. "Let's table this discussion. I, for one, am starving and don't want the work of the elves who have so graciously made this meal for us to go to waste."

Heart, calm. Nervousness, reduced. I picked up my coffee, giving the Queen a moment to grab her fork and move as if to eat before taking a sip. The first whisper of liquid bliss had just hit my tongue when Santa obviously chose to ignore the plea of the Queen.

"Well, I, for one, am glad we get to spend some time together, Jericho. Perhaps tonight, you can skip fraternizing with my factory workers, though. Last time you came to town, I had two or three who missed work because of your antics. I need the ladies on my crew focused, not flittering about as if you actually think they matter."

"Santa," the Queen hissed, looking much like a viper ready to strike. I didn't get to see Jericho's face because he had his shoulder turned to me again, blocking me off. Leaving me alone at the table.

"She's not—" Jericho stopped, the rage in his voice forming a wall between him and his brother. "Liam, she is not just a factory worker. Her job doesn't even matter to me."

But as Santa—whose real name was Liam apparently, something I would not soon forget—began to argue with his brother, I sat back in my chair. Alone. Ignored. Just another factory worker Jericho had brought home. I waited a few minutes as the two men grew louder, anxiously biding my time until Jericho told his brother that I was more than just a one-night fling. That I was his mate. That we were something true.

That moment never came.

It was a concerned look from the Queen that put me into motion. I would not have such a woman pity me for the path the fates had put me on. And if Jericho thought keeping me a secret was an option, he was about to find out how mistaken that assumption was.

I rose to my feet and slipped out the back of the room, not waiting for Jericho to notice my retreat. Not caring if he did. In that second, all I wanted to do was go home, hide in my house, and forget about what had just happened.

Perhaps even forget about being mated to Jericho.

# 9

# JERICHO

Oh please," my brother said, the disdain in his voice riling me up even further. "You've been doing the same dance through my workers since puberty, while I've had to clean up your messes."

"Just because you couldn't get a woman if you dropped to your knees—"

"I'm sure you two would prefer to keep arguing, but I feel as if I should let Jericho know that she's gone."

It took me a solid ten seconds to understand what the Queen had just said. I jerked around, only then realizing my mistake. Sitting beside Zira had been for her protection—so I could be there with her during the meal. Unfortunately, it had forced me to turn my back on her when speaking to my brother. I had ignored her during the argument, a massive failing on my part, and now she was gone.

"Shit." I jumped to my feet, ready to chase after her, but my brother just had to make the moment about him.

"What did I say?" he asked, hands up as if he had no idea how insulting he had been.

It was the Queen who answered him, pure encapsulated fury in her tone. "You treated her like a tissue, Liam."

My brother sat back, mouth open, the use of his given name by Her

Highness obviously not something he was prepared for. "Well, he does go through women quite often. What's so special about this one?"

And that was the moment I realized my even bigger mistake. I had failed to tell my brother why Zira was so important to me, had allowed him to speak of and to her before making sure I had set the ground rules. He would have kept his mouth shut had I just uttered four simple words.

I was an idiot.

"She's my fated mate."

The room went silent and still, the elf in the corner waiting to be needed staring at me. The Queen and Carron both looking shocked. My brother—well, he bumbled for a bit, mouth opening and closing as he tried to find words to right his wrong. I didn't have time to wait for him to catch up.

I was halfway across the room, rushing for the door I had to assume Zira had left through, when I heard him holler, "I am so sorry. I had no idea."

"Go get her, Jericho," the Queen said, sounding almost excited. "We're here to help."

I had no idea what that last part meant, but it didn't matter. I had a woman to track down. I slammed through the door to the dining room and froze, looking left and right. Unsure of where to go. Panicking as I contemplated losing her in the labyrinth of the castle.

The sound of a quiet cough caught my attention and made me spin. There, standing just behind the door I had blasted through, stood one of the castle elves. The young man coughed again then inclined his head to one side.

"Is that... Did she go that way?"

He didn't say a word, just inclined his head again. Something I took as a sign.

"Thank you." I rushed down the hall to the split at the end, once again panicking as I had no clue which way she had gone. Once again running into a quiet elf who turned their head in one direction. Guiding me. I didn't even pause this time, following their motion and picking up speed. At every turn or end, an elf stood guard. Each of them giving me some sort of sign of which direction to choose. Each helping me track down my mate. I was going to have to dig into who each of them was so I could send them presents. Once I found Zira, though. Not a moment before.

In one long hall, I found the elf halfway down the length of it standing in front of a door. I slowed before her, unsure of her intention. Once again, she stayed silent. Instead of words, she simply pushed open the door, one that led to an outside space I had never been in. One I could see my mate through.

"Zira!" I was running before the door closed, rushing across grass and concrete for the woman who did not even pause in her race away from me. "Angel, stop."

"No!" she yelled, not looking back at me. Definitely not slowing down.

I ran all the way to her side, falling in right behind her. Making sure to keep chasing her. "Please. I'm so sorry they—"

My angel spun on me finally, rage and pain both equally visible in her expression. "*They* don't matter to me, Jericho. I'm not mad at them."

She turned as if to leave once more, but I grabbed her arm, unable not to, and pulled her to a stop.

"Wait. Please, Zira. Talk to me."

Thankfully, she did wait, though talking looked off the table if the way she crossed her arms and glared up at me mattered. I had a feeling it did.

"What?" she finally asked, the word hard and almost violent. A challenge. One I had to accept if I wanted to fix this.

"I'm sorry. Not for them, but for me. I was so stunned and so mad at my brother that I didn't react properly to what he said."

"No, you didn't."

"That's totally my fault."

"Yup."

That popped p was a mood in and of itself. One I needed to smooth over.

"I told them you're my mate."

"No. You didn't."

229

I sighed, clinging to her. "I did. Too late, obviously, but when you left, I told them both."

Her arms fell to her sides, her face softening. "You did?"

"Yes, of course. I wasn't keeping it a secret. I was just an idiot who should have realized saying that would have set the rules for the conversation. The error is my fault entirely, though it wasn't intentional." I inched closer to her, reaching for her fingers. Risking her ire for the off chance she might allow me to hold her hand. "You're my first and only mate. I made a mistake by not screaming that I had found you from the rooftops."

"That might have been a little much," she said as she wove her fingers through mine.

I tugged her against me, still only holding her hand. My racing heart beginning to calm just a little bit. "My brother apologized for what he said, if that matters."

"It does," she replied, her voice soft. Her tone a little broken. The sadness there gutted me.

"Angel Zira, I am so—"

"I don't want to be treated like just another woman in your bed."

"I've never had a woman in my bed before you, remember?"

She huffed. "You know what I mean."

"I do, and that definitely will not happen again." I slipped my arm around her back, hugging her close. "You're my mate, Zira. My one true love and fated partner. I would do anything to keep you happy."

She didn't respond, didn't relax into my hold either. The woman stood stiff as a board, holding my hand and staring up at me. Waiting. My mother had once said actions spoke louder than words, something that made a lot of sense in that moment and inspired me to take action. Without another worthless word, I headed for the street on the other side of the enclosure, keeping Zira's hand in mine. She followed me without question through a door and out of the compound. I found myself on a street I had never seen before, one filled with elves in various castle or workshop uniforms. All looking as if they were either going to or coming from work. Zira's peers.

This was about as "scream from the rooftops" as I could get.

I pulled Zira into my arms right there in front of all those elves, giving her a smile when the realization of what I was about to do dawned on her.

"You wouldn't."

I grinned and lifted her clean off her feet, grinning down at her. "I would."

And then I kissed her. Deeply. Soundly. Right there in front of all those people, I gave my mate a kiss that had her arching her body into mine and wrapping her arms around my neck. The world around us went silent and still, reality focusing solely on the two of us in that moment. My mate kissed me back with all she had, making me want to drag her back to my room. Back to my bed. Making me want to strip her naked and hear her moan my name like I had the night before.

But first, I had a point to make.

I broke the kiss, both of us breathing hard, before bringing my head back and looking over the crowd. The elves had all stopped to stare at us, as if waiting for something. Watching the show. It was time for the finale.

"I have found my fated mate in this beautiful woman."

The crowd exploded into cheers, clapping and whistling at the two of us. Zira laughed and tucked herself into my side as if to hide. The other elves would have none of that, though. They approached with joy on their faces, all stopping to congratulate the two of us. All forcing us to move as the crowd built behind us. We ended up on Tinsel Trail, where the owner of the coffee shop came rushing out with two cappuccinos, each with hearts in the foam. The candy shoppe owner also appeared, bringing us peanut brittle and a box of truffles. All celebrating with us. All happy to see a mating happen in their midst.

As the crowd began to sing and celebrate right there in the middle of the street, I leaned down to whisper to Zira. "This whole being mated thing isn't so bad."

She rolled her eyes at me, her smile bright and beautiful. "You're ridiculous."

"Ridiculously adoring of my mate."

"That doesn't even make sense."

"Does anything anymore?" I leaned closer to kiss her, keeping it a little more public-appropriate this time. Still wanting to drag her back to my place and get her naked. "Do you forgive me?"

"Maybe."

"I'll take a maybe if it means you don't run from me again."

She gripped my hand and tucked herself in against me. "It does."

And that was about the most I could hope for.

For the moment, at least.

# EPILOGUE

## ZIRA

Elves could knit. Like *really* knit.

"We need about fifty more pairs of socks and a handful of mittens," I said as I rushed across the room Jericho had set up as our home base.

Dahnearys, my partner in Necessities and Needles, nodded once then turned to address the other elves. "You heard the lady. More socks and mittens before Mr. Jericho flies out. We want children to have warm hands and feet, don't we?"

The knitters—a hundred elves who had volunteered their time for our noble cause—cheered and kept knitting. The sounds in the room were joyous and energetic, everyone working toward the same goal. Everyone wanting to give the children with the most need something they could truly use.

My mate had made my dream come true, and we were going to get to see him fly off in a sleigh behind his brother tomorrow as he began delivering the things children needed. Jericho had turned the nightmare of those letters into something good that Santa and the Queen were thrilled about. Our little knitting-and-delivering sock adventure looked as if it was going to be a hit.

Charisma, still Jericho's personal elf and someone I was getting to know much better, came whipping into the room with bright eyes and a blush on her cheeks.

"Charisma? Are you okay?"

"He's coming."

"Who?"

She didn't get a chance to answer me, but when the door opened, I fully understood her excitement...and her blush. Jericho Claus walked into the room in a suit much like Santa's but made of purple velvet instead of red. Deep, luscious purple that hugged his toned body perfectly. There was no bowl full of jelly with this particular Claus brother.

"There she is," he said, beelining it toward me with a smile on his ridiculously handsome face. "How is my sweet mate?"

I tried to answer, I really did, but instead choked on my spit and coughed.

"This isn't fair," I finally managed to get out just in time to grab hold of his fur-trimmed coat. "This is the opposite of fair."

Jericho—ever the observant one—herded me to the back of the room, tucking the two of us in behind the mound of already wrapped socks and mittens.

"So...should I take that to mean you like my suit?"

This man. "It's velvet."

"I know."

I ran my hands up his arms, a shiver making me tremble right there. "You know how much I love velvet."

Jericho leaned down and nuzzled my neck, dropping a sucking kiss before whispering, "I do know. Why do you think we have a velvet blanket on our bed?"

"Naughty boy."

He grabbed my ass and pulled me up against him, lifting me right off my feet. "Are you complaining?"

"Not in the least."

"Good." And with that, he kissed me. Deep, passionate kisses that had my body melting against his. That had me writhing in his arms and wishing we had a few hours alone. Kisses that did not go unnoticed.

"Ah-hem." Charisma fake coughed behind us, giving me a knowing smile when I broke free of Jericho. "It's time to begin loading, Mr. Jericho."

My mate sighed, pulling me in tight. "I have to work now."

"I know."

"Which means I'll be flying out soon."

I wrapped my arms around him a little tighter. "I know that, too. But I'll be here when you get back."

He sighed again, finally letting me drop back to my feet. "At least I'll have the image of you under our velvet blanket in our bed to keep me company."

I grinned, pulling him back into the workroom. "I'll be under the blanket but on the couch."

"Why?"

"If you don't sleep in that bed alone, then neither do I."

"Zira, you don't—"

"And, Jericho?" I spun, rising up on the balls of my feet to reach him. To drop a kiss next to his ear before whispering, "I'll be naked."

He stared at me, silent, his jaw locked and his eyes on fire. Moving in with the man had been one of the greatest decisions I had ever made. Loving him had been even better. Being loved by him was a gift I did not take advantage of. This was my mate, my forever. And we had so much to look forward to.

Including our first reunion after he spent a few days delivering presents to needy children.

"You're a little naughty," he said, his fingers clutching my sides. Obviously trying to keep from grabbing me in more obvious ways.

I couldn't hold back my grin. "And you think that's nice."

"I do."

"Good. Now go do amazing things. We can be naughty together when you get back."

Because the second that sleigh touched back down in North Pole, it was on. We would be spending a few days under that velvet blanket in and out of the bed. The man would be deserving of a reward for sure, and I would make certain he got one.

"I'm taking that as a promise," Jericho said before raising his voice to address the room. "Let's get to delivering socks and mittens!"

The room exploded in cheers, the final sets of knitted items being tossed at the wrappers who would make sure they looked beautiful. I had no idea how I'd gotten so lucky, but there was no doubt in my mind —Jericho Claus was a dream come true. One I hadn't been creative enough to even think possible.

"Come on, mate," Jericho said before slapping me on the ass. "Let's load up."

A dream that still made me work now and again. But at least it was for a good cause.

# ABOUT THE AUTHOR

A storyteller from the time she could talk, Ellis grew up among family legends of hauntings, psychics, and love spanning decades. Those stories didn't always have the happiest of endings, so they inspired her to write about real life, real love, and the difficulties therein. From farmers to werewolves, store clerks to witches—if there's love to be found, she'll write about it. Ellis lives in the Chicago area with her two daughters and a German Shepherd that never leaves her side.

When she's not writing paranormal romance, Ellis Leigh can be found writing romantic suspense as Kristin Harte and erotic shorts as London Hale.

Sign up for Ellis Leigh's newsletter for release information, promotions, swag opportunities, and early access to free reads!

www.ellisleigh.com/newsletter.

For new release announcements only, follow Ellis on Bookbub.

Come join my reader group for fun, snippets, secret handshakes, and discussions of what I'm working on and when that next book will be out.

Ellis' Elite Reader Group

CPSIA information can be obtained
at www.ICGtesting.com
Printed in the USA
BVHW072355180123
656596BV00015B/52